"Hi, I'm Libby Taylor and I can't thank you enough for returning Wags to us."

Nick stared at the creamy white skin of her delicate hand for a moment. Although he always scrubbed his when he finished a job, motor oil and grease were a part of his life, hazards of his job as a mechanic. His motorcycle repair and restoration business might be successful and entice cycle enthusiasts from across the state to seek him out, but that didn't change the fact he was often covered in dirt and grease. And here she stood dressed in that pristine white sweater. He was almost afraid to stand next to her for fear of transferring grease and oil on to her somehow.

What is wrong with you, Cabot?

He wasn't blushing. Marines, even former ones, did not blush. No way. Of course, marines didn't stutter either, but he had been doing just that a few moments ago.

Dear Reader,

For me, stories evolve from one thing or many things. I save up human interest stories or personal experiences and put them away in the back of my mind to be explored later. They are sometimes matched with something else I've seen, heard or experienced.

A writer friend, Tina, texted me a picture, suggesting that I might be able to use it for inspiration. And boy, did I ever. Messages flew back and forth between us as she helped me brainstorm the characters and basic plot for what would become *His Unlikely Homecoming*.

Nick and Libby's story was born that afternoon and went to the head of my queue for stories I wanted to write. What was the picture? It was a tough-looking guy with tattoos and biker gear holding kittens. The picture reminded me of a real-life event that I had stored in the back of my mind for later use: I was at the vet waiting to pick up my cat. As I waited, I stood next to a guy with tattoos, piercings and leather. I was expecting them to bring out a Rottweiler or some other fierce-looking dog. Instead, the vet tech brought out a sweet kitten. He cradled the kitten to his chest and told it how much he'd missed his baby that day. The writer in me was intrigued and I never forgot that incident. Seeing the picture prodded the incident and Nick was born.

I hope you enjoy his story. Let me know what you think. I love hearing from readers. You can reach me at authorcarrienichols@gmail.com.

Carrie

His Unlikely Homecoming

CARRIE NICHOLS

HARLEQUIN
SPECIAL
EDITION

ISBN-13: 978-1-335-59425-9

His Unlikely Homecoming

Harlequin Enterprises ULC
22 Adelaide St. West, 41st Floor
Toronto, Ontario M5H 4E3, Canada
www.Harlequin.com

Printed in U.S.A.

Carrie Nichols grew up in New England but moved south and traded snow for central AC. She loves to travel, is addicted to British crime dramas and knows a *Seinfeld* quote appropriate for every occasion.

A 2016 RWA Golden Heart® Award winner and two-time Maggie Award for Excellence winner, she has one tolerant husband, two grown sons and two critical cats. To her dismay, Carrie's characters—like her family—often ignore the wisdom and guidance she offers.

Books by Carrie Nichols

Harlequin Special Edition

Small-Town Sweethearts

The Marine's Secret Daughter
The Sergeant's Unexpected Family
His Unexpected Twins
The Scrooge of Loon Lake
The Sergeant's Matchmaking Dog
The Hero Next Door
A Hero and His Dog

Visit the Author Profile page
at Harlequin.com for more titles.

This one is for my friend Tina Medlock, who gave me the idea and helped me form it into a story.

Chapter One

"Why in the world would you want to run away from a sweet setup like this?" Nick Cabot asked his passenger as he eased his restored classic 69 Ford Ranger to the curb in front of a pale yellow two-story home.

The only response from Nick's passenger was a whine deep in his throat.

He liked to think that the noise sounded repentant. "Maybe your little adventure will help you appreciate how lucky you are."

Turning back to the house, he studied the well-maintained exterior. The home and the quiet tree-lined street in Loon Lake, Vermont, was not just a continent away but an entire world apart from the crime-riddled area where he'd grown up.

The Cape Cod–style home had dormers above a

porch that ran the width of the house. The residence, separated from the road by a public sidewalk and a small grass-covered front yard, had six wooden steps leading to a blue-painted front door. Smooth round columns, painted bright white, held up the porch's roof, and four lush Boston ferns, spaced between the columns, hung from the rafters. The porch railings, pickets and step risers were also painted bright white. Blue ceramic pots overflowing with colorful flowers lined one side of the steps and flanked the front door.

He double-checked the house number with the one he'd scribbled on a scrap of paper. Yep, it was correct. In an uncharacteristic flight of fancy, he decided the wholesome picture before him matched the voice of the woman who'd answered his call. He'd been drawn to that melodious voice despite knowing that girl-next-door types were only interested in guys like him for a temporary walk on the wild side. He'd been used in the past and had no plans to revisit that.

His passenger, a fluffy miniature American shepherd who'd been sitting quietly at attention during the ride, began to squirm and whine, drawing Nick's attention back to the matter at hand.

"Yeah, yeah, time to get you back to where you belong," he told the dog. The woman he'd spoken to over the phone had said her five-year-old daughter had been inconsolable over the missing pup. "I know for a fact they will be grateful to get you back."

The dog turned to look at him with a how-can-you-doubt-it expression, causing Nick to laugh and rub the fluff around the floppy ears. "Damn, but you are pretty sweet."

As their name—*miniature*—implied, the dog breed was smaller than their sheep-herding Aussie cousins, but Nick knew they possessed the same drive and intelligence. That intelligence—along with a good dose of mischief—was apparent in this guy's mismatched eyes. The pup's left eye was a bright blue and the right a deep brown. Heterochromia. That was what the condition was called. Nick had looked it up along with more information on the dog's breed. Apparently, mismatched eyes weren't all that unusual.

If the eyes weren't cute enough, the dog's coat looked as if a child had splashed watercolor paints all over him. Although predominantly brown and white, the fur had splashes of black, tan, red and gray in no discernible pattern.

Nick turned his attention back to the home as the front door burst open. A girl came racing down the steps, brown pigtails flying out behind her as she ran toward the truck. He noticed she had Down syndrome.

The dog's entire body shook as he watched his little mistress's approach, and Nick hustled out of the pickup with the puppy on his heels. He sidestepped out of the way to avoid getting knocked over by the eager dog, who bounded toward the child.

"You're home safe. I missed you so much," the girl said, her arms outstretched, a glowing smile on her face.

The dog leaped, and the girl caught the wiggling dynamo but stumbled back before landing on her butt on the grass next to the sidewalk.

Nick had started forward when the girl fell but stopped when she began to giggle, deciding she must not be hurt. She continued to laugh while the puppy showered her with slobbery kisses.

"Mommy says you was very naughty running away like that," she scolded the dog but continued giving him kisses and love pats.

Grinning, Nick wondered who was more excited to see whom. He had to admit that seeing this joyful reunion was worth the ribbing he'd get from some of his customers when they heard about another successful lost-pet reunion.

How or why errant pets found their way to his motorcycle repair business was beyond his understanding. Of course, he had to see to it that the animals were reunited with their rightful owners. Why would anyone find that small thing such a big deal?

His niece, Oakley, hadn't helped the situation. She might live all the way across the country, but that didn't seem to matter because she'd found out about his Loon Lake reputation and had promoted it on social media. Local resident Gabe Bishop, an acquaintance from Nick's Marine Corps days, had found the post, so now the whole town knew about it.

Damn Gabe and his big mouth.

The girl scrambled to her feet, and Nick refocused his attention on her and the pet.

"Thank you, mister, for finding my Wags and bringing him home. I was so worried about him," she said and gave Nick a cheerful smile.

"More like he found me," he said.

The dog, tired and thirsty, had shown up at Nick's place as if road signs had directed him there.

Before he could prepare, the girl ran forward and

threw her arms around him in a hug as exuberant as the one she'd given the dog. Accustomed to most people judging him by his outward appearance, Nick was flummoxed by the girl's unbridled enthusiasm. Most people stepped back to give him space. A hug was the last thing he came to expect from people meeting him for the first time. And that was fine by him. He wouldn't call himself a people person anyway.

Looking up at him with dark brown eyes, the sweet girl said, "I asked Mommy why you was bringing my doggie home, and she said you must be a Good Samaritan. I never met one of those a'fore. But Pastor Cook talked about them when I went to bacation Bible school, so I heard of them. Is you married?"

Blindsided just as much by the girl's non sequitur question as he was by the hug. Nick gave her an awkward pat on the head and tried to move away as he searched for a response. "W-w-well, I—"

"Rebecca," a woman scolded loudly as she hurried through the open doorway and onto the porch. She wiped her hands on a towel, draped it over the top porch railing, and came down the steps. "Give the man some space."

"But Mommy, I had to thank him for bringing Wags home. I was a-feared I wouldn't ever see him again if something bad happened." the girl said. But she did release Nick and move away.

The puppy play-growled in agreement and jumped up as if his back legs were made of springs, nearly knocking the girl over again.

The woman gave an exasperated sigh. "Wags. Down." But the excited puppy ignored her.

Nick put his hand out palm down and ordered the wriggling puppy to sit in a voice reminiscent of his days as a platoon sergeant in the Marines. The dog made complaining noises but managed to plunk his wiggling butt on the ground.

"Look, Mommy! He did it."

"I see that," the woman said, her tone full of surprise.

The girl scrunched up her face and looked at him. "How did you do that, mister? Mommy has been trying to make him behave since we got him, but he ignores her."

"Seems like I've lost control of everyone," the woman muttered and gave her daughter a stern look. "You were supposed to wait for me before you went outside. We agreed. Remember?"

"But, Mommy, you didn't tell me you was gonna be on the potty when the man got here. I couldn't wait no more. I had to see Wags. And he wanted to see me."

The puppy continued to sit but stared adoringly up at his young mistress as if to confirm she was telling the truth.

"We'll discuss your disobedience later, young lady," the woman admonished, face flushed. She then turned to the dog. "The same goes for you. You gave us quite a fright."

The woman may have scolded, but she reached out and welcomed the dog the same as the girl had done, with loving pats.

With the woman's attention on the pup, Nick took a moment to observe her. He'd spotted her a few times from a distance along Main Street. She'd been either coming or going from the Adventures in Quilting shop, but he hadn't had a chance to see her up close. From a distance she was attractive, but this close she was stunning.

She had dark brown eyes like her daughter and glossy dark hair that shone when the rays of the sun hit it. The hair framed her face and fell past her shoulders. She wore dark blue dress slacks and a white cotton knit sweater that gathered at her trim waist. Yep, she looked like her voice. Very all-American girl next door.

"Mommy was on the potty when you came," the girl turned and told him in a stage whisper.

Nick bit the inside of his cheek to keep from laughing at her candor.

The woman's cheeks turned pink again, making the freckles sprinkled across the bridge of her nose and cheeks stand out more. Embarrassed or not, she stepped forward with a smile that looked forced and held out her hand. "Hi, I'm Libby Taylor and I can't thank you enough for returning Wags to us."

Nick stared at the creamy white skin of her delicate hand for a moment. Although he always scrubbed his when he finished a job, motor oil and grease were a part of his life, hazards of his job as a mechanic. His motorcycle repair and restoration business might be successful and entice cycle enthusiasts from across the state to seek him out, but that didn't change the fact he was often covered in dirt and grease. And here she stood dressed in that pristine white sweater. He was almost afraid to stand next to her for fear of transferring grime onto her aura of perfection.

"You might have caught me in the bathroom, but

I swear I washed my hands," she said into the growing silence.

What is wrong with you, Cabot?

He wasn't blushing. Marines, even former ones, did not blush. No way. Of course, Marines didn't stutter, either, but he had been doing just that a few moments ago.

"Sorry. I didn't mean to give you that impression," he said, finally taking the hand she offered. "I'm Nick Cabot, and I'm usually the one with the dirty hands."

"Oh?" She drew her eyebrows together in confusion.

"I work in a motorcycle repair shop," he explained.

"Oh, yes, now I remember you. From what I've heard, you don't just work there but you own it. And I understand it's quite a successful business," she said.

"I manage to do okay." He shrugged as if it meant nothing, but her words made his chest swell, which was strange because he didn't normally go around looking for validation.

After he dropped her hand, he realized only part of his hesitation had to do with grease. He'd hesitated to touch her. And he'd been right to feel that way. Despite the short duration, that skin-to-skin contact had sent a slight electric charge through him and awoken something. Something best left to sleep because women like Libby Taylor did not fall for tattooed, motorcycle-riding guys who lived above the repair shop. At least not once they came to their senses.

"…already met Rebecca," Libby was saying.

"And you met Wags," Rebecca put in.

Nick hoped if he centered his attention on the girl, Rebecca, he'd have the opportunity to forget the warmth of Libby's skin against his and that little electric pulse.

"Is that his name? Wags?" he asked, setting aside all his inappropriate thoughts.

"Uh-huh. He wags his whole body because his tail is so short. Mommy says his kind of doggy has short tails. It's...it's... What's that word, Mommy?"

"Genetic," her mother supplied, sounding as if they'd been down that road before.

"That's it. My grandpa said I should pick a dog with a *real* tail and eyes that matched, but I wanted Wags. I love him and he's sorta like me."

"I see that your eyes match, so you can't mean that." Nick raised an eyebrow in an exaggerated gesture. "Are you saying you don't have a tail, either?"

"That's silly. People don't have tails." Rebecca giggled but suddenly turned serious. "Do they, Mommy?"

"Not any that I know," Libby said and smiled. This time the smile reached her eyes.

Nick swallowed hard. What would it feel like to have all that warmth and sunshine directed at him? He scolded himself for that thought. This was not the time or place to deal with feelings the woman might create in him.

"See? And Mommy would know because she's really, really smart," Rebecca said.

"Then I stand corrected about the tails," Nick replied with mock seriousness.

"You talk funny, Mr. Nick."

"Rebecca, that's rude." Libby sighed, giving Nick an apologetic look. "I'm sorry."

"No, Mommy, I *like* the way he talks to me."

"You do?" Nick said at the same time as Libby.

"Uh-huh." Rebecca nodded. "Sometimes people talk to me like I'm a baby, but I'm not. I'm five. I got Down syndrome, but I'm not a baby."

Nick's heart clenched at Rebecca's words. He hated the thought of people talking down to her because she had Down syndrome. Squatting on his heels in front of her, he said, "Well, if I ever talk down to you, please tell me because I see you're not a baby."

He glanced at Libby and caught her watching him, her eyes shining, her mouth soft and inviting. Would she taste as sweet as she looked?

Whoa. He needed to stop thinking about her like that, stop thinking about her, period. He wasn't looking for anything serious. And Libby Taylor had serious written all over her. What did he have to bring to a relationship? Apart from some fun times, all he had to offer was an armful of tattoos and a drawer full of military medals. Not exactly relationship material.

What is wrong with you, Cabot? One look at Libby Taylor and you're using the R-word. Cut that out.

He was a man, so of course he'd notice and admire her good looks, but he needed to remember he was here to return the errant puppy. That was all.

Libby's heart melted at the respect Nick Cabot was giving Rebecca, and she regretted any previous thoughts regarding him or his appearance. She'd noted how stiff he'd seemed when Rebecca had been hugging him. Was he simply uncomfortable with spontaneous displays of affection from strangers, or did Rebecca herself make him uncomfortable? Libby had run across that before. Not everyone who looked at her daughter saw a young girl with thoughts, feelings and desires, like all other girls her age. All some people saw was a girl with Down syndrome.

She'd been wrong about Nick. But in her defense, her mom radar had sprung to life when she'd come onto the porch to find Rebecca hugging someone. Not just any someone but a guy in a leather biker vest, black T-shirt, scarred black boots and an arm covered in tattoos. He looked as if he'd stepped off the set of *Sons of Anarchy*. The closest she'd come to someone like that was while watching rerun episodes of that show on a streaming service.

Oh, sure, she'd seen him ride through town on his motorcycle a few times and she'd noticed him sitting by himself at the counter of Aunt Polly's once or twice when she'd been there, but they'd never been formally introduced. She and he were both "flatlanders", a local term for people not native to Vermont. Some people referred to them as being "from away" too.

And yeah, okay, she'd noticed him striding past her shop along Main Street a few times, but she hadn't done anything proactive.

Like what? Run down the street after him and introduce herself? Ask him if he was interested in quilting lessons?

Libby had learned from Addie Bishop that Nick owned the motorcycle repair shop across town, so it would make sense that he rode them, too. According to Addie, her husband, Gabe, and Nick had known one another from the Marines, but Nick normally kept to himself.

Addie had told her that two years ago, after attending the annual Motorcycle Week over in Laconia, New Hampshire, Nick had come to Loon Lake to catch up with Gabe. While visiting, Nick had decided to buy the recently closed motorcycle repair shop from its retired owner. Although Nick had been a Loon Lake resident ever since buying the business, his and Libby's paths rarely crossed, even in a small town like Loon Lake.

Not surprising, since guys that looked like Nick weren't in the habit of frequenting quilt shops. And being a business owner and a single mother severely limited her social life. Not that she minded. Rebecca and Adventures in Quilting were her two passions. She wouldn't change anything, even if she could.

But she had to admit that Nick's clothing and all that ink on his arm were a bit intimidating and, yes, exciting. Despite the bad-boy vibes he gave off, he was an upstanding member of the community according to people who knew him. Was it that dichotomy that made him so intriguing?

Her status-conscious parents wouldn't look past the exterior and certainly wouldn't approve.

Why do you care what they think?

Thirty-three-year-old women didn't worry about what their parents thought. But turning away from a lifetime of habit wasn't easy. Isn't that part of the reason she'd moved almost two hundred miles away from them? She liked having that buffer between them. She'd always been the dutiful daughter and had never had the courage to hook up with a bad boy, even if she'd been tempted. She'd even married the man her parents had approved. Yeah, and that had turned out so well. She would have been better off with being in a relationship with someone like Nick Cabot.

Whoa. Where had that thought come from?

"Mommy, are you going to invite him?" Rebecca asked, her tone impatient as if she may have been asking questions while Libby was lost in her thoughts.

She needed to pay attention and not go off on a tangent about bad boys. Libby blinked as she stared down at her daughter. "Invite him?"

"To stay for supper?" Rebecca turned to Nick. "We're having tur-til soup."

Nick raised an eyebrow. "Turtle soup?"

"Tortellini soup," Libby clarified.

How was she going to get out of this without sounding ungrateful to him for going to all the trouble of returning Wags? Rebecca was a friendly child, and she had excellent radar when it came to people. Libby had come to respect her daughter's instincts, but that didn't mean she felt comfortable inviting the man to supper.

"Yeah, that's it," Rebecca nodded and looked at Libby. "He's not married. I asked."

"Rebecca!" Libby stared at her daughter. Good Lord, what exactly had she been saying to this man before she came out?

Like with the dog, had she ever had control of this? She'd planned on greeting the man himself when he arrived, but they'd been waiting for over an hour, and she'd given in to the call of nature. Of course he'd shown up then.

That was how this whole ordeal had started. Libby had been in the bathroom when their rambunctious puppy had escaped. Libby had left the miniature American shepherd in the backyard while she went inside to use the facilities. Their backyard was fenced, so she'd been convinced no harm would come to the little pup, but when she returned, he'd been gone.

She'd combed the neighborhood, figuring he couldn't have gotten very far, but no luck. Someone had suggested she put a lost dog notice on a neighborhood social media site. A man with a warm baritone voice soon called her. She recalled how the slight rasp roughened the voice and made her tummy do a little tumble.

In person, Nick made her stomach do more than tumble. He—

"But, Mommy, Grandma Joyce said everyone knows you're dee-borced. She says it like it's a bad thing. So maybe if you gots married again, you wouldn't be dee-borced no more. But I heard Mrs. Addie say you can't get married again if you don't meet a man. Mr. Nick is a man, and you met him."

Nick made a choking sound that could have been laughter or outrage. Libby didn't know because she wasn't brave enough to look at him. First, she'd been caught in the bathroom when he arrived, and now this. Could things get any worse?

"Thank you for your kind invitation, Miss Rebecca, but I only came here to return your dog, not to get engaged or married," he said and glanced longingly at his truck. His escape route.

Libby groaned inwardly and sent a message to the universe asking to be swallowed up. Maybe the key to not getting caught in awkward situations was to stay out of the bathroom.

Chapter Two

Three days after returning Wags to his rightful owners, Nick pulled up to Libby Taylor's appealing home
once again and cut the engine. This time he came alone
and at a time when he knew she would be in her shop.

"So much for staying away and minding my own
damn business," Nick muttered as he hopped out of his
truck in front of the tidy yellow house. After declin-
ing all their invitations—Libby's albeit reluctant one
to join them for supper and Rebecca's unsubtle one
that included marriage—he'd escaped and promised
himself he'd steer clear of Libby, her sweet daughter
and their frisky pup.

There wasn't anything there for him because he
wasn't in the market for anything permanent. He was
just hitting his stride with his business and didn't have

time for serious involvement with anyone. And any entanglement with a single mother would have to be considered serious.

Libby being a single mother sounded like a good excuse to stay away. Right? He shook his head at his thoughts as he made his way to the rear of his truck.

He'd reiterated that promise not to get attached even as he enjoyed the tin of homemade cookies they had given him to take home. The chocolate chip cookies had the right amount of chewiness and were loaded with gooey chocolate bits. They were perfection. Women in his world did not bake cookies. His mother had been too busy chasing her next high.

So, what was he doing here?

"You're paying it forward. Just like you promised Dan Ridgeway," he told himself as he let the tailgate down and retrieved the new wooden post from the truck bed.

He'd been seventeen and following a path leading to nothing but trouble. His mom was addicted to that white net crawl—that state of mind brought on by heroin, and Pops, his old man, had been doing a stretch in Corcoran, the state prison in California. Nick had been acting out because of his fear and anger, and to this day, he had no idea why Officer Dan Ridgeway had decided to take an interest in the punk kid he'd been. Dan had taken him to the Marines recruiting station and told him to make a choice: Nick could follow his dad to prison—hey, they could be cellmates—or he could become a man others trusted and respected. The Marines had sounded better than prison even to a streetwise kid.

Whenever he had leave, Nick had made it a point to visit Dan, right up until his savior passed away from pancreatic cancer several years ago.

He shook his head. Enough revisiting the past. He had a job to do. He'd made a trip to the local home improvement store to get supplies for installing new shelves in his kitchen in the apartment above his business and remembered seeing the Taylors' leaning mailbox, so he'd gotten supplies for that, too.

People in Loon Lake helped their neighbors. His desire to fix this for her had nothing to do with those light freckles sprinkled across Libby's nose or the way that nose scrunched up when she laughed. Her laughing at the dog's antics kept creeping into his thoughts. He wasn't sure this was what Dan had meant about paying it forward, but he knew that doing this was being a good neighbor.

Yeah, right. You live clear across town. You wouldn't even know about the wobbly mailbox if not for returning her daughter's dog.

Telling his inner critic to step off, he grabbed his toolbox and set it none too gently next to the new wooden post. He'd replace the rotted post with a new one and be gone. She wouldn't even know he'd been back. And that was what he wanted. Right?

"Excuse me, young man?" someone called. "May I inquire what business you have with Libby's mailbox?"

Young man? He'd been called a lot of things but never that. He hadn't fit that category before becoming a marine and certainly hadn't felt young after his first deployment over twenty years ago.

But, considering he was the only one around, they

must mean him, so Nick turned in the direction of the voice. A man who looked like he was somewhere in his seventies or eighties stood on the porch next door. The elderly man placed his hands on his hips as he confronted Nick. He wore a green United States Marine Corps Vietnam Veteran baseball cap, a blue chambray shirt and denim bibbed overalls.

"You may," Nick responded with a respectful nod to a fellow former marine. "When I was here the other day, I noticed her mailbox needed repairing, so I decided to come by and fix it. Seems a simple enough job."

Nick figured the guy must be the self-appointed neighborhood watch. Not that there was anything wrong with that; it even gave him a measure of reassurance that someone looked out for Libby and Rebecca.

And how was that any of his business? It wasn't. He wasn't getting involved.

The man's snow-white bushy eyebrows drew together. "She hire you?"

"No, sir. The fact is, she doesn't know I'm here." Nick glanced at the man again. "Unless you've already called her."

The man chuckled. "Believe me, son, I thought about it but decided I'd speak with you first. I don't want to be seen as an old fuddy-duddy. Not with such a beautiful neighbor. But keep it under your hat that I called Libby a beauty. Was this supposed to be a surprise of some sort?"

Nick shrugged. "Not really, but I'm not looking for any recognition. I saw it needed some attention and decided to help out."

The man nodded. "She's a single mother and she doesn't seem to be struggling financially—not that I know any of her business, mind you—but the wife shops at her place in town. Even takes some of those classes she teaches. The ones in the morning. Clara and I don't drive much after dark anymore. So my wife is glad she has morning stuff. Anyway, the wife says Libby is even looking to hire someone part-time for the summer. I guess she wants to spend more time with Rebecca."

"Uh-huh," Nick mumbled as he removed the mailbox from the old post. He wasn't sure how he was expected to respond. Or if the old guy even required a response. He sighed, trying not to let his annoyance show. This was probably going to take twice as long.

"As I was saying, Clara seems to think her shop turns a profit and Libby must be doing okay. Even so, running a small business and maintaining a home along with being a single parent can't be easy. Although that Rebecca is a little love and doesn't give her any trouble. Can't say the same for that puppy of hers, but he's a cute bugger, so I guess that makes up for a lot."

Nick nodded and made a sound of agreement in his throat but kept working at removing the old post.

"I might be an old man, but I try to look out for them." The man grabbed on to the railing and slowly made his way down the steps.

"And I'm sure they both appreciate it," Nick said, grunting as he tugged on the old post.

"Name's Hank Jensen."

"Nice to meet you. I'm Nick Cabot."

"Cabot?" The man stroked his chin. "You the one

who took over that cycle repair business when old man Robbins retired?"

"That's me," Nick said, stifling a laugh. "Old man" Fred Robbins, whom Nick had bought the business from, couldn't be more than a half dozen years older than Hank Jensen.

"You done good there. With the shop, I mean. I don't ride myself, but I know a couple of guys from back in the day—I did my duty in the Corps. Heard you did, too. Anyway, what was I saying? Oh, yeah, they swear by your customizations. Say you're the best around."

"Thanks." Nick's irritation melted under the warmth spreading in his chest. He didn't even know the man, and yet, for some inexplicable reason, this guy's praise meant a lot. It wasn't as if he craved anyone's acceptance. If he was feeling unappreciated, all he had to do was open that drawer that held the handful of medals the Marines had insisted on giving him.

The man hitched up his overalls and took short, shuffling steps toward him. "Need some help?"

Not really. The response sprang to Nick's lips, but he noticed the guy's halting gait and shaking hands. Parkinson's? But he also spotted Jensen's hopeful expression and swallowed those words. "Sure. I could use some. Thanks."

"Mommy, look! Someone fix-ed our mailbox." Rebecca bounced in her booster seat as Libby pulled into their driveway.

Libby glanced over. Sure enough, the mailbox post no longer listed to the side like a drunken sailor. Fixing the post had been on her to-do list for quite some time, but the quilt shop kept her busy and she'd been too tired to tackle it. Nor was it easy finding someone who wanted to do such a small job. Sure, she could have called on the husband of one of her friends. She happened to know Addie's husband, Gabe, or Brody Wilson, the husband of the accountant Libby used at tax time for her store, would have come over to fix it, but she hated to ask. Both Gabe and Brody would refuse payment and she didn't like feeling as though she was taking advantage of a friendship, especially for something that wasn't a major issue but more like an eyesore.

"Did you see it, Mommy?"

"Yes, I see that, honey. I wonder who did it?"

Hank Jensen came out onto his porch as she got out of the car and opened Rebecca's door to the back seat. Although Rebecca often complained, Libby obeyed the law and made her sit in the back in a booster seat. Rebecca had been touchy lately about being perceived as a baby.

Was it something someone said? Libby knew her friend's children didn't treat Rebecca any different than any of their other friends. As a matter of fact, Natalie Gallagher's son Sam was nonverbal due to a brain injury, and he was accepted into the group whenever the parents got together for barbecues or play dates. Libby sighed. She'd have to try harder to get to the bottom of it.

Did her mom or dad say something? Her parents truly loved their only grandchild, but Libby's dad wasn't the most enlightened guy and often said things he shouldn't. She worked hard despite their criticisms over her life choices to maintain a relationship with them. It had taken her a long time to recover from the fact they'd sympathized with Will during the divorce. According to them, Libby should have tried harder to make things work. Why couldn't they accept that no amount of work on her part was going to change Will's attitude?

But Rebecca deserved grandparents and Will's parents certainly couldn't be counted on, so Libby did her best to maintain a cordial relationship despite the fact she'd disappointed them when she divorced their good friend's son.

"Mr. J, did you see? Someone fix-ed our mailbox." Rebecca ran over to greet their kindly neighbor with a smile and a hug.

Libby suspected the reason Rebecca always ran to greet Hank when he was outside wasn't all down to her innate friendliness. Hank always carried soft peppermints in his pocket.

At least now they'd find out who replaced the mailbox post because Libby couldn't imagine anyone or anything getting past Hank Jensen. Not that she was complaining. She was grateful for her neighbor's eyes and ears.

Hank patted the front pocket on the flap of his overalls, his way of asking permission to give Rebecca a candy. Appreciating his seeking permission first, she nodded and smiled.

"That motorcycle guy came by today and fixed it," he said, handing out the candy after accepting a hug and giving one in return.

Motorcycle guy? Libby's heart kick-started at the

mention of Nick Cabot. It had to be him, since he was the only man she knew who could be classified as a "motorcycle guy." But why would he do that? "Do you mean Nick Cabot?"

"Yeah, that was his name. Why couldn't I remember that?" Mr. Jensen scratched his cheek before he continued, "Anyway, when I first saw him, I came out to make sure he wasn't trying some funny business with your mail. Clara and I watch the news. I heard about these so-called porch pirates even though I don't think we have anything like that in our town…let alone our street. But you never know."

"Thank you," she said but wasn't sure that his vigilance was necessary when it came to her wonky mailbox. "I told Clara I'll let you know to keep an eye out if we're expecting packages."

"Good. Good. We've all got to look out for one another." Hank hitched up his overalls. "Just so you know. This Nick…he checks out. Former marine. He was with the 2nd Reconnaissance Battalion out of Camp Lejeune down in North Carolina. Said he knows Gabe Bishop. The one that's married to the library lady."

Libby nodded. "Yeah, Addie mentioned Gabe had been at Camp Lejeune at the same time as Nick."

Not that she'd been pumping Addie for information about Nick. After all, he had returned Wags, so it was only natural that his name came up in a conversation. Even if she'd had to work hard to make sure it did.

"Yeah, we swapped war stories as we worked on the repairs," Hank said as he unwrapped a peppermint and popped it in his mouth. He handed Rebecca another one with a wink. "Well, truth be told, it was mainly me doing the talking and him the working."

She could just imagine Hank talking the poor man's ear off as he repaired the mailbox. Hank's wife, Clara, said she came to Libby's quilting classes as much to escape the house as to learn to quilt. She smiled, remembering Clara complaining that to hear Hank, she'd been doing all the cooking and cleaning wrong. "I don't know how I managed all those years before he retired," Clara had grumped just that morning during their quilting session at the store.

"He's a good listener," Hank said. "Most young men these days don't have any patience for us old guys and our war stories."

"Maybe because he's an ex-marine too," Libby suggested.

"Libby." Hank tutted his tongue and shook his head slowly. "Once a marine, always a marine. There's no ex about it."

She pressed the ball of her hand to her forehead. "That's right. I think you mentioned that before."

He shook his finger at her but laughed. "I think you're teasing an old man, young lady."

"So, what did Nick have to say about his time in the Marines?" Libby asked. She should be ashamed for pumping others for information about him, but she couldn't help it. She had to admit that she'd been disappointed that his bringing Wags home seemed to be the end of their dealings with one another. But she'd gotten over it. She was a grown woman, not some lovestruck teen mooning over the cute kid in homeroom.

"He gave 'em twenty the same way I did. Went in

at eighteen the same way I did. Said he was from the West Coast but preferred to settle here after he got out. Was a bit closemouthed about family ties. Don't know what the story was there," Hank said, shaking his head.

Hank's comment had Libby wondering what Nick's story was, too. So much for not thinking about the man. He'd returned their dog and she was grateful. He'd refused her invitation to supper… Okay, that invitation had been extended because Rebecca had insisted, but he'd said no and that was the end of it. She'd given him some cookies, also at her daughter's insistence. But she assumed that would be the end of their interaction. She'd even put the cookies in a disposable container so there was no need to return it.

And yeah, maybe she was a little bit sad at that. There had been something about him that had drawn her. He may have given the appearance of a bad boy, but she had a feeling he had a lot of good underneath the leather and tattoos. Not that leather or tattoos or any combo of those things indicated bad.

Careful, Libby, or you'll end up sounding like your parents.

"Well, thank you for helping to fix our mailbox, Hank. I really appreciate it."

"My pleasure. I enjoyed talking with that young man."

Libby smiled. If Nick Cabot had spent twenty years in the Marines and been out for at least two years, he had to be pushing forty. But she guessed to Hank, who was in his eighties, that was young.

"Mommy, can I take Wags into the backyard with his ball before supper?"

"Sure. Thank Mr. Jensen for the candy."

Libby went into the house and set the oven to pre-heat before changing her clothes. Back in the kitchen, she checked on Rebecca and the dog through the window above the sink. She took the casserole she'd put together that morning out of the refrigerator and popped it into the preheated oven.

She wiped her hands down her jeans and looked around her tidy kitchen to see if anything needed her attention. It was spotless, and supper was cooking in the oven.

Enough procrastinating, Libby. Call the man to thank him. It's the neighborly thing to do.

Telling her conscience to shush, she located the number for Nick's repair shop in her recent calls log. Glancing at the clock, she saw it was after six o'clock, but she decided to chance calling the business. She had no choice since it was the only phone number she had for him. She slowed her breathing as she stared at the number. Why did just the thought of hearing that mellow baritone over the phone make her feel giddy? She'd never had a reason to contact him in the days since he'd returned Wags, but now she was seizing the opportunity to reach out.

He'd definitely occupied her thoughts at various times of the day. Yesterday she'd heard a motorcycle drive past on Main Street while she was in her shop, and she'd scurried to the window to look.

She pressed the call button.

He might not answer if it was after hours.

Was that what she wanted? To leave a quick message to thank him for repairing the mailbox?

That would probably be for the best, she told herself. Except she very much wanted to talk to him. She might be an adult but the feeling in her stomach reminded her of the way she felt talking to a boy she had a crush on in junior high. That might not be the best memory, though, because he'd told her he didn't return her feelings.

"Full Throttle Custom, Cabot speaking."

For a moment she let the mellow baritone wash over her, let it release a swarm of butterflies in her stomach. *Please don't let this be like that memory.*

"Hello? Anybody there?"

His question pushed her out of her stasis, and she cursed herself for acting like that giddy teen she once was. "Ah, yes. It's um... Libby... Libby Taylor."

She winced at the squeak in her voice.

You're a grown woman, a mother, and a business owner. Act like it. Sound like it.

"Nick?" Now it was her turn to speak into the silence. Was he feeling as awkward as she? Was that even possible? He seemed so confident.

Forging ahead, she said, "I'm calling to thank you for fixing my mailbox. You didn't have to do that, but I really appreciate your thoughtfulness."

She winced. Did she always sound that prim? It was either that or start gushing, and she certainly didn't want the latter. What was wrong with her?

"I suppose the guy next door was waiting to tell you as soon as you got home."

Libby laughed at Nick's observation, thinking about her conversation with Hank. "Yeah, pretty much."

Nick's response was a low-throated chuckle, and that

sexy sound in her ear sent an electric thrill vibrating through her. It was impossible but she swore she could feel his breath in her ear. Even over the phone, Nick Cabot had the power to discombobulate her. What was up with that? She wasn't in the market for a relationship and she didn't do casual. She couldn't afford to, with an impressionable daughter. And in a small town like Loon Lake, if she started anything, the whole town would know. She had a business to run, so she didn't relish the thought of being the subject of juicy gossip.

Yeah, you're not losing it over this guy.

She shook her head and pulled it out of the clouds. Enough of that, she scolded herself. Nick was just being a good neighbor and here she was debating the pros and cons of a relationship with him. Relationship? What relationship would that be?

Getting a bit ahead of yourself, aren't you, Libby?

Way too far ahead. She needed to get back on track and thank him for fixing the mailbox. Maybe invite him to supper as a thank-you. If he said no, then that would be the end of it.

"I wanted to—" she began but stopped abruptly at a shout from the backyard.

"Mommy! Come quick!" Rebecca called from the yard.

Chapter Three

"I've got to go," Libby choked out before disconnecting the call.

Her heart threatening to pound out of her chest, she dropped the phone onto the counter with a clatter. She only cared about getting to Rebecca. Why had she let her go into the backyard alone?

Once on the back porch, she scanned the yard, seeking out her daughter. Rebecca stood in the middle of the yard all in one piece, with no sign of blood or evidence of injury.

Exhaling, Libby placed her palm over her aching chest and tried to recover her equilibrium.

"What's wrong?" Libby husked out, still breathless from the fright she'd gotten.

"Wags is gone again." Rebecca lifted her arms in a sweeping motion.

Libby glanced around the relatively small, fenced yard. Rebecca was right. No sign of the puppy. She had overlooked that due to her overwhelming concern for her daughter.

"Damn," she muttered and walked down the three steps to the backyard.

"Uh-oh, Mommy. You said a bad word."

"Yeah, I did." And wouldn't you know Rebecca had heard it. Her daughter had narrowed ear canals due to her Down syndrome, and her hearing wasn't the sharpest. And yet, she always managed to hear the things Libby preferred she didn't. At least Rebecca couldn't hear the words in Libby's head. Those were much more colorful and definitely not for young ears.

How could that dang pup have gotten loose again? She couldn't see any broken spots in the fence. "What happened?"

Libby regretted her question as soon as the words passed her lips. She hadn't meant to sound accusatory, but Rebecca's face crumpled and she began to sob.

"I'm sorry. It's…all…my…fault," Rebecca wailed.

"It's not your fault." Libby squatted in front of her daughter and pulled her into her arms to comfort her. "Just tell me what happened."

"I went to get his Fisbee from the box—" she pointed to the plastic storage container on the porch "—and when I came back, he was gone. I was a-supposed to be watching him. It's all—"

"No. It's not your fault." It was just as much her fault as Rebecca's, because she honestly believed the first escape was due to the gate not latching properly. But she'd fixed it, making sure the latch was secure, and she'd assumed the backyard was now escape-proof. "It's okay, sweetie, I'm sure we'll find him."

"I shouldn't have wanted to play Fisbee with him," Rebecca said between broken sobs. "Maybe he just doesn't like playing with me."

"Oh, sweetheart, no. Wags loves you. I know he does. We'll find him and figure out how he keeps escaping and then we'll talk to somebody about what to do with all the extra energy he has."

"You mean like Mr. Nick? Can we ask him?" Rebecca asked, her expression hopeful.

Looked like maybe her daughter had a little crush on Nick Cabot. *Welcome to the club, kiddo.* She sighed. "Let's concentrate on finding Wags for now."

"Wha-what if we don't find him?"

Libby hugged her tighter, refusing to even think that they might not find him. "Let's walk around the neighborhood before we panic. He couldn't have gotten far."

Rebecca pulled in a ragged breath. "Doesn't Wags like us? Is that why he keeps running away?

Rebecca rubbed her tearstained face against Libby's shoulder. At least Libby hoped tears were the only thing getting rubbed on the clean shirt she'd changed into after work. "Oh, sweetie, you know he does, but it's like Mr. Nick said, Wags is an adventurous dog. That's why you playing Frisbee with him *is* a good idea. It lets him use up some of his excess energy."

"I don't know what *'ventrous* means."

"It means he likes to go exploring." Libby rose. "You know what that means, right?"

She didn't want to let too much time pass since his escape, but she always took the time to explain things to Rebecca. And she wasn't going to stop now. She knew her parents often dismissed their granddaughter's questions with a "you wouldn't understand" no matter how many times Libby told them not to place arbitrary limits on Rebecca.

"You mean like Dora the Es-plorer," Rebecca asked, referring to a favorite animated television series.

"Exactly, and it means it's not your fault. And it means that it's not that he doesn't like us," Libby told her and held out her hand so they could start their search.

"Okay. I believe you, Mommy," Rebecca said and took her hand. "But I still wish he hadn't run away from us again."

"Me too, sweetie, me too."

At least she could take comfort in the fact the streets around their home were relatively quiet. She hated the thought of Wags getting hit by a car. Maybe searching for him with Rebecca wasn't such a good idea after all. She'd hate for Rebecca to come across an injured Wags. Or something worse. Libby debated calling Clara next door to see if she could watch Rebecca for a little bit while she looked for the dog by herself. Clara was always up for babysitting. She and Hank looked upon Rebecca like one of their own grandchildren.

Rebecca tugged on her hand. "I got an idea, Mommy. Why don't we call Mr. Nick?"

"Well, I—"

"He found him last time. Remember? I'm sure

he'd help. He's like a Good Samaritan. You said so, Mommy."

"I did, didn't I?" Libby sighed. She needed to be careful what she said, because for all of her challenges, Rebecca's memory was sharp. "Why don't we see if we can find him ourselves first?"

Rebecca looked up at her with a frown. "Don't you want to find Wags?"

"Of course I do." She hadn't counted on the dog being an escape artist, but she still adored him.

Not to mention you wouldn't have had a chance to meet and speak with Nick Cabot if Wags hadn't run away.

"Then asking Mr. Nick might help us find him faster," Rebecca told her.

Libby sighed. Even if she wanted to, she couldn't argue with logic. And she didn't want to hurt Rebecca's feelings, because she had a good point. Another set of eyes wouldn't hurt. And besides, he had made a special trip and taken the time to fix their mailbox. That must mean something. She just wasn't sure what that something was. "I left my phone in the house. We'll need it if we're going to call him."

And if he didn't want to help, he could simply tell her so. No hard feelings.

They went back into the house to retrieve the phone, only to find it ringing and vibrating on the kitchen table. She picked it up, intending to get rid of whoever was on the other end.

"Libby, talk to me. What is it? What's wrong? Is Rebecca hurt?" Nick asked as soon as the call connected.

"Oh, Nick, I'm so sorry about hanging up like that,

but I wasn't thinking clearly. Rebecca is fine, but Wags has managed to escape again. I swear that dog has some Houdini in him." She sighed. Today had been busy with a class and getting things prepared for her booth at the Founder's Day celebration on the town green. She didn't need this to end her day. "Rebecca and I are going to go looking for him."

"I'll be there as soon as I can," was his terse response before *he* disconnected.

She stared at the phone for a minute. That sounded like genuine concern in his tone. As much as she hated to admit it, she was relieved. She wasn't the kind of woman who felt she needed a man to "take care of things," as her mom would say. What Rebecca had told Nick about her mother's disappointment over Libby's divorce was correct. But that was because her mother was a bit old-school. Libby could take care of things by herself, thank you very much. And she had been, since the divorce.

But face it. It's sure nice to think someone might have your back when things got tough.

"Was that Mr. Nick? Is he coming to help us?" Rebecca pressed her palms together in a prayerful pose.

Libby nodded, her feelings a tangled mixture of relief, hope and misgivings. Was it a mistake to place hope in someone else's hands? The last time she'd done that, she'd been devastated. The man she was supposed to count on had let her down. And broken her heart in the process. Not that she was going to let her heart get involved in anything to do with Nick. She barely knew the guy.

But what she did know appealed to her on two very

different levels. Yes, she felt a physical attraction, but there was something more, something deeper—something she couldn't quite put her finger on.

And that was what frightened her the most.

Nick had been in the process of closing up shop when Libby called. After her abrupt disconnection, he'd abandoned the orderly routine he normally followed and begun dragging things into the garage bays so he could bring the doors down. At the moment, all he cared about was getting things inside. Neatness be damned. He'd tried a couple of times to call her back but there'd been no answer.

By the time he'd gotten in touch with her, he hadn't cared that she hadn't actually asked for his assistance. He was going to be with her and help try and find Rebecca's dog. And, God forbid, if the pup had come to a bad end, he'd be there to lend support.

He had no clue what had happened to his resolve to stay away. There'd be time later to figure that out.

He adjusted his helmet and fired up his silver Indian Scout. At the moment, the motorcycle was the fastest way to get him across town. If he located the dog—and he prayed that he did—the pickup would have been the more practical option. But the truck was currently jacked up in one of the bays waiting for the oil change he'd been planning to do this evening. The bike had been outside, ready to go. He'd figure out something if he came across the runaway. If nothing else he could hold on to the dog until they came to him.

Seeing a large canvas backpack, he grabbed it off the hook by the exit, went outside and lowered the garage door behind him. He put the backpack on, swung his leg over the bike and started it up. Despite being in a hurry, he took a couple of precious seconds to let the roar of the engine and the vibration of the powerful bike flow through him.

He shook his head to clear it and, glancing both ways, tore out of the parking lot. The bike thundered as he accelerated away from the shop. Now wasn't the time to examine the inexplicable feelings he had regarding Libby. Or didn't want to explain. Yeah, and when would that time be? Never. He'd help find that dang pup again and put Libby and her sweet daughter out of his thoughts. Out of his life. Living in a small town, he'd probably run into them from time to time but he'd say a friendly hello, and that was it. Just like he'd done after returning the dog the first time.

And how's that working for you?

It's working just fine, he told that annoying, insistent voice as he slowed for the stop sign at the end of the road. He didn't think about Libby's inviting smile that did strange things to his insides. Or the auburn highlights in her glossy, dark hair. Or those generous lips that begged to be kissed. Nope, not thinking about that at all.

Okay, sure, he'd gone over there to fix her mailbox. But he'd chosen a time when she wouldn't be at home. That had to count for something.

Before he could delve any further into his psyche, he spotted a fluffy, multicolored puppy gallivanting along the side of the road. The pooch was halfway between his shop and Libby's home. How the heck had the dog made it this far already? Was Wags on his way back to Full Throttle Custom? Probably just a coincidence. But it still gave him pause.

Now was not the time to ponder that. Nick down-shifted to slow the bike and brought it over to the shoulder, all the while hoping the noise of the bike didn't spook the dog. That was all he needed, to have the mutt run off again. Wags had stopped to watch him, his head tilted to one side, those canine eyes curious. But his body language telegraphed wariness, too. Probably ready to dash off if Nick made a wrong move. At the moment there was no other traffic along the two-lane country road, but he couldn't count on that for long.

He didn't want anything to happen to the dog. No matter how much trouble he'd caused, Nick had a soft spot for him.

He stopped the bike and engaged the kickstand. Removing his helmet and hopping off, he squatted and called to Wags. The dog must've recognized him, because he immediately came galloping over, tongue hanging out of the side of his mouth. As soon as the pup got close enough, Nick grabbed his collar to prevent an escape. Past performance proved the dog was adept at slipping away. At least Libby had attached an ID tag to the dog's collar. That, along with a microchip, would help ensure the dog's safe return if he ran away once more.

"How did you get away from them again?" he asked the canine as he tightened his grip on the collar and tried to decide what to do.

Keeping his hand around the collar, he used the other to undo his leather belt. Pulling it loose from the belt loops on his jeans, he removed it and looped it through the collar.

Holding the dog secure, he took his phone out of the pocket of his jacket and called Libby.

"I found him," he said as soon as she answered. Easing her and Rebecca's worry was at the top of his mind. He imagined them both sick with anxiety for the mischievous pup.

"Oh, thank you." She heaved a big sigh into the phone. "Is…is he okay?"

He glanced down at the dog, who smiled up at him in response. "Yeah, he's totally fine. I'm on the bike but I'll see if I can bring him to you."

"On your bike?" She paused. "Oh, you mean a motorcycle."

He grinned. "Yeah, the motorcycle."

"Look, I don't want you getting hurt. I can come and get him if that's easier."

He shook his head even though she couldn't see him. "Returning him is no problem. I'll be there in a few."

"Please, Nick, don't take any chances. I would never forgive myself if anything happened to you. Your safety is the most important thing. Honest."

Her words stirred something deep in his belly, but he couldn't stop to examine that now. He needed to get the dog back to them so they could see for themselves he was unharmed. And he'd like to check out the situation in their backyard to see if he could figure out how the dog had gotten away again.

"I have an idea. If it doesn't work, I'll call you and you can come to me. How's that for a compromise?"

She hesitated, then sighed. "If you're sure…"

"I am," he assured her, wishing he felt as confident as he sounded.

Face it, you want an excuse to go over there again.

If she came here, he'd simply hand the dog over, and they'd go their separate ways. Could that be what she wanted? No, she'd sounded genuinely concerned about him...hence those feelings unleashed in his gut.

He sighed and unzipped the backpack. Picking up the pup, he removed his belt from around the collar and nestled him safely inside. A tight fit but manageable. He zipped it up around the dog, leaving his head free and careful not to catch the dog's fur in the zipper's teeth. He replaced his belt and adjusted the backpack, wearing it in the front so he could have more control over the dog. Plus, he wanted to keep his eyes on the little rascal. Other than showering Nick's chin with slobbery kisses, Wags seemed perfectly content where he was and with his new adventure.

Of course, the real test would come when Nick started the bike. Making sure the backpack was secure, he started the motorcycle and waited for Wags's reaction. The dog startled for a moment but Nick kept reassuring him with soft words and ear rubs. It must've worked, because the pup didn't panic or try to escape.

"Well, here goes nothing," Nick muttered as he put his helmet back on and eased away from the side of the road.

Nick drove much slower than normal the rest of the way to Libby's home. Taking the turn onto her quiet street, he spotted mother and daughter waiting on the front porch of the pretty, yellow house. Rebecca had started forward, but Libby placed a hand on her shoulder and stopped her. Wags whined and barked as soon as he saw them. Nick stopped the bike, engaged the kickstand and loosened the straps to remove the pack.

"You seem pretty happy to see them, which is why I don't understand why you ran off again," he told the dog and unzipped him once he set the backpack on the ground and looped the strap of his helmet over the handlebars.

"Don't you know you've got it made here?" he asked softly as the dog wiggled around, trying to free himself.

"Mommy, look, look. Mr. Nick carried Wags inside his backpack." Rebecca turned to Libby. "That looks like fun."

"Looks dangerous to me," she said, and her gaze met his as he approached the porch.

Nick winced. He didn't want Libby to consider him a bad influence. "I only did it because it was necessary to get him home to you," he assured her.

He turned to Rebecca with as stern a look as he could muster without scaring the child. "You promise not to try anything like that?"

Rebecca gave him a solemn nod and made an *X* on her chest. "Cross my heart."

"Good." Nick nodded.

He pulled the puppy out of the backpack, and as soon as he set him on the ground, Wags ran to Rebecca. They showered one another with hugs and kisses.

"Kinda feels like déjà vu," Nick said, and chuckling in an attempt to lighten the mood, which seemed to have suddenly changed. He might not be the most sensitive guy, but even he could feel the sudden tension.

She smiled, but it didn't reach her eyes. Did she consider his behavior reckless? "I was very careful. I've been riding since I was fourteen. I know what I'm doing."

"Fourteen? That's not even legal," she sputtered, her cheeks flushed.

He shook his head. "Didn't matter to me."

"What about your parents? Did they find out? What did they do?"

How was he supposed to answer that? Tell her his father encouraged him so he could assist him in whatever scheme he had going? That Pops considered his juvenile son an easy sacrifice in case they got caught. Thank goodness they hadn't, or Nick's career as a marine would never have happened. He'd probably have died or been incarcerated by now instead of being a business owner and a respected member of this town.

"They weren't exactly the rule-following or hovering type. And if it benefited my dad, that's all he cared about." he finally told her.

"Oh," was all she said.

Had he revealed too much? His gut tightened, imagining her reaction to the things he'd done—some at the instigation of his dad—before joining the Marines, before deciding he didn't want to spend his life skirting the law like his old man.

Was that disapproval he saw in her face, heard in her voice? Was his confession the death knell on something that hadn't even started yet?

Chapter Four

Libby hated that she was sounding and acting like her mother. She honestly hadn't meant to sound so disapproving and judgmental because he chose to bring the puppy on his motorcycle. She could tell that Wags had been secure in the backpack and she didn't doubt that Nick knew what he was doing and was an excellent rider.

No, truthfully, that wasn't what had upset her. What he'd told her about his parents disturbed her. She hated the thought he might have had neglectful or even toxic parents. He certainly didn't look like a guy who needed a hug. Or would welcome one. But it still made her want to give him one for reasons she hesitated to examine.

And why was that?

Despite her concern for him over what he'd let slip about his parents, she had to admit that he'd made quite an enticing picture when he came roaring up on the motorbike. The puppy's head peeking out of the backpack across his broad chest had jump-started and melted her heart simultaneously. She wouldn't have thought that possible, but there it was. And his parents' actions weren't his fault. All she needed to do was look at her own.

She was also concerned because accidents happened all the time. Motorcyclists were at a disadvantage when tangling with a car. And while she would of course be upset if anything untoward happened to Wags, her first concern was for Nick and his safety.

She may have only just met him, but she liked him. A lot. She looked forward to getting to know him better. Even if what they might share turned out to be nothing more than a friendship. That thought made her frown. She'd like something a bit more than friendship, but she had no idea how he felt about her. At this point, she could only hope.

She wasn't even sure that was a good idea, because she was a single mother who taught quilting classes. Not exactly biker chick material. At least not from what she'd seen on television or in the movies. Well, if she was considering what qualities motorcycle guys looked for, she certainly wasn't sounding like her mother anymore. Joyce Langston would be mortified if she knew a daughter of hers was mourning the fact she might not be biker chick material.

So much for not examining her feelings.

"Rebecca, I think you need to thank Mr. Nick for

bringing Wags home. Again," she said in an effort to get her mind on the situation at hand and away from her suitability as Nick's girlfriend.

Whoa. How had she jumped from thanking him for bringing Wags home and thinking in terms of being in a relationship?

Rebecca bounded over to Nick and threw her arms around him. "Thank you for bringing Wags home to me, Mr. Nick."

"You're very welcome, Rebecca."

Unlike the first time, he seemed prepared for her exuberant display and even returned the hug with one of his own, making Libby smile.

"Now we have to find out how he keeps escaping," he said.

"Mommy says Wags is like Dora the Es-plorer."

"I don't know who or what that is, but it sounds like your mommy might be right." Nick chuckled.

Libby tried in vain to control her body's reaction to that low-throated chuckle. She was a grown woman—a divorcée and a mother, for crying out loud—not some teen in the throes of first love. Yeah, try telling her hormones that. Her palms felt sweaty, her knees weak, and a flush seemed to be creeping up her face.

"Dora the Es-plorer is one of my favorite-ist TV shows. Dora likes to es-plore," Rebecca told him. "And you know what? So do I. But Mommy lets me use her tablet because I has to do it at home. Does you want to see?"

"I'd love to, but first I think we need to find out how Wags keeps escaping," he said, frowning slightly as he glanced at Libby.

Damn her pale skin. Libby shifted her feet. What could she say? *I'm blushing because I'm having all sorts of inappropriate thoughts about you.*

"Oh," Rebecca said and dropped her head.

He squatted down in front of Rebecca and touched her chin with his thumb. "I promise you can show me your adventures after we find out how Wags got out. It will be better to look for his escape route before it gets dark. Don't you think so?"

His tenderness with her daughter made tears well up in Libby's eyes, and she quickly blinked them away, hoping he hadn't noticed *those*. "Mr. Nick is right. You don't want to go through losing Wags again, do you?"

A calculating expression was on Rebecca's face as her gaze darted between the two of them. "Does that mean Mr. Nick can stay for supper with us?"

"What?" Libby stared open-mouthed at Rebecca.

"Well, I…" Nick began.

"Puh-leez." Rebecca folded her hands and rocked up and down on the balls of her feet.

Evidently her pleading was contagious, because the dog began to bark and dance around in a circle. Although Libby had been caught off guard by her daughter's request, she couldn't help but laugh at the dog's antics.

Giving in to the inevitable, Libby glanced at Nick. "Will you join us? It's just spaghetti Bolognese but I've been told it's palatable."

"My grandpa says that to Mommy about her cooking. She says that word means it's yummy," Rebecca told him with a giggle. "See? I know some big words, don't I, Mommy?"

"You sure do, sweetie." Libby smiled at her daughter, unsure if Rebecca's backhanded endorsement was tempting Nick or warning him off. She looked back at Nick and raised her eyebrows. "So you'll stay?"

He gazed at her for several seconds, as if weighing his options. "Sure," he finally said.

"Yippee," Rebecca clapped her hands and bounced on her toes.

"Glad that's settled," Libby said, feeling as giddy as Rebecca but trying not to let it show.

The dog put his two cents in with a yip and a body wiggle.

His lips twitching, Nick gave Libby an expectant look after the enthusiastic reaction of the other two. He was going to be waiting a long time if he was hoping for her to bounce or wiggle.

"I'm extremely delighted you've accepted our invitation, but I'm trying to exhibit some restraint," she said, teasing him, trying to sound prim. But she spoiled it by bursting out laughing.

"I guess that's acceptable. And just so you know, I'm looking forward to palatable pasta," he said with a grin. "I haven't had a home-cooked meal in ages. I don't think those microwave dinners for one that I nuke count."

Rebecca scrunched up her nose. "What does that mean?"

He chuckled and playfully tugged on one of her pigtails. "It means I can't cook."

"That's okay, cuz my mommy is a very, very good cook."

Libby turned her attention to Rebecca, hoping Nick

wouldn't notice her flustered appearance. That chuckle was going to be the death of her. But at least she'd die happy, in a contented puddle of hormones at his feet.

"Sweetie, why don't we take Wags into the house and let Mr. Nick look to see if he can find how Wags is getting out." And she'd take the time away from his presence to compose herself.

She couldn't remember ever reacting this strongly or this quickly to a guy.

"Before you go in, do you have any idea how he might be escaping?" Nick asked, shifting from one foot to the other. No matter how tempting the food and the company, he shouldn't have agreed to stay for supper. If he were smart, he wouldn't drag this out or get involved. He'd only end up disappointing them at some point. Maybe not tonight. Maybe not tomorrow. But someday in the future.

His mission was to find out how the dog had escaped, plug the escape route if he could, then go home. And that was exactly what he should be doing.

Libby and Rebecca are not part of your plans. How hard was that for his wayward brain to understand? Evidently pretty hard, because he'd agreed to stay and was looking forward to it.

The fact she'd been blushing had his heart skipping a few beats. He couldn't remember the last time he'd made a grown woman blush, and he found he quite liked the way it made him feel. And he wasn't even certain what was making her blush but she seemed to do it while looking at him. Could she be experiencing the same feelings about him as he was about her?

His question about how the dog might be getting out had been a delaying tactic. Yes, it was information he might find useful. But he also had a need to prolong their encounter, if only by a minute or two. With this woman, every minute spent with her seemed precious.

Oh man, he was in trouble. He should have realized it when he found himself accepting her invitation to supper against his better judgment. The word *yes* had come out of his mouth despite the rational part of his brain urging him to say no.

"After the first escape, I replaced the locking mechanism on the gate, but I guess that wasn't the problem. Or, if it was, he found a new way to escape. For a crazy dog, he seems pretty smart."

He nodded. "Yeah, those herding dogs are reputed to be some of the smartest."

"I believe it," she said.

Where had he been going with this? He couldn't remember what point he was trying to make. "Okay, well, I'll figure it out. I'd hate to let a dog outsmart me."

"If you need any tools, there are some basic ones on the bench in the back of the garage." She hitched her chin toward the open door to a detached one-car garage with a late-model Toyota Corolla parked inside. "Or we can borrow from Mr. Jensen if you need something I don't have."

He nodded but was thinking about those lips. How would they taste? Would they be soft or firm?

Pay attention, Cabot, she's using that mouth to talk.

He cleared his throat and did his best to stand perfectly still. Marines didn't fidget.

"Sure thing," he said, hoping he'd gotten the gist of what she had been saying.

Strolling to the open door of the house, she put her hand on the doorjamb and turned with a teasing look. "Maybe I *should* let Wags out to help, him being so smart and all. Maybe he'll save you some time and show you how he got out if you say please."

"Ha ha," he said as she turned to go back inside. Still, he couldn't help grinning like a lovestruck teen at her. Damn, but he was getting in more and more trouble here.

"Mr. Nick?"

"Hmm?" He reluctantly tore his thoughts away from the image in his head of Libby's disappearing backside to see Rebecca had taken her mother's place in the open doorway.

You should be ashamed of yourself for your thoughts in front of her young daughter.

"I heard Mommy and I think she was teasing you. That means she likes you," Rebecca told him.

"Oh?" Now she had his full attention. Maybe he wasn't as alone in this as he'd feared.

The girl nodded. "Mr. Jensen next door is always saying stuff like 'I think you're teasing me, young lady,' to her and I know she likes him cuz she told me she does. So I think teasing means you like someone."

"Is that so?" He opened the door.

"Yeah, but Mr. Jensen says he already gots one wife and doesn't want any more. He points his finger like this—" she demonstrated by wagging her finger "—and says 'one is more than enough,' and then he winks at me."

After spending a few hours with the old codger, Nick could plainly hear Hank in Rebecca's imitation of him. "Yeah, I think the state frowns on bigamy."

"Big-a-what?" She scrunched her face into a frown. "You sure say lots of stuff I don't understand."

"Sorry. Bigamy means having more than one wife at a time, and it is against the law."

"Does against the law mean if you do it, Fiona Cooper's daddy will come and 'under arrest' you like on TV?"

"Yes, it does," he agreed, chuckling to himself. She must have been referring to Riley Cooper's daughter. Riley, a sheriff's deputy, was an acquaintance. Because he too was a fellow marine and not because Nick was on the wrong side of the law in Loon Lake.

Although he'd overcome his past, he was never really out from under its shadow. He probably never would be…not completely. If he got involved with Libby, he'd have to tell her more about his family. He didn't miss how appalled she'd been to simply learn that he'd been allowed to ride a motorcycle while underage.

Oh, sure, all that had happened long ago and he'd lived a different life since joining the Marines. He now lived by the Marines code of honor, but he felt the taint from his past hung around his shoulders like the stink of a skunk. The animal might be long gone but the scent lingered. But the code of conduct that he now adhered to meant he would have to tell her about his less-than-squeaky-clean background. Marines didn't lie and they honored their promises, so he'd stay for supper. But then he'd do his best to stay away, because riding a motorcycle at fourteen was nothing compared to some of the things he'd done as a kid. He'd been trying to impress his father and earn his respect. He'd mistakenly thought that if he did that, he could get him to listen when he pleaded with him to help his mom get off drugs.

"Are you going to find the hole Wags escapes from, Mr. Nick?"

Rebecca's question brought him out of his head, and he did his best to summon up a smile for her. "That's the plan."

"Rebecca," Libby called from in the house. "Come in here and let Mr. Nick get to work, please."

"Uh-oh," the little girl said and giggled.

He smiled at her. "You better get inside before you get in trouble."

Nick walked around the perimeter of the backyard, checking all the posts and pickets on the wooden fence. Halfway around he located a loose board. It wasn't noticeable, but when he pushed on it, it gave just enough for a dog the size of Wags to squeeze through.

"You wily little cuss," he muttered as he examined the dog's escape route. How had the dog found that spot?

He laughed at the picture of the puppy going around the yard testing each of the boards to see if they were loose.

He went back into the garage and found a hammer and some nails. Poking around, he located a couple of pieces of extra wood that looked like they had been left over from when the fence was originally installed.

Smart on Libby's part to save it, he thought, and went back to fix the problem.

Satisfied with the repair, he put the tools away and went back to the spot to double-check his handiwork. The new board didn't match the older ones that had been in the elements, but that could be remedied by pressure washing and staining all the boards.

Looking for more excuses to come back? What happened to his resolve not to get involved again after this? He shook his head at the thought. He could suggest it to her if the mismatched boards bothered her. That didn't automatically mean she'd want him to do the job, if she even wanted it done. Although, considering the pristine condition of the house and yard, even the old garage, she'd probably want it to look nice. He'd suggest it, and if she took him up on the offer, he'd do it.

All a part of being a good neighbor. He shook his head at that last thought. Next, he'd be answering all those emails from princes needing just a little financial assistance to access their lavish inheritances.

Rather than going back around to the front of the house, he climbed the three steps to the screened-in back porch. Voices drifted out from the kitchen as he reached the top step. He could see the inner door to the house standing open.

"Mommy, can Good Samaritans be boyfriends, too?"

Rebecca's question had him pausing before reaching for the door handle. Eavesdropping was not polite, but curiosity had him rooted to the spot. Was Rebecca trying to matchmake? Nick knew from town gossip that Libby was divorced and the ex was not involved in Rebecca's life. What sort of man walked away from a woman like Libby? Or his own child? Nick shook his head, hoping to dislodge that thought. None of this was his business. He should—

"Why would you ask something like that, sweetie?" Libby's tone sounded suspicious, as if she'd been thinking the same thing as he about the matchmaking.

"Mr. Jensen was in his yard this morning when I was out with Wags, and he asked me if your boyfriend finished fixing stuff around the house. Was he talking about Mr. Nick?"

"I suspect he was, but Mr. Nick is not my boyfriend no matter what Mr. Jensen calls him, sweetie."

Nick coughed into his free hand to announce his presence before pushing open the door. Of course he'd never mistake himself for Libby Taylor's boyfriend. He'd made a mistake like that once and sworn to never let that happen again. He and popular head cheerleader Melody Hampton had lost their virginity together, but when he'd asked her to the prom she'd been appalled. He learned then he wasn't the kind of guy "nice" girls took home to their mothers. The twenty years he'd spent in the Marines had only honed that bad-ass persona and he'd done nothing since retiring from the Corps to dispel that impression. Although for some reason the good people of Loon Lake didn't seem put off no matter how many tattoos he had or how much he glowered.

"Mr. Nick." Rebecca ran to him with Wags hot on her heels. "Is the fence fixed so that Wags can't run away again?"

"I think so. I fixed the loose one and checked all

the others. I don't think he can get out now unless he levitates over the fence," he said.

His gaze met Libby's across the kitchen, and she rewarded him with one of her smiles. That smile was a comfortable pleasure. He'd never given a whole lot of thought to a woman's smile and wasn't that a shame? He didn't realize how much he'd been missing. Of course it might just be Libby's smile that gave him pause.

"What does that word mean?" Rebecca asked, drawing his attention away from his thoughts.

"Levitate? It means he'd have to fly over the fence," he told Rebecca and winked at Libby, making color rise in her cheeks again. He liked that he had the ability to do that to her. After all, it was only fair, since she managed to fluster him with a smile.

Rebecca giggled. "Did you hear that, Mommy? He said Wags would have to fly to get over the fence."

"I sure did. Why don't you show Mr. Nick where he can wash up before supper."

"Okay." Rebecca started down the hallway, Wags once again at her heels.

Nick couldn't help glancing back as he fell into step behind them. She was already bending over to remove something from the oven.

Yep, he admired that fine—

"Here it is, Mr. Nick." She stopped in front of a half bath painted a pale mint green, with white lace curtains hanging in the small window.

Caught. Thank goodness Rebecca was too young to understand.

"And let Mr. Nick have some privacy, young lady,"

Libby called from in the kitchen. "That goes for you, too, Wags."

"I will. I promise," Rebecca called down the hall and Wags barked.

He winked at Rebecca before shutting the bathroom door. As he washed his hands, he paused to look at himself in the mirror. He looked the same as he had this morning when he'd shaved, but he felt different. Spending this time with Libby and Rebecca made him contemplate things he hadn't realized had been missing from his life.

Chapter Five

Libby removed the garlic bread from the oven and set it on the table before spooning out the pasta and sauce into one of her good serving dishes. She hoped the pasta tasted as good as it looked and smelled.

Unlike her ex, she enjoyed staying home and cooking a satisfying meal. Will had always wanted to be out and about and "seen" by the right kind of people. She'd been a dutiful wife in the beginning, but the endless socializing had grated on her, and she didn't miss it.

Nick came back into the kitchen as she was finishing filling the bowl. She glanced up, noticing he looked as if he'd finger-combed his hair, not that it was very long.

He reached for the bowl. "Here. Let me get that."

His fingers brushed against hers as he took the dish. That little contact made her skin sizzle.

"Careful. The bowl might be hot," she said, striving for normalcy when her nerve endings were still dancing from the skin-to-skin contact.

"No problem. My hands are pretty tough," he said and set the bowl of piping hot pasta Bolognese on the trivet she'd put on the table earlier.

She glanced at his hands but realized immediately that was a mistake. Unlike Will, who did nothing but push papers, Nick had working hands. The nails were neatly trimmed, but she saw cuts and bruises on the fingers. She tried not to imagine what those hands, distinguished in their own way, would feel like in intimate places. It might get embarrassing if she succeeded.

"Need help with anything else?" he asked.

Oh, God. Had he noticed she'd been staring at his hands? "No, I've got it under control. Besides, this is my way of thanking *you* for all you've done for us."

Under control? Ha, that was a joke. Her stomach was a mass of buzzing bees. She turned her back to him and busied herself with slicing the garlic toast and putting them on a plate.

A chair scraped across the floor. "It looks and smells delicious."

Libby turned to put the aromatic bread on the table as Rebecca came skipping into the kitchen, sniffing her hands.

"Rebecca, what are you doing?" Libby got out a pitcher of ice water from the refrigerator.

"Sniffing my hands."

Libby set the pitcher on the table. "Why?"

"So I could smell them."

"Again. Why?" Libby's gaze met Nick's across the

table. He looked as if he was working on trying to keep a straight face as she was.

Her heart did a little jump. Was this what it would be like if she had someone to share her life with? Sharing silly little moments like this with someone else, someone special. While she didn't miss Will or being married to him, she missed being part of a couple. The little intimacies and inside jokes that couples shared. Only she and Nick weren't a couple and Rebecca wasn't theirs, just hers.

"I like the new soap you bought," Rebecca said, sniffing her hands again.

"I'm glad you like it, honey, but sniffing your hands when you come out of the bathroom isn't a good look," Libby said and glanced at Nick again.

He lifted his hand to his face. "She's right. It does smell nice."

"Not you, too." Libby gave an exasperated sigh.

"See? He likes to smell it, too," Rebecca said she held up her hand, and Nick gave her a high five.

"Don't encourage her," Libby scolded.

She paused, and her stomach muscles tightened. If someone had told her two weeks ago she'd be scolding a man who looked like Nick, she'd have told them they were mistaken. And yet here she was, laughing, teasing and sharing supper with him.

Not wanting to be left out, Wags jumped up and started sniffing first Rebecca's hands and then Nick's.

"Oh, come on." Libby threw up her hands. Tsking her tongue, she said, "Let's eat before this gets even more out of hand."

Rebecca turned to Nick. "Mommy said out of hand."

He playfully lifted his elbow and pressed her arm. "She did, didn't she? Do you think she was making a joke?"

"Mommy, don't give up your day job."

Nick burst out laughing, and Libby tried to contain hers and failed. Finally, she recovered enough to speak. "Where in the world did you hear something like that?"

"From Mrs. Tavie. Last time we were at her store and Elliott's daddy told a joke, that's what Mrs. Tavie said and everybody laughed. Just like Mr. Nick," Rebecca said, her face beaming with pride.

Still laughing, Nick caught Libby's eye, and every thought in her head blew away like smoke. He might be rough around the edges, but God, he was sexy. After getting to know him as she was, she considered him the whole package. Not just sexy but capable of tenderness with Rebecca, and that made him all the more appealing.

"I don't know about you two, but I'm going to eat before it gets cold," Libby said when she finally found her voice. She dished out a helping of pasta for Rebecca and then for herself.

She shooed Wags away, and he eventually gave up and lay under the table with a huge doggy sigh.

Nick helped himself and took a bite. He practically hummed his approval. "This is delicious. Rebecca was right. You're a wonderful cook."

Warmth spread through her, and she preened under the praise because she could tell he was sincere. "Thanks."

He gazed at her for a second and opened his mouth as if to say something but changed his mind and turned instead to Rebecca. "So, does anyone call you Becky? Or maybe Becca?"

She scrunched up her nose and studied him before answering. "Why would they do that? My name is Rebecca, not those other ones. I don't *like* those other ones."

He rubbed his hand across his mouth and looked toward Libby as if for help, but she was busy sorting through all the things he was making her feel. Still, she should help him by—

He cleared his throat. "I see your point, and it's such a pretty name."

"Mommy says she named me after...after... What was she, Mommy?"

"My great-aunt, my father's mother's sister."

"I don't know 'xactly what that is, but it sounds important," she told him as if confiding in him.

"I agree because *you* seem very important, Miss Rebecca," he said, giving the information the importance it deserved.

"Uh-oh, that's what Mommy calls me when she's angry."

He pulled his head back in mock outrage. "I can't imagine why anyone would be angry with you."

"It's true," she said in a serious tone and turned to Libby, "Huh, Mommy?"

"Only sometimes," Libby told her. "Like if you say you brushed your teeth and didn't."

"Oh, that is a serious offense," Nick told Rebecca and helped himself to more pasta.

"Does you think Fiona's daddy will 'under arrest' me?"

"Well, if he tries, I will protect you," he said.

That simple teasing statement was like a seismic shift in Libby. Rebecca's biological father had basically rejected her and here was this wonderful man vowing to protect her. Yes, it was a throwaway comment to a silly remark, but it meant so much more to her. If she had been questioning her burgeoning feelings for Nick, she wasn't any longer. Whether he felt even a small amount of what she was feeling didn't matter.

Nick shifted in his seat. What he'd said had been a offhand comment but he found he truly meant he'd protect this little girl from harm. And those feelings had nothing to with how appealing he found the mother. Yes, he was definitely interested in Libby. Sitting in her kitchen, eating her cooking, talking and laughing about what amounted to nothing felt right. As if a missing puzzle piece had been found and put in place.

That didn't make sense, he argued with himself, because nothing was missing. Well, save for some home-cooked meals, he was doing fine.

But fine is just a little bit better with Libby, that voice told him.

"Mr. Nick? You asked me about my name, so can I ask about that arm picture?" Rebecca looked up at him, a solemn expression on her face.

He refocused his attention. "Arm picture? Oh, did you mean my tattoo?"

She pointed to his newest tattoo. Although it was almost four years old, it was still the latest. The elaborate and colorful Ouroboros wrapped around his left forearm.

"What's that for?" she asked. "It looks like a dragon.

Did you see *How to Train Your Dragon*? Is that why you got it painted on your arm? Mommy and I watched that movie and she bought me a copy for my very own because I liked it so much."

"Yes, it's a dragon." He smiled at her little monologue. "And no, I haven't seen the movie."

"You can watch mine if you want."

"Thank you, I'll consider your offer if I ever want to see that movie," he said, although he didn't think he'd have a sudden urge to watch a kids' movie. Unless watching the movie included watching it with Libby, sitting next to her, maybe putting an arm around her shoulders, and— Whoa. Where was all this coming from? He'd agreed to supper. That was all. He'd make sure the dog was secure in the backyard, then he'd walk away no matter how much Libby interested him.

"It looks like the dragon got its tail in his mouth." Rebecca shook her head. "That's weird."

He was aware of Rebecca talking but was still trying to dispel the image of Libby sitting cuddled up next to him. He shouldn't be thinking—

"Mr Nick? Is you listening? I asked why the dragon was doing that?"

He chased away the enticing image and concentrated on Rebecca. "That's the dragon's tail, and it's called an Ouroboros."

"A what?" She shook her head. "I don't understand what you're saying."

Nick sighed. How was he supposed to explain an ancient symbol of the eternal cycle of destruction and re-creation to a five-year-old? He barely understood why he'd felt the need for that particular symbol after he'd lost men in that ambush. Was it to honor them or punish himself with the constant reminder? "Well, I…"

She scowled. "Is it because I got Down syndrome that you don't want to tell me? I can understand things, you know."

"Rebecca," Libby said in a tone that sounded part admonishment and part concern.

Now he felt like a complete ass. "I know you can. It's hard to explain what the symbol means. But I can tell you I got it because I want to remember some people I used to know that died."

"So if you start to forget, you can look at it and remember? Like when Mommy writes notes, so she doesn't forget things."

"Yes, exactly." He admired her logic.

"See. I understand things," she said with her amazing smile.

He returned her smile and caught Libby's look of relief out of the corner of his eye. "Yes, you do."

"Why did you think I wouldn't?" she demanded, scowling.

"I guess because sometimes I don't understand." He shrugged. May as well be honest with her. The kid deserved that much from him.

Her face smoothed out. "But you's all growed up."

"Yeah, well, that doesn't mean I understand everything." Like his time in the Corps. He still had a mass of contradictory feelings regarding that time that had saved his ass and made him who he was today. But he hadn't been able to protect all the men under his command, and that weighed heavy on his conscience.

Another dragon, even more elaborate, was on his

back and continued over his shoulder to the front. He'd gotten that when he was stationed in Okinawa. The Japanese considered dragons a symbol of protection for the family and home. His family and home at the time had been the Marines, so it had seemed appropriate.

Libby listened to their conversation and watched the expressions on Nick's face. There was a story behind the Ouroboros and the other tattoos. She knew it. But it wasn't her place to ask. Maybe it never would be. Her stomach knotted at that sad thought.

"That's okay, Mr. Nick, cuz I still like you even if you don't know everything." Rebecca reached over and patted his arm. "You got lots of pictures on your arm. Does you have any others anywhere else?"

"I have one on the back of my shoulder that continues around to the front," he told her and frowned as if the thought were painful.

Maybe he was thinking about the physical discomfort of receiving a tattoo. Although she'd never personally received one, she imagined it would be painful. Or maybe remembered pain came from the reason for the tattoo, because she knew people got tattooed for very personal reasons.

Or maybe she was letting her imagination run wild.

"Can I see them?"

It took a moment for Rebecca's words to sink in. "Rebecca, we asked Mr. Nick for supper, not to take his clothes off."

At least not right now, she thought and choked back a laugh that bordered on the hysterical.

"Maybe some other time," Nick said and flicked his finger across the end of Rebecca's nose.

"We'll have dessert after I clear away the dirty dishes," Libby said and stood up. She needed to do something physical to dispel the tension gathering in her at the thought of a shirtless Nick.

"Can I get the tablet and show Mr. Nick how to go es-ploring with it?"

Libby nodded, and Rebecca ran from the room with the dog on her heels.

"Let me help," he said and jumped up.

"But you're our guest." Libby carried plates to the sink to rinse before putting them in the dishwasher. Did he feel that tension, too?

"You rinse, and I'll stack them in the dishwasher. And I really mean it when I say that was delicious. It went way beyond simply palatable."

"Thanks." She handed him a plate.

He slotted it into a spot in the dishwasher. "You know, you're pretty trusting, feeding me before I showed you the repair I made."

"I trust you." And she did. "And you did an excellent job with the mailbox."

"Thanks, but I do have to mention that the new boards don't match exactly. You might want to fix that."

"Right now just keeping that dog from escaping is my top priority."

"Mr. Nick, I want to show you." Rebecca came back in with the tablet.

"Sit at the table with it," Libby told her. "I can make some coffee to go with dessert."

"Sounds good," he said and took a seat next to Rebecca.

"See? I know how to find it," she told him and called up the YouTube channel she loved so much. "Sometimes Mommy fixes it so we can watch it on the TV. Maybe we can do that later."

Libby dried her hands on a dish towel and watched Rebecca show Nick her latest obsession.

"It's from all over the world," Rebecca told him proudly. "As soon as I learn how to read, I won't have to ask Mommy where all the places are."

"They're live streaming webcams," Nick said as he watched.

Libby held her breath, worried he might say something derisive, but his fascination seemed genuine.

"That's very cool. Looks like the owner of the channel put them all together so they run on a loop, spending a certain amount of time on each before moving on to the next," he said.

Libby exhaled. "It's just people within camera range going about their daily lives, but it's oddly addicting. It's fun to watch a street in Amsterdam or a ski area near the Arctic circle."

"I'm very impressed," he told Rebecca, who beamed under the praise.

"My grandpa says it's silly just to watch it cuz I can't visit," she told him.

"But someday you might get to visit yourself," he said, his gaze still on the tablet.

"That's what Mommy says. I can't read yet, but I has some of the places memorized." She pointed her finger. "That's someplace called Oxford. Mommy says it's a school and it's dark there because it's nighttime. Did you know that sometimes when it's daytime here, it's nighttime someplace else?"

He smiled and nodded. "I had heard that. These are fun to watch, huh?"

"Uh-huh."

"I love watching these with you but I need to show your mommy where I fixed the fence. Gotta make sure she approves."

"Can I stay here and watch?" Rebecca asked, her attention riveted on the tablet.

"Sure. We'll just be out in the yard if you need us," Libby said.

"Okay, Mommy."

Nick led the way out the door and held it open for Libby. "She really likes those."

"She does. I try not to allow too much screen time, but she's actually learning some geography because she wants to look at the maps to see where these places are. So I think it's pretty harmless."

They descended the steps to the yard from the porch and walked side by side across to the fence. A few times their arms accidentally bumped, and her pulse increased each time.

"I hope it was okay that she asked about your tattoos. I'm still teaching her about personal boundaries."

He shrugged and once again their arms touched. "Don't give it a second thought. I don't mind."

"Have you had those tattoos a long time?" she asked and winced. Was she too stepping over personal boundaries?

"They're a mixture. Some I've had for ages, but the

Ouroboros is the newest. It's less than five years old. Like I said, the rest are pretty old."

"How old is old?" She was as bad as Rebecca, unable to contain her curiosity, but she was old enough to know better.

"I got some when I was a kid."

"You mean like when you first rode a motorcycle?" The thought made her queasy. Where were his parents?

"A little after that, yeah." He stared at her as if gauging her reaction.

"Like fourteen or fifteen?" She tried not to sound horrified. "Isn't that illegal?"

"Not if you find the right person. Let's just say my father knew the right people." He put his hands in the front pockets of his jeans.

That lack of parenting had her wanting to put her arms around him to offer comfort. Considering his age, that gesture was twenty-five years too late, but still the urge was there. She knew there was a lot more to the story of his childhood than the few ambiguous comments he'd made.

As judgmental and narrow-minded as her parents were, she couldn't imagine growing up without someone who cared about what she was doing or what happened to her. She hated to think Nick might never have had that.

"I'm sorry," she murmured as much to herself as to him.

His eyes widened, then narrowed as he stared at her. "What are you sorry for?"

Yeah, what was she sorry for? How could she explain it without sounding as if she pitied him? She didn't think he'd appreciate that sentiment. She knew she wouldn't. And pity wasn't what she felt. Not really. If what he'd said were true, and she had no reason to believe it wasn't, he'd turned himself into a well-respected, successful man. And, according to many, a decorated war veteran.

He raised an eyebrow as if letting her know he was waiting for her response.

"I'm not sure," she admitted. Honesty seemed the best policy in this situation. "Maybe because it sounds like you might have had a tough childhood."

"What makes you think that? Because I was allowed to ride a motorcycle at fourteen? Or get tattooed at fifteen?"

She shuddered. Fifteen? She couldn't fathom letting a kid—because in her mind at that age he'd been a kid—get marked for life. Not to mention going to a shady tattoo artist. "You have to admit that sounds… dangerous."

"It probably was…but as you can see, I survived."

He shrugged as if it didn't matter, but Libby saw the tightening of his jaw muscles and the slight tick of a muscle in his right cheek. She sensed the situation held a lot more significance than that indifferent shrug would have her believe. It made her want to know more about Nick Cabot. What had he overcome to get where he was today? How much of a part did his past play in the image he projected? She'd perfected a bland countenance as a form of protection when strangers made insensitive comments about Rebecca. So she knew about not exposing a soft underbelly to the world.

Chapter Six

Nick stared at his feet and rubbed the back of his neck. He was a survivor all right, he thought bitterly. He'd survived, mostly unscathed, a childhood surrounded by neglect, drugs and criminal activity long enough to join the Marines. But what would Libby think of him if she knew he'd led his men, the men whose lives he was responsible for, straight into an ambush?

"Mommy, I'm done watching the YouTube places. Can Wags and I come out to play in the yard?" Rebecca called from the doorway to the kitchen.

Libby turned to him and he nodded. All the staining supplies were put away and the fencing was dry enough to avoid any problems.

"All the escape routes are plugged," he added.

"Good. I don't want her blaming herself for his escaping," Libby said, a slight frown marring her brow.

"Did she?" He hated the thought of that sweet girl taking on the blame.

"It's okay, she's fine now. She's pretty resilient."

"Good."

"Is what you experienced in the past part of why you chose to settle here in Loon Lake?" she asked and clamped her mouth shut.

Away from your family. He heard the unspoken part of her question.

She blushed and rushed on. "I'm sorry. It's really none of my business."

"The short answer is yes. And Tavie at the general store has mentioned before that you're a 'flatlander' like me so I assume you didn't grow up in Loon Lake, either," he pointed out, turning the tables on her. "How did *you* come to settle here?"

"Several reasons. I wanted a fresh start after my divorce. My great-aunt and Rebecca's namesake happened to be the previous owner of the quilt shop. She wanted to cut back before retiring altogether. So I came to help her with the business. I remembered how much I loved Loon Lake from visits with her as a child. I also thought it would be a good place to raise Rebecca. I felt at home in Loon Lake, so I bought my great-aunt's store when she wanted to retire full-time. I also purchased this home and settled permanently."

"You moved here by yourself?" he asked, curious about the ex.

Admit it, Cabot, you're also a bit jealous. But that

didn't make sense, because that was her past. And he should be the last person to fault someone for their past.

She nodded and he continued, "May I ask how long you've been divorced?"

"Five years."

His gaze went to Rebecca tossing the ball in the tidy yard and swung back to her. He gave her a speculative glance but didn't say what was on his mind.

"Yeah," she said even though he hadn't asked. "He couldn't handle the *complications* Rebecca represented." She practically spat that word. "All Will talked about was how everything that happened after Rebecca's birth affected him. Never mind that we had a baby that needed our help and support. He was busy acting as if things had happened to foil the life plans he'd laid out for us."

Angry on her behalf, he frowned, letting his gaze roam over her face. "Maybe I shouldn't say this, but it sounds like you might be better off without him."

"Oh, believe me, we definitely are." She nodded with a slight upturn on her lips. "And nice deflection, by the way."

He rubbed a hand over his scalp. "You caught that, huh?"

"Not even denying it?"

He lifted a shoulder and gave her a sheepish grin. "Why bother?"

She returned his grin with her own. "You don't have to say anything about your background if you don't want to. It's probably none of my business anyway."

"Let's just say I didn't win the lottery when it came

to parents, but I survived," he said with a twist of his lips.

"And according to Hank Jensen you survived several deployments to the Middle East during the height of the conflict."

"Yeah, that's me…a survivor."

His tone of voice must've betrayed him, because her eyes narrowed as she studied him, but she didn't say anything else.

Her obvious reaction to his confession of riding a motorcycle as a fourteen-year-old and getting tattooed at too early an age taunted him. He considered those things minor compared to the fact that for the longest time, he hadn't realized—or hadn't wanted to face— that his father was the one who'd supplied Nick's mother's drugs. That went way past being an enabler. How could he confess something like that?

What would Libby's reaction be to that bit of information about his family? She didn't have to say anything because he simply knew her background and her life experiences weren't anything like his. He should say something now, warn her, so she could decide if she wanted to get any further involved. But then she smiled at him and he felt as if he'd been awarded a prize. Her smile was an unexpected, and addicting, pleasure. For a moment, he was at a loss for words and they simply stared at one another, an underlying tension beginning to build between them.

The color in her cheeks deepened. Did she feel it, too? He hated to think he might be in this, whatever *this* was, alone, as he had often been in the past. Maybe his background wouldn't be the barrier he imagined. Did he dare believe?

"Were you going to show me the mended fence? You know, before it gets dark," she said, her lips twitching.

"Oh…yeah." Damn, but she had the ability to fluster him.

He pointed out the new boards, explaining how he'd found the extras in the garage.

"I know the boards don't match, but I think if you stain them all, they'll all blend in. I tried to nail the original boards back in place but they'd warped just enough that they split. Sorry I couldn't make the repair using them."

"No. No. That's fine. I'm just so grateful you were able to fix it at all. I'd hate for Wags to keep getting out. If he does, I'm afraid of what could happen to him. Rebecca would be devastated. So would I, for that matter."

"Then we have to make sure he doesn't escape again." *What's with the "we" business? This is Libby's house, Libby's life. She hasn't invited you to be a part of it.* Besides, would he want to be? He glanced around the kind of backyard he would have envied as a kid. Kid? Heck, he envied it now. Living above the garage was convenient but not exactly an advertisement for *Home & Garden*.

"What kind of stain would you recommend I get?"

"Depends on your preference. You could get solid or semitransparent or…" He stopped. "I can get some samples, and we can try them out before you decide. If… I mean…if you want."

"I want." She nodded vigorously.

"Then it's a deal. I'll check weather reports to avoid

rainy spells." He looked around at the fencing. "Your yard isn't huge, so it shouldn't take me long."

Her eyes widened. "You're offering to do the staining, too?"

Was he? He'd made it sound as if he was. "Depends… Are you offering to feed me again?"

"I'll feed you again even if you don't stain the fence," she said and then looked embarrassed. As if she'd revealed something.

"You've got yourself a deal."

Later that night as he rode home on the bike, he thought about the enjoyment he'd had during the evening with Libby and Rebecca. Strange, because he'd repaired a fence, eaten supper, and later watched live webcams from around the world. Not quite earth-shattering entertainment, but he wouldn't trade the evening he'd just had for a glamorous date with any other woman.

Good thing he had on a helmet, because he was probably grinning like a fool as he drove through the quiet streets of Loon Lake. Maybe Gabe was on to something when he traded his bachelorhood for family life.

Libby stood transfixed, staring out the window over her sink into the backyard. Only a week had passed since Nick's offer to stain her fence, and now he was out there working in a late June heat wave.

Shirtless.

Her tummy had fluttered at just the thought and now did somersaults as she stood watching the real thing.

He had what looked like from this distance a large,

colorful dragon crawling over his back and up over his shoulder. She assumed it continued to the other side. Did he have a fascination with dragons? She understood that those images usually represented something highly personal to the one getting the tattoo. What did that mythical creature represent to Nick?

"Oh, my, please turn around," she whispered as she leaned against the sink to be closer to the window.

She had the urge to touch that exposed skin. Press her lips to all that ink. Would the skin feel any different? Would it—

"Mommy!" Rebecca's voice dragged Libby away from her fantasies.

Libby sighed and gathered herself together. She was a mother, for crying out loud. A mother with responsibilities, and having such lascivious thoughts about Nick was…what? Natural?

Yes, because despite everything that had happened, she was still a woman. A woman in her thirties. Wasn't that when they said women reached their sexual prime? And she'd been divorced for five long years without so much as a date.

"Mommy? Are you even listening to me?"

Libby shoved all her thoughts aside. "What is it, honey?"

"Is Mr. Nick finished yet? Wags and I want to go outside."

Libby turned back to the window. He was putting the lid on the paint can. And, wouldn't you know it, he'd put his shirt back on. She sighed. How disappointing. "It looks like he is."

"So can we go out now?"

"I guess it will be okay now." Maybe she could go, too. But as that thought crossed her mind, the timer she'd set dinged. She had to finish preparing supper. As disappointing as that thought was, she didn't have a choice. She'd promised to feed him in exchange for staining the fence.

Did being jealous of Rebecca, who'd already left the kitchen, make her a bad mother?

"Ask him first," she called.

"Okay, Mommy."

"Mr. Nick, is it safe for us to come out now?" Rebecca asked, but she and Wags were already running over to him. "Can we teach Wags to play fetch?"

He caught both of them in his outstretched arms when they barreled into him. "I don't think dogs need to be taught that. It comes naturally to them."

"Then can we teach him to drop the ball when he brings it back?"

He laughed. "Maybe we can work on that."

Libby ignored the beeping timer and leaned closer to the window. Yep, no doubt about it, she was jealous of a little girl and a dog.

Nick joined Rebecca in a game of toss the ball and then try to get it away from Wags. As much as he was enjoying playing with them, his gaze kept going to the house. Libby was in there cooking supper. Should he offer to help? Maybe he could—

"Mr. Nick?"

He sighed and turned to Rebecca. He probably *was* helping Libby by keeping these two entertained.

"Could you please tie my shoe?" Rebecca thrust out her bottom lip. "I can't do it."

"Sure." He knelt down, she lifted her foot onto his thigh and he tied the laces.

She heaved a sigh as she put her foot back down. "I wish I could do it myself. One of those Twining twins at Mrs. Addie's liberry said only babies can't tie their shoes. They think because they're six they can call me a baby."

"Maybe your mommy can teach you," he said.

He started to panic at the tears gathering in her dark eyes, eyes that reminded him of Libby's. How old were kids when they learned this task? He'd learned at some point but couldn't remember what age he'd been. Damn. Why had he said anything? He should have done as she asked and tied the shoe. And left it at that. Problem solved.

Rebecca shook her head. "I wanted to, but Mommy says it's hard."

"Yes, it can be difficult but I have every confidence in you. I'm sure you can learn," Nick said and grimaced to himself. What was he doing interfering with Libby's parenting of her daughter? She knew best, and if she figured Rebecca wasn't able to learn to tie her shoes yet, perhaps she was right. What did he know?

It wasn't as if he had the inside track on parenting. He didn't exactly have shining examples from either one of his parents. He might know what *not* to do, but what he should do was another story.

Maybe Rebecca's motor skills were not developed enough for her to tie her shoes. Damn. Why couldn't he have kept his mouth shut? He didn't want to hurt either one of them by stumbling around and making mistakes.

"Did your mom say why she thought it was hard?" He couldn't take back his previous words, but maybe he could mitigate some of the damage he may have done. Find out exactly what the problem was and figure out how to correct his mistakes. If he could fight alongside men in battle, surely he could fix a misstep with a five-year-old.

"She said it was because I don't have the same hands like she does."

He frowned, unsure of her meaning. "I don't understand. Do you mean you use your hands differently?"

She held up her left hand. "I like to use this one more and—" she held up her right one "—Mommy likes to use this one. She said it's because…because…"

Somewhere in the back of his mind he recovered a vague memory of his left-handed aunt teaching him to tie his shoes. "You mean you're left-handed?"

"Yeah. That's what she called it."

He grinned. Relieved that maybe he hadn't totally bungled this and may even represent the solution. "Want to know a secret?"

She leaned forward, nodding enthusiastically. "What is it? I love secrets. I won't tell. I didn't tell Sam Mommy bought him a LEGO set when he invited me to his birthday party. Did you know Sam is non-non… I forget the word but it means he can't talk, but he and Teddy are best friends."

"That was very good of you not to spoil the surprise," he said, unsure if he was expected to comment on the other things. He chose not to. "This isn't really that kind of secret."

She frowned. "What other kind is there?"

"It was more a figure of speech. But never mind that. What I meant was, I'm left-handed, too."

"You mean you use this one, too?" Once again she held up her left hand.

"Yup." He held up his left one.

"I don't think I ever mets one before."

"And now you have. We lefties need to stick together."

She drew her brow together in a frown. "How come?"

He'd have to remember to be more careful of the things he tossed out in front of her. "It's another figure of speech."

"I don't know what that means but you gots lots of them fingers of speech."

He grinned. "Figures. Figures of speech, and yeah, I guess I do. But I also think maybe I can show you how to tie your shoes. Do you want to try?"

She clapped her hands. "Yes. And can we surprise Mommy when I learn?"

"Sure. I think that would be a good kind of surprise."

"She says I shouldn't keep secrets from her. Is this like a secret?"

"Hmm. I agree you shouldn't keep secrets from your mom, but this is more like a surprise…like a gift is a surprise when it's wrapped up." He didn't want to encourage keeping secrets from her mother.

"Like Sam's LEGO set?" she asked, a hopeful expression stamped across her features.

"Exactly."

"Like a present but you can't unwrap it."

"Right." He nodded. "I think your mom will still be pleased."

She clapped her hands. "Me, too. And then I won't have to wear baby shoes."

"Baby shoes?"

"I had some I didn't have to tie. They made a funny noise when you open them."

"Velcro?"

"Yeah, and Tommy and Timmy Twining both called them baby shoes."

"Those Twining boys sound annoying," he muttered, hating that she might have to put up with teasing. Was this normal childish teasing or was Rebecca singled out because of her Down syndrome? He felt a swell of protectiveness rising up in him, and its fierceness surprised him.

What was he getting himself into? He patted his phone in his pocket. He could pretend he'd gotten a text from a customer and had to leave immediately to see to some sort of emergency. He could apologize, leave, and not look back.

But he knew now, that wasn't what he wanted. Sure, he wanted whatever Libby was cooking for supper, but he yearned for everything else she represented that was missing in his life.

Panic started to claw its way up into his throat but he swallowed…hard. He was already in over his head.

* * *

Libby used aluminum foil to cover the corned beef she'd taken out of the pressure cooker. She put the strained cooking liquid back into the pot, added the vegetables and set the controls. Nothing to do but wait while the potatoes, carrots and cabbage cooked. She went back to the window, but they weren't there. What happened?

"Mr. Nick? So, is you gonna teach me to tie my shoelaces like you said?" Rebecca's voice drifted through the screened door.

"Has your mommy ever tried to teach you how to tie your laces?" Nick asked.

She went to the kitchen door. Sure enough, they were sitting side by side on the steps to the porch.

Oh no. Libby's stomach clenched when their conversation penetrated past all those thoughts regarding a shirtless Nick taking up residence in her brain. Was Rebecca trying to get him to teach her to tie her shoelaces?

Libby had tried several times but each session ended in tears. Before trying again, Libby had decided to track down a left-handed friend. If she had any. Who'd have thought it would make such a difference? At least that was the thought she was clinging to. She hated to think Rebecca might fail at that task. No, she wasn't going to give up yet.

"Yeah," Rebecca answered. "We tried and tried before she said it was so hard."

Libby winced at those words. She'd been frustrated when she uttered those regrettable words.

"Okay, so we're not doing something she doesn't want you to do, right?" Nick responded.

She started to open the door but stopped herself. Maybe she'd let it play out a bit more before she went barging in. Rebecca would be going to school soon, and Libby wouldn't be there to always step in.

"Uh-huh. She said she really wanted to teach me and we tried until I cried and she got that look on her face."

Libby smiled sadly at her daughter's honesty. Rebecca had a thing about being seen as a baby, so admitting to Nick that she'd cried meant her daughter must trust him not to laugh at her. She hoped Rebecca's trust wasn't misplaced.

"That look?" Nick asked.

Libby was curious, too.

"Yeah, it's the kinda sad and mad you get when you try but still can't do it. Even if it's something you want to," Rebecca was explaining.

"I think you mean frustrated, and yeah, I know the feeling."

"Fust-stated. Thank you, Mr. Nick. I like learning new stuff and I like it when you talk to me like I'm smart…cuz I am…" There was a pause as if Rebecca waited for him to disagree. He didn't, and she continued, "So can we learn to tie my shoe now?"

"I happen to know you're smart and I also think your mommy will be okay with me teaching you to tie your laces," he told her, sounding as if he was going to do his damnedest to teach her to tie her shoes.

Tears gathered in Libby's eyes but she blinked them away. No matter how the shoe-tying session ended, she'd be forever grateful to Nick.

The timer for the vegetables dinged and she set about finishing supper, trying not to think about her burgeoning feelings for Nick.

Chapter Seven

Nick blew out his breath after another failed attempt. Yeah, he could sympathize with Libby's frustration. But Rebecca was trying her best, and he'd keep his impatience at bay.

The cooking smells coming from Libby's kitchen were tempting. He'd think about that waiting for him. Maybe supper would be ready soon, and they could call a natural halt to the lessons.

Rebecca stuck out her lower lip after the knot fell apart again. "I don't want to hafta wear stupid baby shoes when I go to school."

"If the directive is to learn by school, we have all summer to teach you," Nick said in an effort to defuse the situation.

"You're doing it again." She sighed and rested her elbows on her knees, her chin on her upturned palms.

He stretched his legs out in front of him. "Hmm? Doing what?"

She turned her head to look at him. "Saying stuff I don't understand. Does you talk like that cuz you was a marine?"

"Maybe." He chuckled as the frustration melted away like ice cream on a hot day. Could those smells get any more tempting? "Do you think your mom needs help in the kitchen?"

Wags trotted over and dropped the ball they'd been using while trying to teach him to properly play fetch. He snatched one of Rebecca's sneakers and ran across the yard with his prize before either one could stop him.

"Oh no," Rebecca cried and stood. "He'll chew it up like he did to Mommy's and I haven't even learned to tie it yet."

Nick rose and loped after the puppy. "I'll bet your mom was angry when he chewed up her shoe."

"She shrugged and said that's what puppies do. She said she shouldn't have left it where Wags could get it." Rebecca threw the other sneaker aside and gave chase, too.

Nick spotted a stick lying in the grass, grabbed it and handed it to Rebecca. "Call him and see if you can get him to drop the sneaker in favor of the stick."

She waved the stick around, catching the puppy's attention.

"Toss it," Nick said.

She threw the stick and the puppy dropped the sneaker to give chase.

Nick swooped in and grabbed the sneaker. Holding it aloft, he said, "Got it."

"What's going on here?" Libby stood on the top step, wiping her hands on a towel.

"Wags stole my sneaker cuz I had them off while Mr. Nick was teaching me to tie my laces."

"He was?" Libby tossed the towel over her shoulder.

"Yeah but I didn't learn yet. But Mr. Nick says that's okay. We have all summer because that's the deck-tiv."

Libby gave him a puzzled look.

He grinned and shook his head. "I'll explain later."

"Go in and wash your hands," Libby told Rebecca.

Libby waited for him on the step. "Sorry if it didn't go well."

He shrugged. "She's been a good sport, and I haven't given up yet."

She smiled and leaned over and gave him a peck on the cheek with a murmured "Thanks".

Surprise had him rooted to the spot, fighting the urge to place his fingers where her lips had been. The skin still tingled.

Her face flooded with color and she jumped back. "I uh…er…um… Sorry."

"Don't be," he said, mesmerized by the glow in her dark eyes, her scent clouding his senses. He couldn't identify what it was but it was light and fresh, not cloying.

She reached up and brushed his cheek. "Sorry, I think I got lip gloss on you."

"It's okay. I—"

"Hey, you two, aren't you coming in for supper?" Rebecca called from the kitchen.

"We better go," she said, her voice a breathless squawk.

He nodded, too afraid to speak because his voice would probably be just as bad. Letting her go ahead of him, he stood for a moment to catch his breath.

Only fools expected happy endings, and right now he was their leader.

In the kitchen, Libby draped the towel she'd used to dry her hands over the handle on the oven. She fussed with it, making sure it hung perfectly straight.

Damn. What did she do? It was just a friendly gesture of thanks. A simple peck on the cheek. She'd done that on more than one occasion with Hank next door. And she had done so to Ogle Whatley when he came and gave her car a jump start last winter when her car battery died.

So, what was the big deal?

The big deal was that neither Hank nor Ogle made her heart race the way Nick Cabot did. Nor did she get that fluttery feeling in her stomach when either one of them laughed. Nor did they smell like leather and sandalwood.

Those times she hadn't given her action a second thought when she impulsively gave them a thank-you kiss for some kindness they'd extended to her.

Again, what was the big deal?

The surprised look on his face, the slightly panicked look in his brown eyes when she did it. That was the big deal, a voice in her head chided.

Sighing, she realigned the towel again as if her life depended on it. *Get the towel perfectly straight, or relive the moment her lips had made contact with his skin.* She could still feel his skin under her lips, the beginnings of a five o'clock shadow, the slightly salty taste of his skin.

She took the towel off the handle and tossed it on the counter.

"Mommy, Mr. Nick says those Twining twins were 'nnoying."

"What?" She'd forgotten Rebecca was in the kitchen dishing out some kibble for Wags.

"Mr. Nick called the Twinings 'nnoying," Rebecca repeated.

At last, something other than her own behavior she could concentrate on. She turned and did her best to keep from reacting with laughter or assent to Rebecca's statement, despite agreeing with Nick's assessment totally. "That's not a very nice thing to say, and I hope you won't repeat that."

"But—" Rebecca began to protest.

"I mean it, Rebecca. If I hear one word about you repeating something like that, no YouTube for three days."

"But I wouldn't be able to watch my cameras."

"Then don't say anything like that no matter who says it, understand?"

"Yes, Mommy."

Nick came into the kitchen in time to hear the exchange. He mouthed "sorry" to her, and she smiled to show him she wasn't angry. She didn't think he'd spent much time around kids.

"Let's eat." She set the platter of corned beef and vegetables on the table. "Oh. The water."

Nick waved his hand. "Sit. I'll get it."

He put the pitcher on the table and sat.

"Uh-oh," Rebecca said. "Mr. Nick didn't wash his hands."

"She's right." He jumped up and went to the kitchen sink.

After washing his hands he used a raised eyebrow to check with Libby before grabbing the bunched-up towel on the counter.

She nodded to indicate he could use it and dished out Rebecca's supper. "Do you want me to cut your meat?"

"I wanna try first."

"Of course." She knew the meat was fork-tender. She'd already tested it, not for Rebecca's sake, but because she wanted it to be good before serving it to Nick. What would she have done if it had been as tough as a hockey puck? Fed it to the dog and called for pizza?

She smiled at her last thought and caught him watching her. He slowly returned the gesture. Had he thought she was angry over his comment about those boys?

They carefully avoided discussing annoying twins during the meal. Instead, Rebecca talked about some of the things she'd seen on the live webcams. Nick then told her about some of the things he'd seen and eaten while in Japan. Libby listened, just as rapt as her daughter.

"Another delicious meal," Nick told her after they'd eaten and were cleaning up the kitchen.

Rebecca had excused herself to use the bathroom.

After she'd left the room, he heaved a heavy sigh. "I'm sorry if I opened—or reopened—a can of worms over the shoelaces. I had honestly thought I might be able to help since we're both left-handed. I know a left-handed relative had to teach me."

"To be perfectly honest, I hadn't realized what a difference it would make in me being right-handed until I started trying to teach her."

"As long as I'm being repentant, let me also say how sorry I am about the crack about those boys in her class. I didn't think about her repeating it when I said it."

"She's a sponge. Believe me, I've learned the hard way. Just last month when I took her to story time at the library, Linda Griffin, the new children's librarian, came out after and politely cautioned me. Something I'd said over the phone to my friend Addie was repeated. Talk about embarrassing." She shook her head at the memory. "Anyway, for future reference, be careful what you say."

"Believe me, I will."

She hoped the failed lesson hadn't soured him on spending time with them. To her, he didn't look like someone who embraced failure. "But you speak the truth. Even the preschool teacher says those two are a handful."

"Still, I shouldn't have said anything…at least not out loud."

She laughed. "Yeah, you learn to let most of that sort of thing stay in your head."

"So, don't say the quiet part out loud?"

"Exactly."

Just like she wasn't going to tell him how much she enjoyed kissing him. Kissing? Ha! It was just a peck on the cheek that couldn't be classified as a real kiss. But, dear lord, she'd enjoyed it.

She pushed those thoughts aside for later examination. Still, she had to clear her throat before speaking or risk another one of those embarrassing squawks. "How about some coffee?"

"Sure."

Nick took two mugs off the mug tree Libby kept on the counter and set them on the table. He got the jug of milk from the refrigerator and put the sugar bowl next to it. "Spoons?"

She pointed to one of the drawers. "Thanks."

Frankly, he enjoyed working around the kitchen with her. It felt right. Comfortable. She poured coffee into the mugs and sat across from him.

After adding milk and sugar, he took a sip. "I have to compliment you on all the encouragement you give Rebecca. For example with the live web—"

"Look. I'm going to stop you right there," Libby said, her eyes narrowed. "Why wouldn't I give her encouragement? Why shouldn't her future be limitless? It won't be if I start placing limits on her."

He reached out to touch her arm but she pulled away. The action hurt, but he couldn't blame her. She was in protective mother mode and Nick admired that. But he wasn't about to let her remain under the wrong impression about what was said. He may have gone about it all wrong but he'd make sure to correct that.

"You misunderstood my meaning. I was saying that because there are parents who don't give any at all, some that barely notice their kids let alone instill any sense of worth in them."

"I *did* misunderstand." She reached for him, placing her hand over his where it rested on the table after she'd pulled away. "I'm sorry. I guess I've become sensitive over the years. People aren't always kind even if they think they mean well."

"Your parents?" he asked. Oh man, talk about saying the quiet part out loud. He should have let it drop.

"They were devastated when I left Will. Blamed it all on me. Yes, I did leave, but our relationship had become toxic and I had no choice. I felt like a failure. I didn't need them confirming it."

He squeezed her hand at the pain he saw in the depths of her dark eyes. He couldn't take away that pain, but he could offer some comfort. "I know you and I know Rebecca, and he's the one who is losing out."

"Thanks." She swallowed. "Were you referring to your own parents? You know, before."

He hadn't intended to tell her about his childhood or the sorry excuse he'd had for parental influence, but now he felt he needed to. He was doing it to clear the air, not to garner any sympathy. "My interest in motorcycles was passed on from my dad."

"But that's—"

"I haven't finished yet. He didn't simply ride motorcycles. It was his way of life."

She frowned. "I'm not sure I understand. That doesn't sound so bad. My dad treats golf like it's a way of life."

He was going to have to spell it out for her. For anyone else, he wouldn't have done it, but he would for Libby. "He was in a motorcycle club and not the good kind. Not like the ones who ride for charities or deliver Christmas gifts to underprivileged children. The kind that breaks the law, peddles drugs, stuff like that. He used me as much as he could because of my age. He figured that worked in my favor. And his."

"But what about your mother? Didn't she protect you?"

"She was one of the gang's biggest customers for drugs," he admitted and tried to swallow the shame that statement conjured up.

"What happened to her?"

"She overdosed while I was on my first deployment." He managed to get the words out through his clenched jaw.

"Oh, Nick, I'm so sorry." She reached out with both hands and squeezed his arm.

"I don't need sympathy. I survived." As much as he craved her touch, he was afraid to want it too much.

"I'd say you more than survived. You excelled."

He freed one hand and used it to cover both of hers, the warmth from her skin seeping into him. "Well, that's debatable but I did survive. No small thanks to the Marines."

"How did you end up enlisting?"

"I hate to admit this but I was heading down the same path as the old man. Just a street kid trying to act tougher than I was, when a beat cop, Dan Ridgeway, took an interest in me. I can't imagine what he saw in that punk." Nick shook his head. He owed his life to him, and only hoped he was now living a life Dan could be proud of. He hadn't turned away from motorcycles but did his best to show others that good people rode. He did all the things his father hadn't, such as the holiday toy drives.

"I understand what he saw because I see it, too. I'm sure it was always there. And everyone else in Loon Lake who knows you can see it."

Despite the sincerity in her tone, he made a derisive noise by expelling air through his lips. "Ogle Whatley insisted I help him out with some of the younger vets. He gets us all together on a regular basis. He was at Khe Sanh in '68. Man, talk about traumatic."

She nodded. "Yeah, he and Tavie do a lot for this town. People can meddle in your business in a small town like this, but in the end everyone is very helpful and friendly."

"Tell me about it. I've tried to scare them off but they're a stubborn bunch." He huffed out a laugh. He had to admit that the way the town had taken him in made him feel like he had found where he belonged. After leaving the Corps, he hadn't been sure he'd ever find that again.

"It's true. Hank Jensen can't say enough good things about you."

"Mommy, maybe Mr. Nick can be your boyfriend?" Rebecca said from the doorway. "He's not too old like Mr. Jensen."

"What's Mr. Jensen got to do with it?" Libby asked.

"I asked him if he'd be your boyfriend, and he said he'd love to but that he was way too old and that Mrs. Jensen might not like it. And Mr. Nick said Fiona's daddy would under arrest Mr. Jensen if he married you."

"Good grief, Rebecca, what in the world are you talking about?"

Nick couldn't help but laugh. "Hank told her he

didn't want two wives, and I explained to Rebecca about bigamy."

"That still doesn't explain why you're going around trying to find me a husband."

"Because Phoebe told me how happy her mommy is now that she and Mr. Mitch got married. And she said Mr. Mitch's mommy is happy, too, because she married Phoebe's grandpa. See? Everyone who gets married gets happy."

"But, Rebecca, people can also be happy without being married. Isn't that right, Mr. Nick?"

She was looking at him as if she expected him to help out. What could he say without stepping on a hidden land mine? "Being married doesn't *always* lead to happiness. Married people can be unhappy, too."

"Is that why you aren't married to my daddy anymore? Cuz he didn't make you happy?"

Nick saw the cornered look on Libby's face. From what he understood, her ex wasn't involved in his daughter's life. He didn't know the details but he hated that agonized expression in his Libby's bright eyes, so he jumped into the breach. "Other people can't make you happy, Rebecca. You have to want to be happy by yourself first. People can add to your happiness but they can't create it. Do you understand?"

Rebecca threw her arms around Nick. "But you made me happy when you found my Wags."

He brushed a hand over the girl's dark hair, enjoying her eager display of affection, but he hoped he hadn't messed up trying to explain happiness to her.

"I think Mr. Nick means you were happy before Wags got lost and sad only while he was lost."

"So Wags made me happy?"

Libby laughed and shrugged. "I guess he did, but we were happy before we got him, too."

"But happier with him and with Mr. Nick," Rebecca said. "I just hope Wags doesn't try to run away because then we would be sad again. I don't like that he likes to es-plore away from home."

"That's the nature of the breed. Naturally curious and scarily smart, but I fixed the fence rail and pickets blocking that escape route. May I make a suggestion for the future?"

"Yes, please," Libby said.

Rebecca scrunched up her face. "What does that mean?"

"It means I'm asking your mommy if I can give her some advice," he explained.

"Why do you haf to ask? Why can't you just tell her what to do… That's what my grandpa does," Rebecca said.

Pink stained Libby's cheeks. There was a story there but Nick chose not to add to Libby's discomfort and stepped in. "I'd like to put up a dog run so you can tie him up."

The dog whined as if he understood, and Rebecca patted his head. "Wags doesn't want to be tied up. He likes to run around the yard."

"He'll still be able to do that," Nick explained. "If it's okay with your mom, I'll run the overhead wire the length of the yard, and I have a long length of chain. So he'll have plenty of room to exercise. And you have the perfect backyard for it. Not a lot of obstacles to trip up the chain links."

"You just happen to have all that?" Libby asked with raised eyebrows.

"Well… I, uh…" he cleared his throat. Had he over-stepped his bounds? Was the gleam in Libby's eyes mischief or annoyance? He normally didn't have a problem reading people. Ha! Mostly because he wasn't concerned with being an annoyance to them. But Libby was different.

"Yes, thank you. That would add to my peace of mind and make me very, very happy," Libby said.

Could he add to their happiness? He hadn't been enough for his mother to give up the smack. Nor had he been enough to prevent his guys from walking into that ambush. Sure, he'd been able to save some of his men but he didn't feel that could ever make up for those he'd lost. Could he be enough for Libby and Rebecca?

He found he wanted that more than anything.

Chapter Eight

Nick ran water in the sink at the end of one of the garage bays. He'd put up the dog run at Libby's to give them all peace of mind. Unfortunately, he'd had to do it when she wasn't home. They'd had trouble coordinating their schedules. She'd been busy getting things ready for a quilt show and he'd been extra busy, too. Boy, did he miss her.

Of course, Hank had been ready and eager to assist him with the dog run. It was as if the old guy had been waiting for Nick to appear. Libby or Rebecca may have mentioned Nick's plans for the dog.

"Riding up on a bike is hardly traveling in stealth mode," he muttered to himself as he soaped up his hands. The guy wasn't much help but Nick liked him. So he even stayed longer than necessary to shoot the breeze. Like Ogle, the guy had seen some serious action in Vietnam, so Nick had a lot of respect for him.

He rinsed his hands and shook them out before reaching for a paper towel.

"Mr. Cabot? Uh, I'm gonna shove off now. Unless you need me for something else. Then I can stay. It's, uh, like no problem."

Tossing the paper towel in the trash, Nick turned to Kevin Thompson, his new employee. At least he'd accomplished something productive this past week other than missing Libby.

"Kevin, I told you, you're allowed to call me Nick. I thought I heard you say you had a date tonight."

Kevin shoved his hands in the front pockets of his dark blue work pants. "Yeah, but it's just a casual thing. We were gonna watch a movie in her parents' basement. No big deal."

"Netflix and chill?" Nick asked and raised an eyebrow at his employee.

"Oh, hey, I never said, uh…" Twin spots of color appeared on Kevin's cheeks.

"Go. See you tomorrow." Nick waved him off. "Have fun but be safe."

"Oh, I would never—"

"I'm pulling your chain, Kevin. I'm not so old that I don't remember being your age. But I mean it about being safe."

Kevin grinned. "Gee, thanks. See you tomorrow, Mr., uh, Nick."

Nick watched Kevin hurry over to his motorcycle, hop on and roar off. Probably wanting to get away before Nick started lecturing him on being a responsible partner. Not that Nick blamed him. The kid didn't need his boss lecturing him about his love life, but Nick knew Kevin's father was very uninvolved with his son's life, so he was determined to take an interest.

He walked around, checking to be sure everything had been cleaned up and put away, a holdover habit from his military days. Satisfied that it was all in order, Nick switched off the lights inside the garage bays. Then he lowered the metal doors and headed around the side of the building to the exterior staircase that led to his apartment.

Although they hadn't served together, Nick had approached former Marine Riley Cooper, now sheriff's deputy, when he realized he needed some extra help in the garage. He wanted a decent mechanic, but at the same time, he'd wanted to give someone a helping hand if possible. Cooper had recommended Kevin, a youth he and his wife, Meg, had mentored. Riley said Kevin was a good kid, and they'd kept him on the straight and narrow despite an abysmal home life.

That sounded familiar, Nick thought as he climbed the stairs. His saving grace had been Dan, and Nick was pretty sure this was what Dan had meant about paying it forward. So far Kevin had proved himself to be a hard worker and eager to please.

Nick knew Kevin was taking classes at the nearby community college and deciding whether a career in the military was for him. Nick was doing his best to offer advice. But he also wanted to show Kevin he had more than one option. Whereas Nick had had none. He never regretted his decision to join the Marines, but he wanted Kevin to know the military wasn't his only path forward.

He made a mental note to thank Riley for recommending the kid.

"I must be getting old calling a twenty-year-old a kid," he muttered to himself as he removed his greasy work boots before entering the apartment. He chuckled because two months shy of hitting forty probably *was* old to someone Kevin's age.

And what about Libby? Does she see you as old?

He shook his head. Back to her again? He probably had six or seven years on her, so not exactly a wide age gap. It was definitely workable. Workable? Now, where had that thought come from? Damn, but it seemed like lately his thoughts were turning to Libby and her daughter more and more. He wasn't sure what he had to offer Libby, but she seemed to like him and he wasn't so noble he'd throw the chance to prove himself to her.

He didn't know what he could do, because he'd bet that Libby's dad hadn't spent the better part of his adult life a guest of the state. Her mother was probably the type to bake cookies and attend parent conferences at the school. Nick recalled Tavie Whatley, proprietor of the Loon Lake General Store, who had an encyclopedic knowledge of everyone and everything to do with the town, mentioning that. Libby might be "from away" as people here would say, but residents of Loon Lake had accepted her and Rebecca as their own. So Tavie had made it her business to know as much as possible about Libby's background. And Tavie had mentioned to him that Libby's parents were what some might call "the country club set." Had she been trying to warn him off Libby? Or just gossiping?

Nick was pretty sure many people knew about his background, too, but no one seemed to hold it against him. Gabe Bishop had told him the residents respected him for his service to his country.

Letting himself into the apartment, he slammed the door behind him. He had no business feeling sorry for himself. Considering where he came from, he'd made a decent, successful life. So what if his background wasn't in the same stratosphere as Libby's? Or that of her parents? She hadn't held it against him.

He dropped his dirty boots on a mat he kept by the door. Padding across the floor in sock-clad feet, he got out a frozen dinner and popped it into the microwave. While he waited for dinner to cook, he checked the plastic tub Libby had filled with homemade cookies for him to take home the last time he'd been there. Nothing but crumbs left. Maybe if he returned her tub, she'd refill it. That thought made him smile. Boy, he had it bad. Standing alone in his kitchen grinning his fool head off at the mere thought of a woman.

Ah, but not just any woman. A very special one.

The microwave dinged at the same time a hesitant knock sounded at the door.

He glanced at the microwave that held his dinner and grumbled as he made his way to see who it was. It wasn't Kevin, because he would have heard the bike. Who'd be visiting him now? He knew Libby had quilting classes tonight.

Maybe he ought to get a dog to discourage visitors. Of course, to accomplish that he'd need one that at least sounded fierce. Not some fluffy, friendly thing like Wags. That thought led to him thinking about Rebecca. And Libby. And her glossy hair, expressive eyes and lips that begged to be kissed.

As much as he liked Rebecca and the three of them spending time together, he needed to start thinking about how to get Libby alone so he could explore that enticing mouth.

He pulled the door open and stood staring, finding it hard to believe what— No, make that who he was seeing.

How in the world? He shook his head, thinking he must be seeing things. But no, he wasn't.

"Surprise, Uncle Nick." A girl, dressed in a black T-shirt and ratty jeans, stood staring expectantly at him from the other side of the doorway.

Nick blinked, barely recognizing his fifteen-year-old niece, Oakley. Exactly how long had it been since he'd seen her? Three years? Was this what fifteen looked like these days? She had on, in his opinion, way too much makeup, and was that an eyebrow piercing? Or had she had some sort of accident with an earring? And that hair. It was unnaturally black, with bright red tips. What happened to the sweet little blonde girl who loved pink and used to drag stuffed animals around?

"Oakley?"

She crossed her arms over her chest, revealing a tattoo on her wrist. It was a cat with angel wings and the name Aldo in fancy script underneath. "So you do remember me."

He was assaulted with guilt. He hadn't gone back home after getting out of the Marines because he hadn't wanted to deal with what returning to that environment entailed, hadn't wanted to get sucked into the life he'd escaped. He could see now that was pure selfishness on his part. He was stronger than that. But at that time he'd been mourning the loss of the men from his squad along with the loss of Dan, and hadn't trusted himself to make good decisions about his future.

Pulling himself together, he glanced past Oakley, expecting to see his sister, Beth. But no one stood behind Oakley. Just empty space. No Beth ready to jump out and yell surprise. Surely Oakley couldn't have come all the way across the country by herself, could she? "Where's your mother?"

Oakley shrugged as if it didn't matter, but the look in her eyes told a different story. "Probably picking up litter by the side of the road."

"*What?* What are you talking about?" He didn't like the sound of this. Not one bit. What had been happening to his sister and niece while he was hiding out in Loon Lake?

Hiding out? No, that wasn't what he'd been doing. He'd been making a life for himself. A decent life. A respectable life.

"Isn't that what people who are sentenced to community service do?" She shuffled her feet and suddenly, despite the clothes, makeup and hair, she looked like a lost little girl.

"Damn," he muttered and reached out to pull her in for a hug. No matter how she was dressed, no matter how much makeup she wore, he could spot the scared girl under the disguise. Wasn't that what he'd done? Worn a tough disguise to survive. Heck, maybe he still did. Only there'd been no one to give him a hug. Until Rebecca. She was a great dispenser of hugs.

He'd been close to Dan, but they hadn't been into physical displays of affection. As much as he loved the guy, as much as he owed him, he'd never given him a hug until the guy was diagnosed with terminal cancer. Wasn't that a shame? Now it was too late to rectify that. He wouldn't make the same mistake with his niece.

"Uncle Nick? Aren't you going to invite me in?" she asked in a muffled voice as she buried her face in his shoulder and hugged him just as tightly.

He released her and stepped aside so she could enter first. "C'mon in."

Once inside, she turned to face him. "I thought maybe you had a hot date in here you need to get rid of first."

"No. No hot dates." Despite his words to the contrary, an image of Libby flashed into his mind. She was hot but not a date. Not tonight, anyway. He shoved those thoughts aside. He had his niece to deal with at the moment.

"Is that your microwave dinging?" She glanced around his cramped but spotlessly clean and organized kitchen.

Muttering to himself, he went to the microwave and removed what had been going to be his dinner and set it on the counter.

She raised an eyebrow, the one with the piercing, at the sight of his frozen dinner. "Looks like you're really living the exciting bachelor lifestyle."

"Something like that." His mind went to the nights he'd shared home-cooked meals with Libby and Rebecca. Time and food was all they shared but those evenings were special, whereas the last time he'd had a proper date with anyone was just a fuzzy memory.

Glancing around, she nodded. "Spotless. Looks like the Marines rubbed off on you. I like the retro look."

"Thanks." As he recalled, his sister had been a bit of a slob. Probably still was. Of course he'd know that if he'd gone home. Fresh guilt gutted him.

Seeing Oakley's glance linger on his dinner, he asked, "Would you like that?"

"Do you mind? I'm not too proud to admit I'm starved." She fingered the strap of her backpack.

"Sit." He put the dinner on the table and got out utensils. He ripped off a strip from the paper towel dispenser and put them on the table.

Oakley pulled off the backpack and set it on the table with a thump. She began eating as soon as she got the fork in her hand.

He pulled out a chair and sat across from her.

She paused with the fork halfway to her mouth. "I'm sorry. Did I take your last one?"

He waved away her comment. "Don't worry about it."

The processed turkey and gravy dinner couldn't compare to anything Libby might have given him. He'd have to take Oakley to meet Libby and get a decent meal.

Getting a little ahead of yourself, aren't you?

He ignored those thoughts. "How did you find me?"

"Why? Were you trying to stay hidden?" Oakley narrowed her eyes as she chased peas around the small container.

He shook his head but his lips twitched with the need to smile. "If I was, it obviously didn't work."

"Yeah, some nice old lady with a hairdo straight outta the sixties at the general store was only too pleased to tell me where to find you."

"That must've been Tavie, and don't let her catch you referring to her as an old lady. She practically runs this town and can make life unpleasant," he warned.

"Oh? Sounds like you speak from experience." She spooned apple dessert into her mouth.

"Actually I was given that advice when I first came," he said, remembering how Gabe had cautioned him when Nick had mentioned he was considering staying permanently in Loon Lake.

"Ah, the whole 'we Marines stick together' thing, I suppose." She set the spoon next to the empty TV dinner tray and tapped the ancient, teal-colored Formica and metal kitchen table. "I see you're into the vintage look, Uncle Nick."

"I believe it's called mid-century modern," he told her, his tongue firmly in his cheek. The guy he'd bought the business from had left most of the apartment furnishings behind and Nick hadn't gotten around to updating them. What the guy had left behind was serviceable and that worked fine for Nick. He'd replaced a few things like the microwave and refrigerator and bought a big-screen television with a decent sound system. A man had to have priorities.

"I have to admit," she said, her gaze roaming around the kitchen, "the set works with what you've got going on here. A definite fifties or sixties vibe. Sorta like the lady at the general store and her beehive hair. What's up with that?"

He shrugged because he'd had the same question but never worked up the nerve to inquire. "That's something best left alone. Tavie must have been full of questions. Did you tell her why you were looking for me?"

And why did you come looking for me?

Fresh guilt assailed him. He jumped up and took the empty food container and tossed it in the trash. He winced, thinking he should have rinsed it out first. There were a lot of things he should have done and didn't. Like after leaving the Marines, he should have done a sitrep and personally checked on his sister and niece. He should have—

"I told her I was your illegitimate daughter from your brief but scorching affair with that porn star," Oakley said and sat back, waiting for his reaction.

"You what?" Oh man, he could just imagine something like that getting around town. What would Libby think? She wouldn't believe it. Would she?

"Would you rather have had me tell her I was the underage wife you'd married in Vegas and then deserted when you sobered up?"

He put his hands on his hips and tried for a stern look. "Oakley, of all the—"

"Calm down. I asked where the motorcycle repair shop was and she pointed me in your direction. She was full of questions especially since I wasn't riding a bike. I told her I needed to get here before you closed so I didn't have time to give her answers. But I assured her I would be happy to at a later date. She told me that you closing up shop wouldn't be a problem because you lived over the business and would most likely be home. She seemed to be under the impression you didn't get out much. Anyway, I didn't give her a straight answer, and she gave up."

"That was just a reprieve." He snort laughed. "Tavie doesn't give up, believe me."

He was surprised Tavie hadn't called him by now to try and gather information. She was so good that she could have been recruited by the CIA.

"Aren't you going to eat?" Oakley asked, rubbing her finger on the tabletop.

He had a few more dinners in the freezer, but those didn't hold any appeal. "You still hungry?"

She shrugged. "Well…"

"How about I order a pizza, and you tell me what's going on."

"Deal."

"But you're going to tell me the truth. The whole truth," he said, trying again to sound stern.

"And nothing but the truth. So help me, God."

"Oakley."

"Sorry."

He took his phone off the charger on the counter. "Supreme okay?"

"Sure, I can pick off what I don't like," she said and studied her fingernails.

He sighed. "What don't you like?"

"Mushrooms, anchovies, peppers, onions—"

He held up his hand. "I'll get pepperoni. Is that okay?"

"Sure. I can—"

"Half cheese and half pepperoni it is." He checked

for the number on his phone and ordered a pizza to be delivered.

"I guess this town isn't as backward as I thought if it has pizza delivery," Oakley said.

"Yeah, we have indoor plumbing and everything." Funny, but he'd had some of the same thoughts when he'd first come to town to visit Gabe. And yet now, he wouldn't want to be anywhere else. And that was due in part to his business. But not completely, *not since you met a certain single mother*, a voice in his head reminded him.

He also recalled thinking how contented Gabe was with his life as a husband and father figure to Addie's younger brother Teddy. Nick's mind immediately went to Libby and Rebecca, but he pushed all those thoughts to the back of his mind. He had a more pressing situation to deal with first. Like finding out how and why Oakley had come across the country by herself.

"Pizza is ordered. Now tell me how you got here."

He sat and tried to prepare himself for hearing things he already knew he wasn't going to like.

Chapter Nine

"Oakley? I'm waiting," he said, drumming his fingers on the table.

She gave him a mulish look and held up her thumb.

He pushed back his chair, the metal legs scraping on the cheap vinyl. He swore, using that all-encompassing word that could be used as a verb, noun or adjective, depending on the situation.

"Whoa. Language, Uncle Nick."

"Never mind my language. Tell me you did not hitchhike all the way here from California," he said through gritted teeth.

All his protective instincts bubbled to the surface. He felt conflicting emotions, too many to untangle. So much for leaving those feelings behind when he left the Corps. He wasn't sure whether to hug her again or take her over his knee. *Corporal punishment isn't allowed, Cabot.* But he could tell her to drop and give him twenty. Yeah, like a set of pushups would go over big.

"Um, Uncle Nick?" She glanced at his face and grimaced. "If you must know, I took the bus."

"The bus?" he echoed.

"Yeah, you know, a large motor vehicle that carries passengers on a fixed route for money."

"Don't get cute." Nick inhaled and prayed for patience. "You came all this way all by yourself? What were you—"

"What do you mean *all by myself*? Who was I supposed to bring with me? My mother who keeps saying she's getting her act together but never does, or Pops, who's a guest of the state. Again."

He pinched the bridge of his nose. So his dad, or Pops, as everyone referred to him, was back in jail? "What did Pops do this time?"

"Let's just say there was a dispute over the motorcycle parts he was selling to repair shops. It seems they fell off the back of a truck." She used air quotes around that last sentence.

How could he fault her for wanting to escape that madness? Hell, he hadn't even gone back after his time with the Marines was up. No, he couldn't blame her. "I wish you'd called me."

"I thought about it and…"

"And what?"

She shrugged, looking sheepish. "I was afraid you'd say no. You know that saying 'better to beg forgiveness than ask permission.'"

He rubbed his eyes. Would he have said no? He liked to think he wouldn't have, but he would have at least contacted his sister first. Who knows what kind of garbage she would have fed him. And it was a toss-up whether he'd have believed her over a fifteen-year-old.

Damn, but he wasn't liking himself very much right now. His first instinct was to phone Libby, but he wanted to get a handle on this situation first. He didn't want her to think he hadn't taken care of his family as he should.

"How long before the pizza?"

"The what? Oh, um, twenty minutes, maybe."

"Did you say you had indoor plumbing?" Oakley asked in a hopeful tone.

"Why? Do you need to use the bathroom?"

She smirked. "Since I've sworn to tell the truth, I'd kill for a shower."

"How long did it take for you to get here anyway?" he asked, feeling as though Libby would have all of this under control if she were here. God, he wished she were here to help. He was probably handling this whole situation wrong.

"Three and a half days."

"Damn," he muttered. The thought of a fifteen-year-old girl traveling across the country for three days blew his mind. So many things could have happened to her. Libby had been beside herself worrying over Wags traveling across town.

"I'll make it quick before the pizza gets here," she said in a small voice.

Hearing that tone had him feeling like an ass. He was pretty sure Libby would be calm and reassuring.

"Take as long as you need. I can keep the pizza hot if it gets here before you're done. There are clean towels in the cabinet and soap and shampoo in the shower. Sorry, it's just basic guy stuff."

"What? No choice of lavender or honeysuckle?"

He snorted. "I don't even know what honeysuckle is."

Unless…could that have been the scent of Libby's soap that had Rebecca sniffing her hands? That thought had his mind traveling back to that night. The food and the teasing and—

"Um, Uncle Nick?"

He shook off the memory. "What?"

"It's just…" She made a circling motion with her hand. "All of a sudden, you got this look on your face."

"A look?"

"Yeah, it's like— OMG, who is she?"

Great. He knew he'd been acting like a lovestruck adolescent. But he looked like one, too? He conjured up his scariest glower. "Shower?"

"I'm going. I'm going," she said but cackled with laughter as she shut the door.

"Mommy?"

"Hmm?" Libby looked up from the book she was attempting to read. Attempting because her mind kept going to Nick.

She hadn't seen him in almost a week, and she missed him. Part of that was her fault because she'd been traveling back and forth between Loon Lake and Montpelier for a quilt show. Adventures in Quilting was a vendor at the event, so she'd had to set up and work the show. When she'd finally had free time, Nick had been busy.

"How come you didn't invite Mr. Nick for dinner after he put up the wire for Wags?"

Hearing his name, the dog got up from his spot in front of the unlit fireplace and ambled over. He sat and looked expectantly at Libby.

She patted the dog. "I was out of town for the quilt show and you were with Grandma and Grandpa, remember?"

Rebecca frowned. "Grandpa made Wags stay in the sunroom."

Wags made a noise that sounded like a protest.

"And I heard you went and slept in the sunroom," Libby said but didn't scold.

"He was lonesome. We should have left him with Mr. Nick. I'll bet he wouldn't make Wags sleep in the sunroom all night."

"Maybe next time," Libby said and gave Rebecca a hug.

"Remember when I wanted to play with Phoebe and you said I should just call and ask her mommy?"

"Yes," Libby said, dragging out the word. What was Rebecca getting at?

"Maybe we can just call and ask Mr. Nick."

Ask him if he wants to come and play with us?

Libby pushed that thought aside with an inner laugh that she contained because it could easily have become a little hysterical if she let it out. Not having a man in her life had worked just fine since the divorce. So, why now? What was it about this particular man that had her thinking about things she thought she didn't need in her life?

Sure, Nick was handsome in a rough, unpolished way. The polar opposite of her ex and maybe that was the reason for the strong attraction. But, truth be told, her attraction to him went beyond anything purely physical and—

"Mommy? Are you listening to me?" Rebecca patted her leg. "Can we call him and ask him? Maybe he'll come even if he doesn't have to fix anything."

Libby laughed. Her heart skipped a beat. What if that were true? Well, the only way to find out was to ask. And much better than breaking something on purpose. "Okay, but he might be busy. He runs his own business."

"Mrs. Addie said he fixes lots of moto-sicles."

"When did she…? Never mind." Libby shook her head. Rebecca enjoyed talking with Addie Bishop whenever they went to the library, and sometimes Libby wandered off to look at the books, knowing her daughter was in safe hands. But maybe from now on she should hang around and find out exactly what her daughter discussed with others.

And to find out what Addie might know about Nick?

Yeah, pumping Addie or anyone in town for information on Nick Cabot would set Loon Lake tongues wagging. She didn't relish the thought of being the subject of town gossip. And what would happen if it got back to Nick? Imagining he might return her interest might all be wishful thinking on her part. Talk about humiliation if he found out and didn't return her feelings. But if he did…

"What if he *isn't* busy? What if he is home wishing for some of your sketti? Sometimes I wish we can have sketti and then we have it. Maybe that will happen to him, too."

"But he's already had my spaghetti," Libby pointed out, smiling at Rebecca's logic. Her daughter gave her affection freely, not worrying whether or not it was going to be returned. Maybe she should strive to be more like that. If it didn't work out, so be it. It wasn't the end of the world.

"Then we really should call him and ask him what else he likes."

"I suppose we could do that." After that peck on the cheek she'd given him, she'd been dreaming about what the real thing might feel like. "I'll tell you what. We'll invite him, but if he says no, we'll accept his answer."

"A-cept it? What do you mean?"

"I mean if he says no, we'll say thank-you and leave him alone." Was that why she hadn't called him? Because she was afraid he might say no? He might not be thinking about that almost kiss the same way she was.

Rebecca scowled. "Why do we have to say thank-you if he doesn't want to come?"

Yeah, why? Libby sighed. "Because we want to be polite."

"And maybe if we're po-lite he will change his mind and want to come."

Libby laughed. "Maybe."

She had to admit that Rebecca was one of the most optimistic people she knew. Grabbing her purse, she dug her phone out and tapped to call Nick.

"Libby?"

Libby had prepared herself for all the things Nick's voice would do to her. Or thought she had.

"Libby? Is everything okay?" he asked.

"Oh, yes, I just... I wanted to invite you—"

"Me too, say me too," Rebecca said, tapping her leg. Wags let out a yip.

She smiled at her audience. "*We* wanted to invite you to dinner."

"Tonight? Well, I can't..." He paused when someone said something in the background.

Libby's stomach sank to her knees, and her eyes stung. That was definitely a woman's voice she heard. She tried to swallow past the growing knot in her throat. "Sounds like you're busy. I can call back some other time."

"Wait! No," he shouted into the phone.

She froze.

"You still there?" he asked, sounding desperate. "That's my niece."

"Niece?" she asked as relief washed over her.

"Yeah, my sister's kid."

She heard a squawk in the background before he came back on. "Correction. She's my sister's teenager."

"Ah." Libby smiled, but her lips still trembled.

"Bratty teenager," he whispered into the phone.

Libby flushed, imagining his lips close to the phone. "Is there any other kind?"

His chuckle sent her senses spinning again.

"Mommy? Is he coming? Is he?" Rebecca bounced, and Wags did his wiggly butt thing.

Libby waved her hand to quiet the peanut gallery.

"So, uh, how about tomorrow night? Teens have to eat, too."

"They sure do. She just inhaled a frozen dinner and now we're waiting on a pizza."

There was more protesting on the other end, and Libby laughed. "What does she like?"

"Evidently anything that doesn't include mush-rooms, anchovies, peppers, onions or pepperonis."

"I thought you said you were waiting on a pizza delivery?"

"We are," he said with a sigh. "Oh, wait. I have further information. That only applies to pizza. Go figure."

"Go figure," she repeated.

"Just cook whatever you want and she'll eat it."

Libby laughed because she heard the implied threat in his voice. She found she was looking forward to meeting his niece. They made arrangements for the following evening before disconnecting.

"So, is he coming?" Rebecca asked as soon as she set the phone down.

"He is, and he's bringing someone."

"Who?"

"His niece."

"Will she like us? Do you think she'll like Wags? Will she play with me? Will she play with Wags?"

"I don't know, sweetie, but we'll make her feel wel-come no matter what," Libby told her and smiled. She imagined her tone was a bit like Nick's when he said his niece would eat what she cooked. But she didn't need to threaten Rebecca, because she was so naturally friendly. Of course, she hadn't hit those teen years yet.

"How do we do that?" Rebecca asked.

"Do what?"

"That thing you said…about welcome."

"Well, I guess we'll just have to be nice."

Libby got up to look in her recipe book to see if she could come up with something a teen might like.

As she flipped through the pages, she wondered what his niece was like. She had pretty much the same questions as Rebecca. This girl—jeez, she should have asked her name—was Nick's family and Libby wanted her to like them. He might have sounded a bit exasperated on the phone, but Libby caught the affection in his tone, too.

Yeah, she wanted her to like them. She shuddered at the thought of how unpleasant and critical her parents would be upon meeting Nick. She didn't like burying her head in the sand but she'd worry about that another time. Right now, she needed to find something to feed them.

"So, was that the woman who put that goofy look on your face?"

Nick rolled his eyes at his niece, but he was too content to argue with her. He still had to deal with Oakley, but talking to Libby had set him back on an even keel. "She's invited us to supper tomorrow night."

"You're doing it again," she said.

"Doing what?"

She pointed a finger at him. "Getting that look on your face."

"And you're deflecting. We are going to discuss this

situation first and foremost. You'll get to meet Libby and Rebecca tomorrow night."

"Libby *and* Rebecca? This isn't some sort of kinky thing, is it?"

He clicked his tongue against the back of his front teeth. "Rebecca is her five-year-old daughter."

"A single mother? At least I'm assuming she's—"

"Oakley. Don't." He pinched the bridge of his nose between his thumb and forefinger. He knew she was deflecting, but he missed the sweet kid she used to be.

Maybe if he'd gone back home, she still would be. Would Libby see his not going back as selfish? Would he be able to explain how he'd been afraid of getting sucked into something he might not be able to walk away from a second time? Did he want to admit this and be seen as weak?

"Uncle Nick? I'm sorry. It seems you really like this woman and I didn't mean to…well, you know." She shrugged.

Yeah, he knew. "It's okay, but we will be setting ground rules. Where are your dirty clothes? I'll start a load in the washer."

She jumped up from the chair. "I left them in the bathroom. Let me get them. I have some in my backpack that need washing, too. I did my best to keep clean when the bus stopped at rest areas or truck stops."

Truck stops? He had a few choice words for his sister and her conduct toward her daughter.

While Oakley was in the bathroom, he picked up her shabby backpack. He made a mental note to take her shopping tomorrow to a mall in one of the bigger surrounding towns.

"And what do we have here?" Nick asked as he reached in and pulled out a scruffy-looking blue stuffed rabbit. "Could this possibly be Blue Bunny?"

"Hey. Give me that," she snarled, making a grab for the item. "Talk about boundaries."

He easily pulled it out of reach. "This looks familiar... Isn't this the one I bought you when I came back on leave to meet you for the first time?"

She'd been nearly two, and the guilt from not going back sooner still stabbed him in the gut. How could he have waited that long to see her? He must be the worst uncle on the planet.

"It might be." Oakley stuck out her chin. "So what if it is?"

"I'm honored you kept it."

"Yeah...well." She shrugged.

He went with his gut and pulled her in for a hug.

She returned the hug before pushing away. "Hey, hey, let's not get carried away. Since when have we been a family prone to displays of affection?"

"Since right now. So get used to it."

Oakley grinned. "I guess this Libby really is rubbing off on you."

"Libby is an off-limits topic until we discuss you, young lady."

"I thought you were going to wash clothes."

"Sit yourself down in that chair. I'll throw these in and be right back."

After throwing Oakley's clothes in the washer, he dealt with the pizza delivery.

"He called you by name. Order pizza much?" Oakley asked.

"It's a small town. Everyone knows everyone," he said. Half the town probably already knew about his guest—and her pizza preference.

He set the pizza box in center of the table and they ate in silence for a few minutes before he decided he needed answers.

"So, what did your mom say when you told her you were coming to find me?" he asked. If Beth was going to show up, too, he needed to be prepared. Oakley didn't answer and he set his slice of pizza back on the plate. "Does she know you're here?"

"Like I said, she probably hasn't noticed I'm gone. We got kicked out of the apartment for nonpayment of rent. I could stay in a fleabag motel with her or stay with a…a friend."

What the hell was wrong with his sister? She had a daughter. He thought about Libby and how protective she was of Rebecca. He couldn't imagine Libby letting Oakley travel across the country by herself. "Who were you staying with?"

"His name is Ramon, and no, it's not like that. We're friends. That's all."

"What about your mother? How did she feel about that?"

Oakley snorted. "Like I said, I'm not sure she noticed. Beth has more issues than National Geographic."

"That's no way to talk about your mother," he scolded. Even if it was the truth. And what was with Oakley calling her mother by her first name?

Damn. He felt a tightening in the pit of his stomach. Why hadn't he gone back and settled closer to family once he got out? He should have kept closer tabs on

Oakley. And his sister, for that matter. Instead, he'd stayed in Loon Lake, hoping the small town and its people would help him heal. God, he was such a selfish bastard.

His sister hadn't had the benefit of someone like Dan to give her a chance to turn her life around. If he'd stayed, he could have been that stable person for her. Or he might have gotten sucked into the abyss like his sister and mother.

"You really should have called me. I would have sent money for the train or a plane."

She made a derisive sound with her tongue against her teeth. "Yeah, right. You would have told me to patch things up with Beth. Suck it up, kid."

"I would nev—" he started and broke off. "Okay. I would have urged you to work things out with your mom."

He looked at Oakley and had to acknowledge that maybe it was past time for working things out. He'd find out what was going on with his sister, but in the meantime he'd make sure Oakley was clean, fed and safe.

He pushed a hand through his short hair. Those all sounded so…so basic. His heart ached for his niece. She should be hanging out at the mall with her friends or getting manicures or whatever it was that girls her age liked to do.

Maybe Libby would have some answers. He'd known her for a short time but she was fast becoming a crucial part of his life. She featured in his decisions and he thought of her when he needed answers.

Chapter Ten

"So, are you going to spill?" Oakley asked Nick as they got into his truck to drive over to Libby's the next evening.

"Spill what?" Nick countered, trying to sound like this was no big deal. And it wasn't, was it?

"Like what's going on with the two of you."

"Nothing's going on."

"Uh-huh," Oakley said in a tone laced with skepticism.

"What makes you think this is more than a casual friend inviting us to supper. People do that, you know."

"Uh-huh."

"Oakley," he said with a note of warning.

"Well, for one thing you showered."

"I was working in the shop all day. I shower most evenings."

"And you shaved. And..." She leaned over and sniffed. "You're wearing aftershave or cologne or something. And looks like those are new jeans."

"So I cleaned up a little," he grumbled. "You're wearing new jeans, too. At least mine aren't riddled with holes and tears."

She laughed. "Nice deflection but it won't work. Tell me about her."

He sighed. As much as he was looking forward to seeing Libby again, he didn't appreciate the third degree from his niece. It wouldn't matter except he had a feeling he might reveal too much. Since she'd mentioned it, he'd been mindful of his facial expressions when thinking of Libby.

"How old did you say Rebecca was?" Oakley asked.

"Five." If Nick didn't know better, he'd say Oakley was nervous about meeting them.

Well, why not? He was nervous about this meeting, too. He wanted Libby to like Oakley and vice versa. After the conversation—if you could call it that—he'd had with his sister last night, he knew Oakley would be staying with him for the foreseeable future. He wouldn't send her back to a toxic environment. He'd waited until Oakley had gone to bed to call, and he was glad he had.

Beth kept promising she was getting her act together but Nick suspected she was high even as they spoke. She seemed surprised when he told her Oakley was with him. She'd asked why he hadn't come to see her if he was in California. He wasn't sure she understood when he tried to explain that he wasn't, that Oakley was with him in Loon Lake. He'd hung up in disgust and contacted Gabe to request information about a family attorney. Nick knew Gabe's wife, Addie, had applied for permanent guardianship for her much younger brother. Nick would follow the steps for applying for guardianship over Oakley. He wasn't going to let anything happen to her on his watch.

"And Libby's a single mother?"

Oakley's question broke into his thoughts. "Yeah. I've already told you all this."

"I'm just verifying your story."

"It's not a story. It's the truth," he said through his clenched jaw.

"The whole truth and nothing but the— Okay. Okay." She threw up her hands when he glared at her. "And how did you meet?"

Damn. He should have driven them over on the motorcycle and avoided the interrogation. "Libby owns a quilt shop."

Oakley stared at him from the passenger side. "And you've taken up quilting?"

"Ha ha. I returned Rebecca's lost dog."

"And the pet finder strikes again," she said with a lighthearted laugh. "Did she find you from the internet?"

"No, her dog found me. But she'd posted on the site, and I contacted her."

"That must have been touching scene. Is that why she's inviting you, I mean us, for supper?"

He made a sound of agreement in his throat. He needed to admit this would be his third time dining with Libby and Rebecca, because it would come out. He didn't want to make it seem like he was hiding anything.

"Gee, Uncle Nick, something makes me think there's more to this story than what you're telling me."

"The dog likes to escape and Libby likes to cook to show her appreciation."

"Uh-huh."

"We're here," he said and pulled into her driveway.

"What a cute house. Does she cook as good as the house indicates?"

"Yeah, she—" he started but broke off when he detected a note of…what? Something in Oakley's voice and the way she was staring at the home. It reminded him of his reaction the first time he saw Libby's house. "What does her house have to do with her ability to cook?"

"I dunno… It just looks so…"

"Like a sixties' family sitcom?"

"Like a dream home. I always wished I could live in a place like this. The kind of place you could bring friends home to, ya know?"

He reached over and took Oakley's hand. "Yes, I know. It's different from what we've been used to. It looks like—"

"Like we don't belong," Oakley whispered.

He squeezed her hand before dropping it. "Sweetheart, don't think like that."

Why not? You did when you first saw it. Still do, if you're being honest.

"You're right, we're as good as everyone else," Oakley said, sounding as if she were trying to reassure herself.

"Damn right," he said, hoping he sounded convincing. He didn't want her to ever feel less.

This might not be the ideal time to bring up two things he'd observed but he forged ahead. The tattoo was important but the reason behind it might be even more important and he'd been ignoring it, not wanting to deal with the fact Oakley's cat had died.

"I see you wore long sleeves," he said and touched the cuff of the shirt she'd bought at the mall he'd taken her to that afternoon. He'd left Kevin in charge while he took Oakley shopping. He did blame the kid for looking askance at him when he'd announced he was leaving early to go to a mall.

"Yeah. So?" she said, her tone defensive.

"You don't have to hide that tattoo from Libby." At least he hoped she didn't.

"I know." She crossed her arms. "I just liked the shirt. Okay?"

He touched her arm. "I'm sorry. About Aldo, I mean."

Considering her age, she'd owned that scrappy orange tabby with the tattered ear for most of her life.

"Like Mom said, he was old and sick," she said, her voice thick.

Nick's eyes stung. Had anyone been there to hold her while she cried over her cat? Once again, he damned his sister. "Doesn't change the fact that it must have sucked."

"Big-time, but that was last year. I'm okay now."

God, he shouldn't have started this now. What a jerk.

He gave her arm a squeeze before letting go. But he couldn't let the subject go that easily.

"Grief doesn't work like that. Some days it doesn't matter if it's been three hours or three years because it all feels the same," he said, thinking of Dan.

"Thanks."

She leaned toward him and he hugged her as best as he could across the bench seat.

"So," she said, pulling away. "Did you say this woman is a good cook?"

"Did I?" he asked, grateful for the change of subject.

"Yeah, you did." She opened her door. "How many times have you been here for supper?"

"A couple of times," he tried to sound as casual as possible.

"Oh?" She turned back before jumping out of the truck.

"If you must know, her dog escaped again and I returned it." He scratched his cheek.

"And?"

"And I repaired the fence so the dog couldn't get out again. And, uh, fixed her mailbox. Stained her fence. Set up a dog run."

"So you're her handyman?" There was a note of amusement in her voice.

Nick muttered under his breath and sighed. "Just be nice. No stories about porn stars or underage wives."

He climbed out of the truck and reached into the back to pull out a box. He handed it to Oakley when she came around to his side. "Here, give them this."

She raised her eyebrows. "Chocolates? And the fancy stuff, too. That's impressive for a handyman."

He grumbled something about respecting your elders. Aloud, he said, "Don't drop them and don't let the dog get them. Chocolate isn't good for dogs."

She mumbled a phrase that included a bodily function and Sherlock, but he let it go. The front door of the pretty, yellow house was already opening.

"Mommy, they're here." Rebecca called from her position at the front windows in the living room.

"Hooray and I'm not even in the bathroom. Will wonders never cease?" Libby said and set the oven mitts on the counter.

She walked out of the kitchen and realized she was still wearing her apron. Quickly untying it, she tossed it over the back of a chair in the living room.

Rebecca and Wags were already on the porch.

"Well, hello, you two," Nick greeted them.

Wags barked and Rebecca rushed to give Nick a hug.

Libby arrived at the door in time to hear his niece say to him, "I understand that huggy thing now."

What did that mean? No time to worry about that now. She smoothed down the lightweight cotton knit sweater she'd chosen for tonight and stepped onto the porch. Rebecca and the dog were jumping around and creating chaos.

"Rebecca, let them at least get in the house before we bombard them."

"Are those for me?" Rebecca pointed to a box his niece was carrying.

"Rebecca, manners," she admonished, but the teenager laughed and turned to her uncle.

"I like her," she told him and handed the candy to Rebecca. "I think you're supposed to share with your mom. But not the dog."

Libby grabbed the dog's collar when he tried started sniffing the box, and Nick spread his arms and herded everyone inside. To anyone watching them, it would look like a typical family scene. Libby's heart squeezed at the thought. If only...

Once inside, Nick closed the door and said, "Libby, I'd like you to meet my niece, Oakley. And this is Rebecca."

"Nice to meet you," Oakley said and shook hands with Libby.

"I like your name," Rebecca said.

"Thank you. I like yours." Oakley said and rubbed the dog's ears when he jumped up on her.

"Wags, down," Libby scolded. "Sorry. We start obedience training next week."

"Can I give you a hug?" Rebecca handed the chocolates to Libby and threw her arms around Oakley. After releasing Oakley, she turned to Libby. "See, Mommy? I asked first."

"But you didn't wait for her to answer," Libby pointed out. "C'mon in and we'll sit in the living room. Dinner isn't ready yet."

"Yeah, we're a bit early," Nick said, sounding sheepish.

"I'm glad. We can get a chance to chat before we eat," Libby told him. Had he been as eager to see her as she'd been to see him?

They went into the living room. Wags followed but kept a close eye on the box of chocolates, so Libby set them on the fireplace mantel out of the dog's reach. She sat in a chair opposite the couch where Nick and his niece sat.

"How come you gots Oakley with you?" Rebecca asked Nick.

"She's, uh, visiting for a while," he said.

"He means I ran away from home," Oakley put in.

Nick sighed. "Oakley, please."

Libby laughed. She liked the girl already. "Who gets through childhood without wanting to run away from home at least once? I recall wanting to join the traveling carnival that had come to town."

"What stopped you?" Oakley asked.

Libby laughed at the memory. "Mostly it was because I was only eight and my dad refused to give me a ride to the parking lot where they were set up."

Oakley chuckled. "Wow, how lame is that? Asking your dad for a ride so you could run away?"

Nick rolled his eyes. "Oakley, please."

"Oops. Sorry." She looked from him to Libby.

Libby waved her hand at him. "It's okay. I already know I wasn't much of a rebel."

"My doggy likes to run away from home," Rebecca told Oakley.

"I'll bet that's scary," Oakley told her.

Rebecca nodded.

Nick seemed on edge every time Oakley opened her mouth, and Libby wanted to tell him to chill but didn't want to embarrass the girl. He'd already told her enough about his family that she knew it was far from ideal. Oakley had probably come from that same environment. Libby had to admit that the girl, like Nick, was a bit rough around the edges, but she, also like Nick, seemed like a wonderful, caring person.

"We was scared, but Mr. Nick found him and brought him home." Rebecca was telling Oakley. "Two times. That's how we met him. Mr. Nick, not Wags. We already knew Wags cuz he's ours."

"He's a cute dog," Oakley told her.

As if he knew they were talking about him, Wags gave up his vigil with the chocolate box and ambled over to them.

Nick rubbed the dog's ears. "Have you been behaving yourself? Huh?"

Libby watched him with the dog and she fell for him a bit more. She may not have known him long, but her admiration for him kept growing. She suddenly realized they'd never even gone on a date. But that didn't matter. You didn't need formal dates to fall in love with someone.

Fall in love? What? No. She couldn't be. She wasn't. It was too soon. Too...too...too what?

Well, she didn't know what but it was too soon. Yep. Too soon. They hadn't even properly kissed yet. *Yet?*

Nick was looking at her, a frown drawing his brow together. Oh, God, he couldn't read her thoughts, could he? Most guys would go running for the hills if you mentioned the L-word so soon. And she was one with a ready-made family.

"My mommy knows how to fix those," Rebecca told Oakley, pointing to the tears in her jeans.

"Rebecca, maybe—" Libby began and sat up

straighter in the chair. Now who was worried about their child making a faux pas?

"But you do, Mommy. Remember you sewed a pretty patch on mine when I fell and they got a hole and I cried because I liked them so much?" Rebecca quickly glanced from her mom to Oakley. "But that was before…when I was a baby. I'm not a baby anymore."

"I can see that you're a big girl now," Oakley said. "And thank you for the offer."

Nick snorted. "Believe it or not, Rebecca, she bought them like that."

"Can't you return them to the store?" Rebecca asked, looking very concerned. "Mommy gots her money back when she bought a jacket and the zipper broke when she came home. 'Member that, Mommy?"

"I do, sweetie, but I think Oakley likes them like that." The last time Libby had wanted a new pair of jeans, she'd had to search high and low for a pair that didn't look ready for the rag bin.

Rebecca scrunched up her face. "Do you?"

Oakley grinned. "I guess I do since they're the ones I picked out."

Nick playfully elbowed his niece. "Told you those were defective."

She rolled her eyes at him in typical teenage fashion. Libby grinned and her heart inched further over the edge. She abruptly stood. "I better go and check on dinner."

"Whatever it is, it smells good," Oakley said.

"Thanks. It's bourbon chicken, rice and pot stickers."

The girl's eyes widened and she stood. "You mean like those chicken samples they give you on a toothpick at the food court in the mall?"

"That would be them," Libby confirmed. "But no toothpicks, I'm afraid. You get a proper helping on a plate with rice."

"Gosh, could you teach me how to make them sometime?" the girl asked, her aloof teen persona had melted away and left an eager girl in its place.

"Sure. Have your uncle bring you over, but you might want to try mine first before you commit to anything."

"Oh, no." She shook her head. "Uncle Nick has been bragging about what a wonderful cook you are...among other things."

Nick stood up and put an arm around the girl's shoulder. "Thanks bunches."

"What? You did." She elbowed him. "Besides, you made me swear to tell the truth, the whole truth and nothing but the truth."

Libby burst out laughing. "Oh, I'd love to hear the story behind that."

Nick was practically frog-marching Oakley toward the kitchen, but she turned and looked over her shoulder. "Teach me to cook that chicken and those potsticker things and I'll spill all."

Libby laughed but her heart sped up. Did that mean he might be feeling some of the same things that she was?

Or, he just liked her cooking.

No, that was too depressing a thought to entertain.

* * *

Nick had to admit that the evening was going well despite his crappy timing mentioning Oakley's cat. As usual, the food was delicious and Libby was such a gracious host. He only wished that she'd been there last night to greet his niece with him. But maybe he hadn't messed up too badly. He hated to think what he might have done if not for Libby and Rebecca's influence. Yeah, he might have felt some initial embarrassment over greeting Oakley with hugs, but he knew he'd done the right thing.

They finished eating and Oakley carried her empty plate to the sink without being asked. That had to count for something. Maybe his sister wasn't all bad, but no matter what, Oakley was his number one priority. He was going to go ahead with the guardianship thing. Plus, he'd need it if she was going to stay with him. Beth couldn't be counted on to make decisions should Oakley need anything.

"Would you like to watch a movie with us after we eat?" Rebecca asked Oakley, clearly in awe of the older girl.

Nick saw that Libby had tensed. Was she worried Oakley might rebuff Rebecca's tentative offer?

"I got Wallace and Gromit. Don't I, Mommy?"

"You do?" Oakley grinned, her excitement genuine. "I love Wallace and Gromit. Please tell me it's *The Curse of the Were-Rabbit*. I haven't seen that one in such a long time."

"Mommy gots me all the Wallace and Gromit movies because I love them so much. Do you want to see them, too?"

Oakley nodded eagerly. "I would love to."

Warmth spread through Nick's chest as he watched the girls. Thank goodness for this Wallace person, whoever he was. Sounded like he was capable of bridging an age and socioeconomic gap.

"Mr. Nick, does you want to help us look for the movies?"

"Thanks, but I think I'll see if your mom needs help in the kitchen," he said.

"Oh, I'm sure she does," Oakley said with an innocent smile directed at him.

He returned it with one that promised retribution and sauntered off to the kitchen.

"They're busy looking for movies I know nothing about," Nick said as he stood in the doorway to the kitchen. "Nothing like a teenager to make you feel old and ignorant."

"I think it's part of their job description." She turned around and took one look at him and said, "Something's wrong. What is it?"

She set the plate she had in her hand on the counter, and wiped her hands on her apron.

"I messed up," he confessed. Quickly adding, "With Oakley."

She started toward him as he moved further into the kitchen. They met in the middle.

"What happened?" she asked, standing before him.

"She has it covered with her shirt, but she has a tattoo on her wrist. It's for her cat. He died." He shook his head, knowing this woman wouldn't have bungled the whole thing.

"And?"

"I waited until just before we came in to mention it. I saw it yesterday and knew what it meant and I avoided the subject."

She touched his arm. "What did you say?"

"I hugged her told her how sorry I was she'd lost her cat. And I came up with a pearl of wisdom like 'that sucks.'" He sighed and leaned into her touch, her warmth filling him up.

"You didn't mess up, Nick," she said, her tone gentle. "That's all you can say. You can't take away someone else's pain. All you can do is be there for them, and that sounds like what you did for Oakley."

She put her arms around his waist and snuggled close. He reveled in the offer of comfort. Maybe he *had* done his best with Oakley. What had started as comfort morphed into something else.

"Libby?" he whispered, getting lost in the depths of her dark eyes.

He shouldn't be doing this here, now, with the girls in the next room. But her arms were around him, and he was lost. He pulled her even closer, fitting her body to his. The pad of his thumb moved in lazy circles near the corner of her mouth. The anticipation in her gaze had his heart crashing against his ribs.

"Please tell me you feel this, too," he said, anticipation pulsing through him.

"Yes, please."

He wasn't sure what that *please* was for, but he didn't need to be. He fastened his mouth to hers. He used his lips to coax a response from her. He drew the tip of his tongue along the seam of her lips, and they parted. At last, he thought, and his tongue slid inside. Her moan—or was that his?—went straight to his groin.

"Oh...uh... I..." Oakley said from the doorway.

Chapter Eleven

Talk about embarrassing, was Libby's first thought. But she didn't regret the kiss, just the getting caught part. Yeah, no regrets for the kiss.

Does this mean you can fall in love now?

That last thought had her making a choking sound. Searching her face, Nick took hold of her arm.

He frowned. "Oakley—"

"Sorry. Sorry," the girl protested.

"It's okay." Libby patted his chest and looked past him to Oakley. "You have nothing to be sorry for. You didn't do anything wrong."

Oakley didn't look as though she completely believed her, but there was some relief evident on her face. "I was going to say, we found the movie."

"Do you know how to set it up?" she asked. Oakley

nodded and Libby continued, "Tell Rebecca we'll be there in a minute. You can start the movie. I've seen it too many times to count."

"And don't say anything to Rebecca," Nick instructed.

"Duh," Oakley said and did the teen eye roll before she disappeared down the hall.

He shook his head. "Still think I'm not messing up?"

She stood on her toes and gave him a peck on the cheek. "You're doing great."

He grumbled but took Libby by her upper arms and gave her a quick, hard kiss.

"What was that for?" she asked in a breathless squeak.

"For being you."

Warmth rose in her face, but she couldn't wipe the ear-to-ear grin off her face. "You can go catch the movie if you want."

"Nah, clean up will go faster if I help. Besides, my reaction to that kiss was a bit more…um, noticeable."

"Oh."

"Yeah, oh," he said and flicked the end of her nose with his finger.

She loved seeing this playful side of him. "Thank you for bringing your niece over."

"Me? Thank you for inviting us. I confess I feel I'm in over my head with trying to feed her. I can't keep ordering pizza delivery."

"I take it you had to have plain cheese pizza?" she asked and turned on the faucet to hand-wash the things she didn't like putting in the dishwasher. "Will she be staying with you for a while?"

"Looks that way."

Libby caught the way he said it and wondered but didn't ask. He'd tell her what he wanted her to know. "Did you invite her for a visit or something?"

He shook his head. "She just showed up at my door."

"But...but...how did she get here?" She tried to wrap her head around the situation. "I thought you said your family was in California. Or someone said it," she amended.

"That's what I'd like to know. She says she took the bus." He put the last plate in the dishwasher and slammed it shut.

"As opposed to?"

"Hitchhiking."

Libby shuddered at the thought. Poor kid. Things must have been bad for her to undertake such a dangerous trip. But she knew the girl was in good hands now. She was with Nick.

Nick couldn't miss her reaction. *Great.* Now she probably wouldn't want his niece anywhere near Rebecca. He might understand the picture Oakley presented to the world was a front. Hadn't he done the same thing? He hadn't been totally convinced that it was an act until he'd pulled out Blue Bunny from her backpack.

"I'd like to offer her a job at the store."

"What?" He turned to her. Had he heard correctly? She was offering Oakley a job? He'd been expecting her to ask him not to bring his niece around, worried she might be a bad influence on Rebecca with her piercings and her tattoo. He was still upset at his sister for allowing Oakley to do that at her age. She'd been underage, so Beth must've signed consent forms. And if she hadn't, and the work had been done by an unlicensed tattooist, that was even worse.

But then, that's what he'd done so it was a case of do as I say, not as I do. Oakley would probably call him a hypocrite but two and a half decades had changed his perspective on these matters. If that made him hypocritical, so be it.

"I said I'd like to offer her a job, but I wanted to check with you first. It's just part-time and minimum wage, I'm afraid, but it will give her some spending money and something to do all summer. Assuming of course that you agree, and you're letting her stay all summer."

Oh, yeah, he was letting her stay all summer. If the situation with his sister was even half as dire as he suspected, he was giving Oakley a permanent home. He'd gotten things started by calling the attorney Gabe had suggested. Damn, but he should have kept closer tabs on both his sister and his niece. Part of this was his fault. Maybe he could have intervened and Oakley would have been able to stay with her mother.

"So, is it okay?" Libby asked, her tone hesitant. She gnawed on her lower lip.

He mentally shook off his depressing thoughts and smiled at Libby. "Yes. Absolutely. And thank you."

He leaned closer to her, fighting the urge to capture that poor worried lip between his own. Not a good idea. Next time it could be Rebecca interrupting them. Straightening up, he stepped back, away from temptation.

She smiled as if she knew what he was thinking, and her gaze lingered on his mouth.

"That's good," she said and tilted her head to one side as she studied him. "Except I'm sensing something else going on, something you're not saying."

He sighed. "I apologize if she's being a bad influence on Rebecca."

She frowned. "How is she being a bad influence on Rebecca?" She glanced into the family room, listening to the laughter. "Sounds like they're both enjoying the movie."

"I was referring to the tattoo and piercings," he admitted.

"Neither Rebecca nor I live in a sixties' sitcom. We encounter real people every day. Do I want my five-year-old to get a tattoo or a body piercing? Absolutely not. Nor would I let her, but she's going to be grown one day and will make those sorts of decisions for herself. Oakley seems like a lovely girl. So unless you know something you aren't telling me, I'm fine with her being here and with working for me."

She looped her arm through his. "Now let's go watch that movie."

Nick climbed the exterior steps to his apartment, wondering what Oakley was going to try and cook tonight. She'd been with him for two weeks, and, inspired by Libby, insisted on cooking for them on the nights they didn't join Libby and Rebecca.

Oakley had even used money she'd earned from working at the quilt shop to buy some of the cooking gadgets Libby used, including a special pressure cooker. So he did his best to be encouraging.

He toed his boots off outside the door and stepped inside, surprised there wasn't a mess in his kitchen. Usually he came home to a counter littered with dirty bowls and utensil.

"Oakley?"

"In here," she called from her bedroom.

Was she sick or something? He padded down the hall in his socks and walked into her room with its chaos of books, clothes, and who knew what all scattered around. He was doing his best to ignore it as long as she contained the mess to her room and to the kitchen while cooking.

His gaze went to her sitting on the edge of her bed, cradling something in her arms. Something tiny and furry. "What the hell is that?"

Oakley tutted her tongue. "Does Libby allow you to use language like that in front of Rebecca?"

He pinched the skin between his eye sockets because, yeah, he did need to police his language in front of Rebecca. He glanced at his niece and shook his head. "Nice deflection, Oaks, but it's not going to work. What have you got there?"

"It's a kitten." She clutched it to her chest. "I'm keeping it. I don't care what anyone says."

"What are we supposed to do with a kitten?" He entered her room and sat next to her. He reached over and used his finger to rub the fur on its head. The kitten meowed at him and batted at his hand.

"Feed it, love it, keep it alive?" She rubbed her cheek

against the kitten's gray-and-white fur, causing it to come alive with static electricity.

That was what he was afraid of. Didn't she understand he wasn't any good at keeping things alive? He'd lost half his men in some godforsaken desert half a world away...and they were well-trained, battle-hardened men. Not minuscule mewling bits of fur. "Taking on a pet is a huge responsibility, not some spur-of-the-moment decision. You could be looking at a twenty-year commitment."

"You're not the only one in the family who can commit themselves to something. Maybe I take after you instead of the two people who are supposed to be committed to feeding, loving and keeping *me* alive."

Her words made his gut clench. Seeing her holding that small bundle of life reminded him of the little girl she used to be. She was still there, under all that attitude.

"I suppose you're going to tell me it followed you home?"

"Would you believe it if I did?"

"Oakley."

"Okay. Okay. I was at Polly's on Main Street picking up lunch for Libby and me. An electric lineman was in there saying how he'd found a tiny abandoned kitten crying in a field. He said he was gonna bring it some water and pieces of chicken left from his lunch." She held the kitten aloft.

He had to admit it was pretty cute. Damn. Did he have sucker written across his forehead? "So why doesn't *he* have the kitten?"

"He said his wife is highly allergic. I followed him

to the spot and he found a box to keep it in until I could bring it home."

"What did Libby say?" Maybe he could take his cue from her. She was never far from his thoughts. They hadn't had a chance to be alone but Oakley had agreed to babysit Rebecca on Friday so he could take Libby on a real, honest-to-goodness date. Friday couldn't get here soon enough.

"Um." She held the kitten against her cheek as if for protection.

"Yes?"

"She doesn't know. I was afraid she'd call you and there'd be this whole thing. I knew if I brought it home and you saw it, you'd let me keep it. How can you resist that face?"

That was what he'd suspected. He couldn't imagine Libby keeping something like this from him. He couldn't imagine her keeping anything from him.

"We're going to have to take it to the vet and get it checked out, get whatever shots it needs." He started making a mental list, but then a thought occurred to him and he winced. "Uh, you don't happen to know if Libby or Rebecca are allergic to cats?"

"Why would that matter? I'm not bringing the cat to work with me or anything."

Oakley had a point, but it illustrated to him exactly how much Libby and Rebecca had become part of his thinking.

He shrugged and tried for casual. "Just curious, I guess."

"They aren't." She frowned as if she didn't know whether to believe him. "I kinda asked when I got back after lunch. Libby actually said she might get one someday if the puppy ever calms down."

"Really?" Now, he was skeptical.

"Yes, really. Ask her yourself, if you don't believe me."

"I believe you." Did she think he didn't trust her? "Oakley, I—"

"Not another hug." She rolled her eyes and moved away but her attempt to suppress a smile gave her true feelings away.

Grinning, he held up his hands. "No hugs. But I want you to know I really am sorry I wasn't there more for you when you were growing up."

"I survived."

Her words scraped his insides. Yeah, he knew about surviving.

"…and you're here now," she was saying. Giving him a calculated look, she said. "So I get to keep Sparky?"

"Sparky?" He knew he'd been manipulated, but he didn't care. He'd do what he had to keep Oakley safe and make up for all the time he wasn't there. He wanted to show Libby he could be counted on.

She shrugged and the kitten meowed. "I named him that because it seemed appropriate since it was an electric lineman who found hi.

"So it's a boy?"

"I have absolutely no idea." She lifted the kitten toward him. "Do *you* want to check?"

"I'll pass. The vet can tell us. Does all this activity mean I'm not getting any supper?"

"Oh, sh-shenanigans." She jumped up. "I forgot to make something. I'll go and—"

"I'll order pizza." He stood up and rubbed the kitten's head again. "You can pick off what you don't like."

"Sure. Sure."

He ended up ordering half-and-half.

Friday afternoon Libby sat in her kitchen and had to make one of the most disappointing telephone calls she could remember making.

"Full Throttle Custom."

She didn't recognize the voice and assumed it was Nick's employee and asked for Nick.

Nick came on the line and she explained, "I'm afraid I'm not going to be able to make our date tonight. I am just now getting home. I was at the doctor's with Rebecca this afternoon."

"Is something wrong? Is she okay?"

She heard the immediate concern in his voice instead of the disappointment she'd dreaded. *He's not Will*, she scolded herself. *Look what he's doing for his niece.* She knew he'd been meeting with an attorney to formalize guardianship. He cared about those around him.

"Libby?"

"Sorry." She shook her head to clear it. "Nothing too terribly serious. She's got an earache. She's prone to ear infections."

"Isn't that common in kids with Down syndrome because of the narrowed ear canals?"

Libby paused for a moment before answering. "Yes, but how did you know?"

"The internet is an amazing resource."

Her throat felt tight, but she managed to say a few words. "Yes it is."

The fact that he'd taken the time to look up facts about Down syndrome impressed her. Will hadn't taken the time to do anything like that. Even her parents often had preconceived notions and didn't take the time to learn the full truth.

"Is she in a lot of pain?" he asked.

"I think we caught it before it got too bad. We stopped at the pharmacy and filled the prescription for antibiotics. Usually twenty-four hours on those and she's feeling better."

"About tonight…" he began.

She could hear him speaking with someone—she was assuming it was Oakley—but couldn't make out what was being said.

"I'm really sorry to ruin our plans, but I don't want to leave her when she's sick. And it's not that I don't trust Oakley or anything. Please don't let her think that." She hated the thought of hurting the girl's feelings. Oakley might try to come off as tough but she had a soft inner core. A lot like her uncle. "I'm actually doing her a favor. Rebecca can get cranky when she's sick."

"You didn't ruin anything," he said.

Maybe he was glad she'd canceled. Maybe he was glad to grab at an excuse to cancel. Maybe he—

"I have a better idea," he said, interrupting her

angst-filled thoughts. "I'll bring over dinner and some entertainment."

"Entertainment?" she echoed.

He chuckled. "Rated G of course. Leave it to me. Unless you'd rather we didn't come over if Rebecca's not feeling well. We don't want to impose."

"Please come. Rebecca has been upset because she was afraid she wouldn't get to see Oakley tonight. She can't wait to hear all about her new kitten." she said. *And she wasn't the only one upset at the thought of not seeing you tonight.*

"We'll be there. Don't go to any trouble. As I said, we'll supply the food."

"You're welcome to bring the kitten if you want."

He did that deep-throated chuckle that melted her insides. "We'll save you from that chaos, but thanks for the offer."

"Okay, but the offer still stands. See you later." *Love you*, she added silently.

"Looking forward to it."

Long after he'd disconnected the call, she sat with the phone in her hand. Nick hadn't even sounded upset because their plans had been ruined. It wasn't Rebecca's fault, but Libby was pretty sure Will would have been angry. He would have thought only of himself and not Rebecca.

She held the phone and rubbed her thumb across the screen. Nick might not belong to a country club or play golf with bankers and politicians, but he was a great guy. Kind. Loyal. Loving.

And you're in love with him.

She gripped the phone until her knuckles were

white. Denial was futile. She'd fallen in love with the tattooed biker. And she was already halfway in love with his niece.

Standing up, she glanced around her sunny kitchen. Everything was the same, and yet, not. Everything was different. She could see Nick everywhere. She heard his low-throated chuckle, felt his lips on hers, saw the gleam in his dark brown eyes when he teased.

What had she done?

"Oakley! Get in here."

Nick stood, hands on hips, and surveyed the damage. He shook his head. And Libby had invited them to bring the little beast tonight.

Oakley came sauntering into the kitchen and Nick pointed to the ruined bag and the scattered dry kibble. "Look what your kitten did."

"What can I say? He's a troublemaker." She sighed and retrieved the kitten who was sitting in the middle of the mess, happily chomping on his food. She cuddled him to her chest. "Such a troublemaker. I guess it goes to show you really do belong in this family."

He held out his hands. "Give him to me. I'll hang on to him while you clean this up."

She handed him the kitten. "So I guess you'll be kicking us out soon."

She'd said it in a joking manner but he knew that behind that facade she worried. Had he done or said anything to cause her insecurities? He'd have to talk to Libby tonight. Maybe she'd have some advice.

"What are you— Ouch." Little claws dug in as the

kitten scrambled onto Nick's shoulder. "He needs his nails trimmed."

"Oh, good. Thanks."

"What do you mean thanks? I wasn't offering, I was making a suggestion." The kitten snuggled against his neck and he stroked it. How could anyone be so heartless as to dump a defenseless kitten? His thoughts turned to his sister. Hadn't she done that with her daughter?

"And I will take your *suggestion* under advisement."

""When did you get to be such a pain in the—"

"Tut-tut," she said, wagging her finger. "Remember we're watching our language because of Rebecca."

He made a show of looking around. "She's not here."

She lowered her chin and looked at him. He laughed and conceded. "You're right. We need to make it a habit."

She blew on her fingertips, then rubbed them on her shirt, but her smile trembled. The uncertainty in Oakley's brown eyes was like a punch to the gut. Did she really believe he'd kick her out?

She started scooping up the kitten food. "Do you think this is salvageable?"

"He was already eating it off the floor, but if you want we can pick up another bag when we stop at the store."

"Tell me again why we're stopping at the store." She put the largest pile of food onto the opened bag and set it out of reach. She got out the broom to pick up the rest.

"We're bringing one of those dinners that have all the ingredients and you cook it at home."

"That sounds cool."

"I guess we'll find out because you're going to help me. Libby and Rebecca get to be the guests tonight." He only hoped he and Oakley could manage.

"So I get to cook for Libby this time? Cool."

"What did you mean when you said I'd be kicking you out?" Nick asked. He needed to know.

"We seem to be more trouble than we're worth," she mumbled.

"When have I ever said that?" He set the kitten down and crossed the room. Taking the broom from her hands, he made her look at him. "That is not true. You're family, Oakley."

"Yeah. Family." She tutted her tongue. "Isn't that why you're living in Loon Lake…twenty-nine thousand miles away?"

He laughed. "Twenty-nine hundred, not twenty-nine thousand."

She sniffed. "So I'm not good at geography or math or whatever is involved."

He put his arms around her. "Look, I admit I like having a continent between Pops and the others, but I like having you here."

"You mean that?"

"Yep."

"Even if I cramp your style with Libby?"

"How is having you here cramping my style?"

She shrugged. "You can't bring her here for wild trysts."

He hooted with laughter. "Wild trysts? Does this look like the kind of place for wild trysts?"

"I guess not." She suddenly threw her arms around him. "Thanks, Uncle Nick."

He returned her hug as the kitten dug its claws into his jeans and climbed his leg. This was his life now and he found he was okay with that. He only hoped he could count Libby and Rebecca as part of it. Even without any wild trysts.

Well, he wouldn't mind a few wild trysts.

Chapter Twelve

Nick pulled the pickup into Libby's driveway and killed the engine, remembering the first time he'd come here. At that time he'd had no idea how his life was about to change.

He turned to glance at Oakley, who was already undoing her seat belt. "Ready?"

"We got this, Unc."

He grunted. He bet Libby's ex would have hired a caterer or some sort of upscale arrangement. Certainly not a ready-made dinner off the shelf from the local grocery store. He felt Oakley's hand on his arm and looked over at her.

"She'll love it, believe me." She squeezed his arm.

"We better get in there," he said, afraid he might embarrass himself. Loaded down with bags, they climbed the steps to her porch.

"What's all this?" Libby asked when she opened the door.

"Delivering on my promise. Dinner and tonight's entertainment. Oakley assures me this game is kid-friendly." He held up a box containing a card game.

Nick wasn't sure how Libby would react. He hoped she'd be pleased with their effort, if nothing else.

"I brought several different games that I think Rebecca will like playing," Oakley told her.

"That's so sweet of you."

Oakley nodded and blushed. "I…uh, actually I had ordered a few games when we first made plans for tonight. To be honest, I've been looking forward to playing, too. I've heard all of these games a lot of fun."

Libby went to her and gave her a hug. "Thank you for being so thoughtful. Rebecca is going to love it."

Nick watched the expressions flitting across Oakley's face. She might be fifteen and surly as hell at times, but he was pretty sure that hug from Libby meant a lot to her.

"Where is she?" Nick was surprised she wasn't at the door.

"She fell asleep earlier watching a movie. I'm sure she'll be awake soon and eager to play if she's feeling better." She took one of the bags from Oakley. "You didn't bring the new kitten? I told your uncle it was okay."

Oakley turned to him. "You didn't tell me she invited Sparky."

He imitated her with an exaggerated eye roll as

Libby led them into the kitchen. They set their bags on the counter and he began unpacking things.

"Such a cute name. Is it a boy or girl?" Libby asked, looking from one to the other.

He cleared his throat. "Uh…"

"We *think* it's a boy. But we're not sure," Oakley said.

"Oh." Libby smiled again.

"He's still quite young," he said, feeling a bit defensive.

"I guess it's not easy to tell when they're that little," Libby said.

"We…uh, we looked it up but neither one of us wanted to palpitate that…uh…that area to find out for sure," Oakley said. Giving him a sly look, she continued, "Uncle Nick seemed especially squeamish."

"I see," Libby said, rubbing a hand over her mouth.

"Go ahead and laugh," he told her. "It's okay. I feel as though I've already been emasculated here."

She turned back and met his gaze and they both burst out laughing. As embarrassing as all this was, sharing a laugh with Libby was worth it. He loved hearing that slightly husky sound. Even if it did do funny things to his insides.

"I'm sure the vet would be able to determine the gender for you," Libby said.

"Yeah, I've got an appointment at the end of the week. It was the earliest I could get," Oakley told her. "Now, you're supposed to sit and do nothing. We got this."

"I'll go check on Rebecca."

Nick was glad he'd chosen the easiest dinner they'd

had at the store. Store-made chicken potpie, dinner rolls, a salad, and brownies for dessert.

Rebecca woke up feeling better and was excited about the card games. Nick wondered if the fact Oakley had picked them out made them more appealing to the younger girl.

After supper, Nick and Oakley cleared away the dirty dishes and brought the games to the table.

"I'm sorry it wasn't the evening you had planned," Libby said after they'd cleaned up the kitchen and sat at the table to share a cup of coffee and some quiet time. The girls had gone into Rebecca's room.

"It was fun," he said, meaning it. He was glad he could do this for Libby and he appreciated Oakley's help. He had to admit his niece had some mad kitchen skills. Did his sister appreciate that? Did she even know?

He recalled the last time he'd talked to Gabe and thought the guy had never looked happier. Gabe had officially adopted Addie's little brother, and now they were expecting a baby.

He looked at Libby and wondered what she'd look like pregnant. The thought made his palms sweat but, to his surprise, he didn't panic as much as he would have expected.

Libby noticed Nick seemed to be deep in thought and she wondered what was on his mind. He honestly didn't seem bothered by the sudden change in their plans for the evening.

"Mommy. Look. Look what Oakley gave me." Rebecca came running into the kitchen. She had bounced back a bit after her nap and a dose of over- the-counter painkillers.

"It's an arm picture just like Mr. Nick and Oakley gots." She held up her hand to show off a temporary tattoo. "It's Wallace and Gromit. My favorite."

Libby took her hand to admire it. "Well, would you look at that."

"See, Mr. Nick," Rebecca said and yawned.

"I see it. That's very pretty," he said but he was scowling.

That scowl didn't escape Oakley's notice, either, because she crossed her arms over her chest. "I hope it didn't make you mad or anything. It washes right off after a few days."

Libby sighed. She knew the girl was scared. No child should feel that insecure. "Oakley, look at my face, please. Do I look angry to you?"

"No, ma'am."

"Oakley?" Rebecca tugged on the other girl's shirt. "Mommy says that to me and it means she's not mad."

Oakley gave Rebecca a hug. "That's good to know, kiddo."

Rebecca yawned again and Libby stood up.

"I think it's someone's bedtime," she said.

Rebecca protested but Libby insisted and took her into her room after she'd said good-night to Nick and Oakley.

"She's my new bestest friend," Rebecca said as they climbed the stairs to her room.

After finally getting Rebecca settled in bed, Libby went back to the kitchen to find Nick and Oakley having a heated conversation.

"Oakley, you should have asked Libby before you gave that tattoo to Rebecca." Nick closed his eyes, pinching the bridge of his nose between his thumb and forefinger. A gesture Libby was coming to recognize.

"What in the world were you thinking?" he asked.

"I was thinking that it was just a silly temporary tattoo. It washes off with soap and water and some scrubbing." Oakley crossed her arms across her chest and thrust her chin out.

Libby recognized the defensive posture for what it was. Oakley was insecure and desperate not to let it show, but Libby saw it even if Nick couldn't. She decided she needed to step in even if she had no desire to come between him and his niece.

"It's okay. No harm done," Libby said and put a comforting hand on the girl's shoulders. She wanted to take her in her arms and tell her everything was going to be okay the way she did with Rebecca, but she didn't want to embarrass the teen in front of her uncle.

She might have left it at that, but she saw Oakley struggling to swallow. The girl looked close to tears. "Nick, could you go check on Wags?"

"What?" He shot her a puzzled look.

"I wanted to be sure he is still safely in the yard," she said and tried her best to communicate her true intentions by giving him a partial eye roll toward the door to the backyard.

"Are you questioning my…" He trailed off. Eyes narrowed, his let his gaze bounce between Libby and his niece.

Libby gave him a slight nod, exhaling when he

seemed to catch on and returned her nod with one of his own.

"You're right. I better go check on that dog. You never know what he could be up to," he said as he slipped out the back door.

Relieved, Libby turned to Oakley and gave her that hug she'd been wanting to. The girl rested her head on Libby's shoulder and quietly cried.

Libby didn't say anything, just held her and rubbed her back as she would have done for Rebecca.

"I'm so sorry," the teen said and pulled away. "I didn't mean to do anything wrong."

"And you didn't. Your uncle overreacted. I'll talk to him."

"You will?" The girl wiped the back of her hand across her cheeks.

"You bet." Libby patted her shoulder. "I'll give him a piece of my mind."

"Oh, don't do that. I don't want him to think I made you angry with him."

Libby laughed. "Don't worry. This is on him, not you. I'll make him understand that. Now, why don't you go use the powder room to clean up."

"Thanks." Oakley gave Libby a quick hug and went to the hall bathroom. "I'll unload the dishwasher, if you'd like."

"That would be great. Thanks." Libby had a feeling the girl wanted to feel needed.

Didn't everyone want to feel needed?

Nick threw the ball again after wrestling it away from Wags. He glanced back at the house, wondering what was going on. Sighing, he sat on the steps. He'd probably messed up again. If he kept doing that, Libby might decide he and Oakley were nothing but trouble. What would he do if he didn't have Libby to turn to for parenting advice?

As if his thoughts had conjured her up, Libby came out and joined him on the steps.

"Where's Oakley?"

"She offered to unload the dishwasher."

He raised an eyebrow. "Punishment?"

"Absolutely not. What she did doesn't deserve punishment. Do I wish she'd asked me first? Yes, but seriously, Nick, it's a temporary tattoo that's meant for kids and washes off. They do that stuff at birthday parties."

He rubbed his face with his palms. "I feel like I'm stumbling in the dark with her. One minute she's needy and the next she's belligerent."

"Hormones," Libby said.

He looked at her and she laughed. "Teenage ones. They're the worst kind."

They fell into a companionable silence, watching the dog romp in the yard, playing ball with himself.

"She worries you'll try to send her back to her mother," Libby said quietly.

"No way. I wouldn't keep her here against her will, but unless I have proof that my sister has cleaned up her act, Oakley stays here with me. She has a home with me for as long as she wants it." He held his breath as he waited for Libby's reaction. Would she prefer it if he didn't have responsibility for his niece?

He figured he may as well lay his cards on the table. "As you already know, I've been meeting with that family law attorney." She nodded and he continued, "I've applied for permanent guardianship, not just temporary."

"Have you told *her* that?"

"Well, no, but—"

"You should," she told him and patted his knee. "It might help make her feel more secure."

"Thanks. I'll do that." Nick felt the relief wash over him.

"I'm glad to hear it. I hope the court awards you custody," she said, looping her arm through his. "She's a good kid."

"A bit exasperating at times, but you're right."

She laughed. "How many times do I have to tell you that's the definition of teenager?"

That laugh did crazy things to his insides. He gave in to his urge and leaned over, planting a kiss on her delectable mouth. And strangely, the kiss had nothing to do with sex. Well…mostly nothing.

He pulled away and squeezed her arm closer to his side. "I have a confession."

"Oh?" She turned her head to meet his gaze with her own.

Damn. Why had he said anything? He was blaming that laugh and the effect it had on his senses. Now she was gazing intently at him, waiting, and he felt obligated to say something, anything. He blamed that sexy laugh for the urge to not only tell her but to tell her the truth. "When I'm confronted with a situation with Oakley that I'm not sure how best to handle, I ask myself 'What would Libby do?'"

"Me?" She looked flabbergasted. "Why would you think that?"

"Why? Look at the wonderful job you're doing with Rebecca. You seem to have everything under control, like you know instinctively what to do."

She shook her head slowly. "I'm flying by the seat of my pants most of the time. You flatter me by thinking otherwise. The only thing I know for sure is that I don't want Rebecca brought up with the same values my parents have and tried to instill in me."

"It couldn't be that bad."

"Oh no? How do you think I ended up married to William Taylor *the Third*? My parents, and his, basically pushed us together. Of course I can't place all the blame on them, since I possess free will."

His gut tightened at the mention of her first husband's name. Even the name sounded classy, something he was not nor ever would be. He couldn't imagine William Taylor the Third's father using him as a lookout or a runner for his drugs. The guy's mother probably didn't miss parent-teacher conferences, probably served on those committees people and places liked to form. Unlike Nick's mom, who was usually stoned by noon.

"Why'd they push you two together?"

"They considered us 'perfect' for one another. Our dads were golfing buddies and our moms served on the same committees together."

Golfing and committees, just as he'd suspected. "You must have felt something, given that you two married…had a child."

He had tagged on that last part and, seeing her reaction, he was sorry he'd said anything at all. Why hadn't he left well enough alone? Why probe the subject like a tongue seeking out a toothache?

"I had a child," she said. "He wanted nothing to do with her. And I wanted nothing to do with him after that. The separation and divorce came as a relief."

He swallowed, taking in that information. Maybe he had a shot at what Gabe had. Stranger things had happened. Right?

"Um, Libby, Uncle Nick? I finished putting the dishes away. I left a couple things on the counter because I wasn't sure where they went. I hope that's okay." Oakley stood in the doorway of the porch.

Wags ran up the steps and greeted her. She rubbed his ears and patted his head. "Hey, boy. It's always good to see you, too."

"Oakley, why don't you join us. I think your uncle has something he wants to say."

Nick didn't appreciate eating crow, but he'd do it for Oakley's sake and for the sake of his relationship with her. And with Libby. "I'm sorry I overreacted about the tattoo."

Oakley shrugged. "Thanks. I realize now I should have asked first. We wanted to surprise you."

"As I said, it's fine." Libby raised her eyebrows at him. "I think he has something else? Unless you'd rather wait until you got home?"

"Now is as good a time as any. Maybe I should have told you sooner anyway. I've… I've hired an attorney to see about obtaining guardianship over you. If that's what you want, I mean. This isn't a kidnapping."

Her face lit up. "So, like, I could live here with

you permanently? Go to school here? And work at the quilt shop?"

Libby had been right. Again. He smiled. "Yeah, all of that."

"And I get to keep Sparky, too?"

"Yes."

Oakley jumped down the steps and gave him a hug, much like Rebecca was always doing. For a guy who was never physically demonstrative, he was mired in it. Was that what came of being surrounded by girls?

He grinned and turned to Libby. "Looks like I have myself a kitten."

Libby laughed and kissed his cheek. "Welcome to pet ownership, Mr. Cabot."

"On that note, I think it's time for us to go home," he said.

"I'll be in the truck," Oakley said and went back into the house.

"I think she is giving us a little privacy," Libby observed.

"An opportunity I plan to take full advantage of," he told her before he captured her mouth for a kiss.

The next morning, Nick stuck his spoon in his instant oatmeal and replayed last night's kiss in his mind while he spooned up cereal. They'd known Oakley was waiting in his pickup, so they'd had to cut it short, but that particular kiss held a promise of more to come. He couldn't say why, but he'd felt it when he'd held her.

Fact was, he was falling for Libby in a big way. And now that he knew getting custody of Oakley wasn't a deal breaker, he saw them taking a step forward.

They'd agreed to wait until Rebecca's ear infection had cleared up to reschedule their date. But Libby had seemed to enjoy their family game night as much as he had.

Sparky came racing into the kitchen, took a flying leap and landed on his lap. The kitten lifted up his paw and snagged the place mat under Nick's cereal bowl. Before he could react, he ended up with a lap full of oatmeal. It had all happened in the blink of an eye.

Jumping up from the chair, he cursed loudly as the bowl crashed to the floor with the kitten following it down. Nick glanced down at the oatmeal and milk dripping from his lap and cursed again. The kitten was in the middle of the mess, happily lapping up the milk and cereal. The chaos he'd created hadn't bothered him one bit.

Oakley came running down the hall. "What's going on? Why are you yelling at Sparky?"

"I'm not yelling *at* him," he defended himself.

She scooped up the squirming and protesting kitten. Sparky obviously wanted to get back to his unexpected breakfast treat. "It sure sounded like it to me."

"I was *protesting* because I had a bowl of oatmeal dumped in my lap. I was angry at the circumstances, not the cat." He inhaled and rubbed at the mess on his pants. "Although the cat did cause the situation."

"It's not his fault. He's just a baby."

"How is it not his fault? He's directly responsible for—"

"Hello?"

The sound of Libby's voice cut Nick off and he turned toward the door. He'd left the metal inner door open since the screen door kept the kitten inside while also letting in fresh air. Plus, the cat enjoyed sitting in front of it and listening to the birds.

Yeah, admit it, you've got a soft spot for the little troublemaker.

"Oh, dear. Have I come at a bad time?" Libby stood on the small landing at the top of the stairs just outside the door. She stepped back and made a vague motion with her hand. "I can come back later if—"

Nick and Oakley yelled "no" at the same time.

"Well…if you're sure."

"Come in." Oakley hurried across the room and un-latched the door to let Libby into Nick's small kitchen.

His niece's actions snapped Nick out of the stasis he was in. Damn. He was glad to see Libby. He was always glad to see her. Just not under these circum-stances. His normally spotless kitchen was a mess. He was a mess with his soggy pants. And she'd probably heard him yelling at a defenseless animal.

Yeah, he'd been yelling.

Why did she always have to catch him at his worst?

Chapter Thirteen

"How's Rebecca today?" Nick asked, trying to gather his wits in front of the woman he… He what? Had feelings for? Wanted to kiss and more?

The and more part, please.

"She's feeling better, but I kept her home from her preschool just in case. Clara next door is going to watch her this morning."

Her answer to his question snapped him out of his inner thoughts, which was for the best, because he didn't want to go there.

"Oh my." Libby reached out to pet the kitten in Oakley's arms. "How adorable."

"Uncle Nick was yelling at him," Oakley said as she shut the door behind Libby.

He threw up his hands in frustration. "I wasn't yelling at him. Not directly."

Nick could hear the damn kitten's motor running from across the room. Not that he blamed him. If Libby had been stroking him like that, he'd probably purr, too. Damn, but he needed to get her alone. For an entire night. Or afternoon, he wasn't fussy.

"…right, Nick?" said Libby.

"What?" He shook his head. *Stay in the game, Cabot.*

Libby frowned. "I said, I'm sure you wouldn't have intentionally scared the cat."

"That's what I've been saying. I was startled when my breakfast landed in my lap," he said, feeling warmth rise in his cheeks because Libby's gaze had gone to the giant wet spot on the front of his pants. The fact his embarrassment probably showed on his face made him angry. "Excuse me for reacting like a normal human being."

"But he's so adorable." Libby said and reached over again to pet the kitten, who was still squirming to get down.

He glowered at his niece. "Don't let him get down until you clean up that mess."

"Me? That is so misogynistic. Why do I have to clean it up? I didn't make the mess."

"Your cat did," he reminded her. "As I recall, you insisted that Sparky was going to be your responsibility."

"Let me take the kitten so you can clean up. I don't think cow's milk is good for them, despite popular lore," Libby said.

Oakley quickly handed Sparky to Libby. "I don't want him to get sick. I'll clean it up."

Nick could plainly see how worried Oakley had become over the idea of the kitten getting sick. "I don't think what little milk he got will do any harm."

"Sorry, I seem to have forgotten my manners," he said, scrambling to pull out a chair for Libby. "Have a seat."

She sat in the seat with the kitten on her lap. "I needed to drop some tax stuff off with my accountant, Mary Wilson. I realized I hadn't gotten Oakley's information for her employment. And I thought since I was going out to Mary's place, Oakley might enjoy seeing their animals. They run Camp Life Launch on their farm."

"What kind of animals do they have on this farm?" Oakley asked as she mopped up the last of the cereal mess.

"I know they have horses because the kids from the camp ride, and Brody, Mary's husband, has a pair of alpacas and—"

Nick decided he'd bow out and so he could change into some dry pants. Getting up, he resisted the urge to kiss Libby because...well, just because. "I'm going to go change, I won't be long."

Libby watched him saunter off, trying to not look as if he hadn't just had a bowl of cereal dumped on his lap by a tiny kitten.

"Did you say you had some paperwork for me to fill out?"

Oakley's question penetrated and Libby snapped to

attention. She dug some papers out of her purse and handed it to the girl.

"I don't have any experience to list or anything," Oakley said as she scanned the paper Libby had handed her.

"Of course not. I don't know of any fifteen-year-olds with job experience. But that's what a first job is for." She really wanted to help the girl and not just because she was Nick's niece. Libby admired her. She only wished she'd had half of Oakley's spunk. Maybe her life would have turned out differently if she'd had the courage to defy her parents. But then, she wouldn't have her precious daughter. All the heartache the end of her marriage had caused was nothing compared to the joy Rebecca gave her.

"So my appearance hasn't turned you off?" Oakley asked.

"What? Why would you say that?"

"It's something Uncle Nick mentioned."

Libby made a noise by blowing air between her lips. "He's one to talk."

Oakley burst out laughing. "He's really not the bad-ass he tries to portray... You know that, right? And for all his bluster he wouldn't hurt Sparky or nothing."

"I know that." Libby smiled to reassure her. Was Oakley hoping to do a bit of matchmaking?

Oakley nodded and went back to filling out the application form.

"Did you want some coffee or something?" Oakley handed over the completed form.

"No, thanks. I had some at breakfast with Rebecca this morning." Libby glanced up from the form Oakley had filled out. "I see Oakley is actually your middle name. What does the *A* stand for?"

The teen pushed her chin out. "Is that important?"

"Well, I do need your full name if I'm going to be paying your wages. I prefer not to get in trouble with the IRS."

"It's Annie."

"Okay. That's a pretty name, too. Nothing to be ashamed of." Libby smiled. "Annie Oak— Oh."

"Yeah, my mom's idea of a joke, I guess. Of course I didn't even know who that was but Darryl Johnson sure did. He told everyone in our third-grade class and no one would let me forget it."

"Well, Oakley, don't feel so bad. Libby is actually short for Elizabeth. So that makes me Elizabeth Taylor."

Oakley frowned. "I don't know who that is."

Libby laughed. "That's because you're too young. She was one of the most famous movie stars of the fifties and sixties."

"So, if no one knows who she is anymore, why does it matter?"

Libby raised an eyebrow. "I could ask you the same thing."

"Oh. Yeah." Oakley blushed, then laughed. "Duh."

Nick came back into the room wearing dry work pants. "If you're going with Libby, put Sparky in his kennel and— I know you don't like *locking* him up, but he's too young to leave unsupervised. We don't want anything happening to him."

Libby couldn't help noticing that Nick had said *we.* Yeah, he really was a wonderful and caring guy.

Hugging the kitten close to her chest, Oakley scurried down the hall. Once she was gone, he leaned over the chair and gave Libby a chaste kiss. But it was loaded with promise.

He pulled back and met her gaze. "You mean to tell me I just kissed Elizabeth Taylor?"

"And if you play your cards right, you may be able to do a lot more," she said, surprised at her own boldness.

"Hold that thought," he said and gave her another quick kiss. Glancing at his watch, he continued, "Because right now, I have to open up the shop."

Admiring his backside, she watched him walk out the door. Maybe Oakley's take-no-prisoners attitude was rubbing off on her.

Later that afternoon, Libby turned into the parking lot of Full Throttle Custom to drop off Oakley. They'd spent most of the day together. After visiting Mary on her farm, Libby had brought Oakley to the store. It was one of the days she closed the shop, so she'd decided it would be a good time to build the girl's confidence. She explained quilting terms while getting her even more comfortable with the specialty merchandise in the shop. Sometimes it seemed as if quilters had a language of their own.

Libby admired how quickly Oakley had caught on to how things worked at the store. In the beginning, she'd seemed a bit intimidated by the point of sale cash register. Libby had explained that most sales were credit card, but they'd practiced counting back change anyway.

"Thanks for today," Oakley said when Libby

brought the car to a stop in front of one of the garage bays. She opened the car door and turned back. "I want to go see Sparky. He probably missed me today. Could you talk to Uncle Nick for me?"

"Don't worry. I'm sure he'll be fine with it." Especially once he understood the ramifications of it.

Oakley nodded and practically flew up the stairs to the apartment. Libby got out of the car and leaned against the driver's door, admiring the way Nick looked crouched next to a mean-looking motorcycle. Why was that so attractive and exciting?

A much younger guy was in the second bay talking with a customer, pointing something out on the bike in front of them.

Nick strolled over, wiping his hands on a rag. "Hey, how'd it go today?"

"Good," she said, feeling like Rebecca when she was eager to share good news.

He came closer and leaned over to give her an all too brief kiss. "I don't want to get you dirty."

"I don't mind a little dirt."

He groaned, his dark eyes taking on a gleam. She loved the power she had to make this wonderful man react.

"What's up? You look like you have something to tell me."

"I do," she nodded and began to explain, "Mary and Brody Wilson run a nonprofit camp for disadvantaged children on their farm on the outskirts of town. They have a wonderful place. It's called Camp Life Launch. They deal mostly with children in the foster system to give them a summer camp experience. It was all Mary's idea, and when she and Brody got together, he jumped on board. It's really taken off and is quite successful."

"That's nice," he said, sounding a little disappointed. "I've heard about the place but haven't been there myself. Is Oakley wanting to volunteer or something?"

Libby shook her head, brimming with excitement but aware that Nick's employee and customer in the second garage bay might overhear. "They're having a special camping jamboree next weekend and they invited Rebecca."

"Oh, well, that's nice. I'm happy for her." Nick continued to wipe his hands on the rag.

"They've invited Oakley, too. She would have told you herself, but she couldn't wait to get back to Sparky."

"I checked on him a couple times," he said casually. Almost too casual. "All right, maybe it was more than just a couple."

"You're a good man, Nick Cabot." She patted his cheek, her fingers lingering until the jingle of a metal tool being dropped came from inside the garage.

"Anyway, she'll be more like a camp counselor for the younger kids, but she can ride the horses and do all the things the camp is famous for. Plus, she'd get paid for helping out," Libby said, her gaze darting to Kevin and the man he was with.

"That's very generous of them." He tossed the rag aside. "You said it's a camp for underprivileged kids? Not some spoiled rich kids. I just don't want anyone trying to say she doesn't fit."

Her heart melted a bit more for him. "She'll be fine.

Mary and Brody really like her and she seems to like them."

He nodded. "That's good."

She sighed. He still hadn't picked up on the best aspect of this whole thing.

"That means both girls would be gone this weekend." Okay, she couldn't put it any plainer than that. Her heart was pounding, and her palms were sweaty. This was like stepping into the void without a safety net. His comment this morning had indicated he wanted to take things to the next level.

She saw the moment the opportunity this news presented occurred to him.

"*Both* girls gone…for the entire weekend?"

She nodded.

"I may be slow on the uptake but I'm there now." He started laughing. "You must have thought I was dense."

"Or not interested," she admitted.

"Oh, I'm interested. Boy, am I ever interested." He glanced to where Kevin stood. "We are talking about the same thing, right?"

"I hope so." Relief rippled through her along with a sexual thrill. They were on the same page. Her heart thudded in her chest. She couldn't see her own face, but she was certain she had a silly grin.

"I know people with kids must manage it all the time." He leaned close. "But I wanted it to be special for you and sneaking around behind the backs of a five- and a fifteen-year-old isn't easy. Or special."

He'd wanted to make it special for her. Yep, they were on the same page. More so if his words were anything to go by.

"There's always the threat of getting interrupted," she said on a more practical note.

"And I plan to take my time with you," he whispered.

"And me with you," she whispered back. "I have had this fantasy involving my tongue and a dragon." He groaned. "I have to get back to work or Kevin and my customers will be getting a show."

The following Friday, they dropped both girls off at the camp together and practically ran back to get in Libby's car. The camp was having a barbecue to kick off the weekend's events. Brody had told them they could stay if they were interested. Libby had held her breath until Nick declined with a nonsensical and mumbled excuse.

"We invite, but strangely enough most decline," Brody said, clapping Nick on the back and waving them off with a laugh. "I remember those days. Have fun, you two."

She giggled as they climbed back in the car. "You'd think we were a couple of teenagers whose parents are gone for the weekend."

"That's how it feels," he said as he started the engine on her Toyota. "Do you want to go somewhere to eat?"

"No, I just want to go home. We can eat later."

"Much later," he said, placing his hand on her thigh.

Back at Libby's, they went inside and he pulled her into his arms as soon as the door was shut. Her back was against the door, the knob sticking into the small of her back.

"You can't imagine how long I've been waiting for this," he said and clamped his mouth over hers.

She brought her arms up to wind around his neck to pull him closer. His tongue demanded entry, and she opened with a moan of pleasure as it danced with hers, cavorting back and forth, sliding and caressing.

A bark sounded from the kitchen.

"Damn, I forgot about Wags. He's in his crate."

"Where?"

"In the kitchen. It's…"

But Nick had already disappeared down the hall.

"Hey, there, boy. I've got something for you. My friend Gabe tells me these are the best toys and you can take it into the backyard and give me a little privacy with Libby."

Amused, she was still standing in the same spot when he got back. "You think of everything."

"Yep," he said, and reached into his pocket to pull out two strips of condoms.

Her eyes widened. "And you're an optimist."

He stopped and stared at her, raising an eyebrow. "The question is, are you?"

"Oh, absolutely." She nodded. "And I—"

What she'd been going to say got lost because he scooped her up and carried her toward the bedroom.

"You already know where it is?"

"I'm a marine, ma'am. I do reconnaissance."

She giggled and put her arms around his neck again. "Very sexy."

In her bedroom, he laid her on her bed. And shucked off his boots before joining her. He brought his mouth down on hers and she opened immediately for him, her tongue meeting his. Without lifting his mouth from hers, he began unbuttoning her blouse, and she wiggled out of it. Still kissing her, he pinched the nipple through the fabric of her bra.

With his other hand behind her, he unclasped her bra and tugged it off, throwing it aside. Once he had it free, his mouth claimed the breast, sucking and teasing with his teeth. Her other breast begged for the same attention and she ground her hips against him.

When his mouth touched the other nipple, she thought she would explode from the pleasure and the longing. He gave that one the same attention, licking, sucking and nipping at the rigid flesh. As he lifted his mouth and blew on the nipple again, her hips twitched and bucked toward his erection.

He leaped off the bed and began tearing off his clothes. While he was getting rid of his, she pulled her jeans off.

She reached up to pull off her red lace panties and he growled, "Leave those on a bit longer."

She immediately dropped her hand. "As long as I can explore that dragon."

"We'll get to that part," he said, his eyes gleaming as he looked at her panties.

"You like red lace?"

"You have no idea," he said, and came back down on the bed.

All her nerve endings humming and sizzling, she reached up and twined her arms around his neck. She pulled him down, reveling in the way his weight felt on top of her. He kissed her with a searing hunger, as if he'd been waiting for her all his life. He feasted on her mouth like a starving man before moving on.

His mouth left hers and he trailed tantalizing kisses over her shoulders, stopping at her breasts to suckle. Then he'd blow his breath onto each one until she moaned wildly. Smiling, he drew his tongue lightly across the underside of her breasts toward her belly button. He kissed a spot on her hip and let his tongue drift over to the waistband of the red panties. He slowly pulled them down with his teeth and admired them.

Good choice with the color.

But that was the last rational thought she had because his mouth was on that spot that had been begging for attention and she exploded.

There was a rustle of foil as reached for one of the packets he'd set on her nightstand.

Should she tell him there'd been no one in the past five years? "It's been a while, so…"

Her tentative admission touched him and he fumbled with the condom wrapper.

Time to fess up. "For me, too, but I'll try to take my time."

He finally got the wrapper open and hoped she didn't notice how much his hands shook.

"May I?" she asked as he started to sheath himself.

He nodded. Her hands shook as she carefully rolled the condom in place. They were in this together, he thought, before moving over her to spread her thighs.

"I'll try to make it last and not hurt you."

"You won't." She shook her head, her eyes dark with pleasure and trust.

She trusted him. He groaned again. "Tell me to stop if it hurts and I will."

He took his time and made sure she was ready again before he pushed in. He pulled out then thrust again. Lifting her legs, she crossed her heels around the small of his back and urged him to keep up his pace. Using his thumb he brought her to the peak and made sure she tumbled over again.

Closing his eyes, he thrust hard and deep one last time before he exploded. This had been unlike anything he'd experienced with anyone before. Maybe if he wasn't so numb with pleasure, he'd be able to figure out the implications of that.

He stretched out next to her and anchored her against him with his arm. But she lifted herself up.

"Now I get to explore the dragon." She caressed his chest, her fingers running along the tattoo.

He kissed the top of her head. "Keep that up and we may need those other condoms."

"That's the plan," she said as she ran her lips over his ink.

They used another condom before dragging themselves out of bed to look for something to eat.

She made some sandwiches while he opened the back door for the dog. Wags came trotting in with a red rubber toy in his mouth.

"I'll have to thank Gabe for his dog toy suggestion."

She stopped with the sandwich halfway to her mouth. "You didn't tell him *why* you were asking, did you?"

He stilled. Was she ashamed of what they were doing? "Would that matter if I had?"

"No, except the next time I see him he'll…he'll know and I'll get all tongue-tied if asks how Wags liked the toy."

He laughed and grabbed her hand. "Are saying you're a prude?"

"No." She scowled at him.

"You don't think he and Addie…?"

"Of course they do. She's pregnant, isn't she?"

"Is it me?" He had to know.

She leaned over and kissed him. "I'm proud to be with you. I'll announce what happened to the whole world, if you want."

"That won't be necessary," he told her and kissed her.

He didn't notice when the dog grabbed part of his sandwich and trotted off with his tasty prize.

Chapter Fourteen

"You can bring him to my place," Libby suggested.

They'd gone back to his place to check on the kitten.

Nick knew he was being silly, but he'd promised Oakley he'd look after Sparky while she was at Camp Life Launch. So here he was cradling Sparky before putting him back in the comfortable kennel they'd set up with all the kitten essentials plus a special shaggy calming blanket. "Not tonight. I have plans that don't include chaperoning a puppy and a kitten who've never met before. It's not every night I get to sleep with Elizabeth Taylor."

She rolled her eyes but a huge grin split her face. "Do you have any more condoms?"

"Why, do you?"

She blushed and nodded. "When I first found out

about the girls being invited to camp, I might have stocked up."

He raised an eyebrow. "Stocked up?"

"I was out of town and decided to take advantage. You know how gossip is in this town. If we'd both been seen stocking up."

Once again, he had that niggling in the back of his mind. Was she ashamed or just easily embarrassed? He felt too good not to go with embarrassment. After all, she had a business and a young daughter to think about.

Later than evening, they lazed on her couch, a movie playing in the background. But Libby would have been hard-pressed to name the movie.

They'd been talking about everything and nothing. And kissing. A lot of that. Necking on the couch like a couple of teens. Except with no parents to worry about catching them.

She didn't want to ruin the mood, but curiosity got the better of her. "Oakley told me you have a bunch of medals from your time in the Marines. How come you don't talk about it? You hardly ever talk about your time in the military."

He snorted. "It was hardly a distinguished career like Ogle and Hank."

"That's not what I heard." She pressed her mouth to the dragon coming over his shoulder.

"Heard? Who have you heard from?"

"According to Gabe, you—"

"You spoke with Gabe Bishop about me?"

"No. I wouldn't do something like that. I saw him at the general store. He and Ogle were trading war stories.

He mentioned how you had won a boatload of medals for heroism. That your actions during an ambush attack saved a lot of men." She didn't tell him the rest of the things Gabe had told her. How Nick blamed himself for the whole fiasco. Gabe had also said that it was faulty information on the ground that was responsible.

"Yeah, after leading them into the attack in the first place."

Well, at least that verified what Gabe had told her.

She hated that he might feel responsible for something out of his control, something that had happened during the fog of war. "I know you probably don't want to hear this, but I think you need to. And you've probably even heard all this before, but maybe this will be the time it sticks."

"Libby—"

She held up her hand, determined to have her say. "Please, let me say this. I need to say it maybe even more than you need to hear it."

He sighed but nodded.

"I know you feel responsible for what happened to your men, but the definition of ambush is 'surprise attack.'"

"I know what the definition of ambush is," he snapped.

Libby smoothed her palm across his chest, enjoying the ink covering his warm skin. She rested her hand over his heart.

He reached up and wrapped his hand around hers. "Sorry."

"It's okay. I knew I was wading into dicey territory

when I brought up the subject. But I couldn't not say anything. And I'm not doing it to hurt you by bringing up the past."

Nick squeezed her hand, wishing he could ignore the whole conversation, go back to kissing and not talking. "Those men were my responsibility. I let them down."

"I don't believe that for one second." A furrow appeared in her forehead from her fierce frown.

"Don't people say you're supposed to pay attention when people tell you who they are?"

"That's when people *show* you who they are. And you've shown me who you are, Nick. Numerous times."

"And you haven't run away yet?" He tried to make light of the conversation. He *needed* to make light of the conversation. Needed to because this was Libby and he cared what she thought. As much as he might try to deny it, his feelings for this woman ran deep... more than they had for any other woman before her.

"Nope. And you want to know why?" Libby looked into his eyes.

"Dare I ask?" He was still trying to act like what she was going to say didn't matter, wouldn't change things. But he was only fooling himself by thinking that. He cared what she thought. And that was why he hadn't wanted to get involved. Because she would matter. And Rebecca. How could she not matter, too?

"You returned Wags...twice."

"That was—"

She pressed her fingers against his lips. "Shh. I'm not finished yet."

Her fingers fell away from his lips but she continued to stare at his mouth. He should kiss her. Kissing was better than talking.

As if sensing where his mind had gone, she held up that hand like a traffic cop. "Where was I? Ah yes, the dog. You not only returned him but you made sure he was safe and secure in the backyard. You didn't have to do that, but you did. And you went the extra mile with the dog run."

"I know how much Rebecca loves that mutt," he said, again trying to inject a note of levity.

"And you are looking after your niece. Going to the trouble of hiring an attorney to secure guardianship so you can properly take care of her, make sure she's safe. And most importantly, you're showing her she's loved."

"She's worth loving."

"Exactly."

"I couldn't ship her back home to a toxic environment." He wouldn't be able to forgive himself if he sent Oakley back to her mother and something happened. Maybe if he hadn't left in the first place, his sister wouldn't have followed in their mother's footsteps.

"See? That shows me you care about your family."

He wanted to believe her but she didn't know the whole story. "If I cared so much, why did I choose to be selfish?"

"How do you figure that?"

"I deserted them."

"Deserted? I don't understand."

"I joined the Marines. I chose to save myself rather than stay and try to help my mother get off drugs. If I'd stayed maybe I could have helped. Helped her, helped my sister. At least it's not too late for Oakley."

"How were you supposed to help her? Do you mean financially? Couldn't you do that while in the Marines?"

"I made sure she had a roof over her head but sending money to my mother would have been a huge mistake, so I paid her rent." And when she got behind, he paid for the electricity and the water, but he didn't say any of that. He wasn't looking for pity or praise. Didn't deserve either.

"Why would sending her money have been a mistake?"

"Because she would have spent it on booze and drugs."

"Oh."

"Yeah. Oh."

Maybe now she got it. But that thought made his stomach burn. "I should have stayed to help her."

"Sounds like she was an addict."

"She was." No sense lying about it.

"Then you couldn't have helped her."

"Why do you say that? If I had set aside my—"

"C'mon, Nick. You're a smart guy. You can't really believe that. Addicts have to want to help themselves. You can support an addict who wants to get clean, who seeks help, but you can't make them get clean. Did she want to get clean? Truly?"

He sighed. "She talked about it, but when push came to shove she refused. Just like my sister. If she had agreed to treatment, I would have done everything in my power to see that she got help."

"Then how can you blame yourself?"

Nick didn't answer. She might have a point, but it

wasn't easy to throw off almost two decades of guilt. "How about we get back to our other forms of communication?"

"Yeah, we have a lot of condoms to use up before the girls get back."

"Let me put Wags in his crate. Don't move."

She saluted him. "Yes sir."

He flicked his finger off the end of her nose and escorted a reluctant Wags to the crate. But he had one more trick up his sleeve. He picked the favored red rubber dog toy and tossed it into the crate. Wags jumped in after it.

"Sorry, bud," he said and shut the door.

Libby was waiting He took her hand and led her down the hall to the bedroom and shut that door.

On Sunday, Libby had accompanied Nick to Camp Life Launch to pick up the girls. Now they were driving back home with two exhausted but still chattering girls in the back seat of her Corolla.

Almost like a real family, she thought, and glanced at Nick. He must have felt her gaze on him, because he turned a questioning look to her. She smiled and he returned it. Yep, almost like a real family.

"And Mr. Brody offered Oakley a job at the camp for the summer," Rebecca was saying.

"It's just temporary, and only if it's okay with you, Uncle Nick. I can learn to work as a camp counselor for the younger kids."

Libby glanced into the back seat. Oakley's foot jiggled while she waited for Nick's response. She really did look to her uncle for guidance. Libby hoped it would help him heal from the self-inflicted wounds regarding his family.

"I think it all sounds exciting," he said, glancing into the rearview mirror.

"I can still help you out at the shop," the girl assured Libby. "Mary said we'd work around my schedule. I told her I'd already accepted a job with you. I wouldn't leave you high and dry."

"I know you wouldn't. We'll work it out."

"Yippee," Rebecca clapped. "And a boy at the camp kept smiling at Oakley."

Nick snapped to attention. "What?"

Oakley made that exaggerated eye roll, but her cheeks bloomed with color. "It was nothing."

"I'll be the judge of that," he said.

Oakley thrust her chin out. "Before you go all Neanderthal, he's just a friend."

Libby lightly touched Nick's shoulder. "I'm sure once your uncle meets this boy, he'll be very happy for you. Now, what does everyone want for supper?"

Nick grumbled but grinned when Libby squeezed his arm and gave him a look.

Was this what being in a true relationship felt like? Each one supporting the other? She knew now that her relationship with Will had been doomed from the start. After urging Nick to forgive himself, maybe it was time she did that for herself.

"Here, Mommy, Grandma wants to talk to you now." Rebecca handed Libby the phone.

Libby sighed. A week had passed since the weekend at Camp Life Launch, and Rebecca had been bugging her to call her grandmother. She wanted to tell her about all her adventures. Libby had dragged her feet because she'd been in a contented bubble with her life. Oakley had offered to babysit so she and Nick could finally share a real date.

"Mommy." Rebecca waved the phone in front of Libby.

She had to face reality at some point. Cutting off her parents wasn't a solution.

Sighing, Libby took the phone. "Hello, Mother."

"Who is this Nick person Rebecca has been talking about?"

She should have anticipated this. Of course, Rebecca was going to talk about him. He and Oakley were her favorite people. And why should have to tell her daughter not to talk about them? "He's a…friend."

"Huh, well, from the way Rebecca talked, he sounds like a bit more than that."

So what if he is? Libby thought angrily. She was an adult and didn't need permission from her parents to…to what? Like Nick? Oh, she liked him. More than that. She loved him. It was too late to stop it even if she wanted to. And she found that she didn't want to. She might not have any idea where they were going with this relationship, but she wanted to find out. There was a wonderful, caring man beneath the tough exterior he liked to project. If her parents didn't see that, then tough.

"Elizabeth? What have you got to say for yourself?" her mother demanded from the side of the phone.

"I'm not sure what you want to hear. Rebecca and I like Nick…a lot." So there.

"*Humph.* Rebecca makes it sound like he'd practically living there."

"Mom, she's five. Her perception of things can be skewed." Why was she always trying to appease them?

"And she told me that his arm is covered in tattoos. What will people think?"

"Who cares?"

"What? How can you say that? You have a daughter to think of and a business to run. Although why you'd want to work in a poky little shop is beyond me. If you'd stayed with Will you wouldn't have to worry about finances. You wouldn't have to send Rebecca to some charity camp."

To say the conversation went downhill from there was an understatement.

Two days after the horrible phone call with her mother, Libby was closing up shop and thinking about what to cook for supper. She'd invited Nick and Oakley and was looking forward to seeing them. Once again, their schedules had been clashing and she hadn't seen him. Even Oakley hadn't come in because she was out at the camp. She and Nick had talked on the phone, but it wasn't the same. She missed being able to see and touch him.

She locked the door to the shop and turned. As soon as she stepped onto the sidewalk she spotted the black Cadillac, and her heart stuttered. It couldn't be. But it was, and they hadn't even called to tell her of their plans. Her parents were here. Talk about an ambush.

"Surprise," her mother said, getting out of the car. "We came to take our two girls to supper."

Chapter Fifteen

Nick drove out to the camp to pick up Oakley, that itchy feeling keeping him company. The same feeling he'd had when Libby had acted embarrassed to have people know about them.

He'd been looking forward to spending the evening with Libby but she'd called just before he'd left and begged off. He tried to find out why, but she just kept saying "something" had come up.

Oakley jumped into the car when he pulled up. "Are we going to Libby's tonight? I've been working with Rebecca on tying her shoes. I think she's almost there and we were going to surprise her mother. That sort of surprise is okay, isn't it? Not like the tattoo thing."

"That's a good surprise. I'm sure Libby will be pleased."

"Cool. I'll work with Rebecca some more tonight."

"Uh, we're not going."

"What? Why not? Does Rebecca have another ear infection?"

He shrugged. Libby had assured him that Rebecca was fine. "No, she just said something's come up and she couldn't make it."

"Oh," Oakley said, disappointment evident in her tone.

"How about we go somewhere for supper? The two of us." He hated hearing that disappointment.

"But I missed Sparky today. Can we get it to go and eat at home?"

"Sure. Call Polly's and order what you want. I'll pick it up."

"Great. Can you drop me at home so I can play with Sparky?"

"Sure."

Oakley ordered fried chicken for both of them, and continued to chatter away about her day at camp. Nick barely listened as the feeling he had kept growing. He didn't understand it, but the last time he'd ignored it, he'd walked into an ambush.

After dropping Oakley off, Nick went to the popular restaurant on the town green to pick up their supper. He was standing at the cashier when he glanced over at a booth by the window.

He blinked. It was Libby and Rebecca sitting with an older couple. Her parents? She happened to glance over and made eye contact. Her eyes widened, so he knew she'd seen him.

Surely, she'd wave him over. But instead of acknowledging him, she looked away. Nick felt as if she'd sliced him open with a KA-BAR knife.

"Here's your supper, Mr. Cabot," the girl manning the cash register handed him the bag.

He grabbed the bag and managed to smile and thank the girl. He'd ridden the bike, so he put the bag in the saddlebag.

Libby came running out of the restaurant, waving at him. A little too late.

But he paused before putting on his helmet and starting the bike.

"You don't understand," she said, her eyes frantic.

"What don't I understand? It was clear you didn't want to introduce me to your parents. I got that message loud and clear."

"Yes. I mean no."

"Which is it. Libby?"

She glanced back at the restaurant. "I don't know. I just…"

He put the helmet on and jammed his foot down hard to start the Scout. He roared off, leaving her standing on the sidewalk.

Whatever she had to say, he wasn't interested. She was ashamed to introduce him to her parents. Did she feel that way about Oakley, too? Well, he was not going to give her an opportunity to hurt his niece.

He tried to act normal during supper but Oakley asked a few times if anything was wrong.

"No, all good," he told her.

Luckily, Oakley had the kitten to keep her entertained, and he could brood in silence.

After they'd cleaned up from supper, he told Oakley

he had some paperwork to take care of and went down to the shop. He had an unopened bottle of whiskey there. A present from a customer, but with his family history, he'd left it in the drawer.

He sat with his feet on his desk but didn't open the bottle. He'd be damned if he let her drive him to drink. Glanced at the ceiling and the apartment upstairs.

"I wouldn't do that to you, kid."

A car pulled into the driveway, the tires crunching on the gravel. He looked at the bottle again, wishing he'd opened it.

Libby jumped out of the car. "Nick, I need to explain."

He didn't get up, just sat with his feet on the desk, the whiskey bottle next to his foot.

When he didn't say anything, she hesitated.

"I'm not ashamed of you, if that's what you think. I'm ashamed of *them*. I didn't want to expose you to their vitriol." She seemed to collapse in on herself. "They were in rare form tonight. I didn't want…"

"I get it. You didn't want. Is that all?"

"What do you mean? Is that all?"

"I mean is that what you came to tell me?" he enunciated each word as if he had drunk the bottle next to his foot.

"I love you, damn it."

He dropped his feet off the desk. "Where's Rebecca?"

"She's with Clara." Libby waved her hands. "Did you hear what I said?"

"I heard. You're speaking loud enough to raise the dead."

"Haven't you anything to say?"

"Yeah, that kind of love, I don't need." He'd been doing his best not to let her words affect him, but his hand started to shake, and he rose. "If you'll excuse me, I need to get back upstairs."

He left her standing in the parking lot. Damn, he should have taken the bottle with him.

"It's obvious that you love her," Oakley said for the umpteenth time since he'd had to confess that they'd split. And why.

"Is that so?" Nick asked, shaking his head at himself.

What are you, twelve? a voice asked, because he was certainly acting like it with that response.

It had been a week since he'd walked out on Libby that night. He'd had time to think about what she'd said. Maybe expecting her to introduce him before she was ready had been unfair. Oakley had told him how Libby said she had trouble standing up to her parents, but she was working on it. Maybe he should have been more understanding.

"Remember that night we went to Libby's for supper?"

"Which night?" he asked, realizing they'd gone dozens of times. Damn, but he missed spending time with her, her cooking, helping her in the kitchen and—No. Not going there.

"I'm talking about the first time." She sighed. "I remember I was nervous because after seeing her house, that nice neighborhood, I was worried. I felt as if I didn't belong because of my background."

"There's no reason you shouldn't belong, no matter where you came from, Oakley. What your mother or your grandparents do is no reflection on you as a person."

"Exactly. So, why shouldn't you be with Libby? You deserve happiness and love as much as anyone. From what I've seen, you make her happy. From what she's confided in me, her first husband was a jerk. No wonder she fell in love with you. You're a good guy, Uncle Nick. No matter where you came from."

"You don't know what happened in—"

"I don't need to know the details of what happened in Afghanistan, because I know you. I *know* you acted with courage and honor. No matter what you might think, you're a hero. You saved lives."

"Yes, but—"

"No! No buts. I know you don't like to talk about it, but I can read and I can do research and I know some of what happened. You saved lives. That's nothing to throw away. Stop doing penance and live your best life. Live your life with Libby."

"When did you get to be so smart."

"I think it was when I decided not to accept what was happening around me and to me and I came to find you."

"I thank God every day that you did." He thought how the attorney had come through with temporary guardianship. Next step was to make it permanent.

"I could have gotten sucked into all that sh—stuff and ruined my life by staying. Even when I came, I wasn't sure if you'd let me stay. I know what you saw when I first appeared on your doorstep."

"I saw that my niece was growing into a beautiful young woman."

She lifted an eyebrow. "Rewrite history much?"

He began to protest and she waved it away. "You saw a girl who was trying to look tough, but you saw the scared girl underneath and gave me a hug. A very welcome hug. How did you know that's what I needed?"

Because when confronted with a situation like that, he imagined what Libby would do. He imagined Libby welcoming the scared young girl with open arms, so that was what he'd done.

"Uncle Nick?"

He shrugged nonchalantly, but he felt warmth rise in his cheeks.

"I see," she said and grinned.

He scowled. "You see what?"

"I see Libby's influence written all over that hug."

He grumbled but didn't contradict her.

She ran to him and gave him a hug. "Go to her. Apologize for acting like a jerk."

"Hey. Why are you assuming the breakup was all my fault?"

She grinned. "I don't know what you did or said, but you're a guy, so I imagine you probably messed up somehow."

"That's very sexist."

"And very true."

He sighed in exasperation, but secretly had to admit she was right. The more thought he had given it, the more he could see he should have given Libby a chance. "I'll talk to her, but she may not forgive me."

Oh, God. What would he do if she didn't? What if

she took one look and slammed the door in his face? Like he'd done to her.

"Then we'll have to be sure she does."

"How do you propose I do that?" Taking advice from a teenager. Yeah, he was that desperate. He'd gone a week without Libby and it was killing him. He couldn't imagine going the rest of his life without her. He might not be able to resist that bottle on his desk. And he had to. Not just for Oakley but himself. And for Dan who'd believed in him when no one else had.

"With a grand gesture."

"With a what?"

"A grand gesture... You know, like when you save her sister's reputation by forcing a louse to marry her and pay off his debts when he does."

"What in the world are you talking about? Libby doesn't have a sister."

"But I happen to know she's a Jane Austen fan."

"You have totally lost me, young lady."

She sighed. "Just bring her some flowers or candy."

"Here. This came for you." She shoved an envelope at him and marched back to her room.

Nick opened the manila envelope and pulled out a note. A letter-sized envelope addressed to him fell out.

He read the handwritten note first.

I apologize for not sending this before now. Somehow it had gotten misplaced in Dan's desk. I haven't read it myself but I know he wanted you to have it. Just let me add, I know how much he cared for you and how proud he was of you for turning your life around.

The note was signed by Dan's widow, Evelyn. Next he took out the smaller note.

I know what happened to your platoon and I know you feel responsible for the men you lost. How do I know this? Because that's how I would feel. I can tell you I could say, "Knock it off and suck it up," but I'm not sure that will help. But I can say this. I know in my heart that you led your men with integrity and that you would have sacrificed yourself for any one of them. But allow them to feel the same. They knew going in what the risks were and they accepted that. The fact that so many survived in those overwhelming odds is down to your leadership and the fact you were willing to sacrifice yourself to save even one of them. You succeeded in saving a dozen men. That's twelve men that wouldn't be here today if not for you. No small feat, Cabot.

I could go on but I think I've gushed enough about your value as a man and a marine. I'm not normally this sentimental but I find that it sneaks in when one is facing his own mortality.

Don't just mourn for me but go and live a good life. Don't let your less than stellar childhood or what happened in Kabul prevent you from being happy and fulfilled.

That's an order, Marine!

Nick tried to swallow past the lump forming in his throat. For him, Dan had been more than a mentor. He'd been a savior. A father figure. A friend.

He thought about Libby and Rebecca. He'd once told Libby that Dan would have liked her, and he still believed that. He could imagine Dan giving him a slap upside the head and calling him dense for letting her slip through his fingers.

He climbed the stairs to the apartment, trying to decide what to do. He went and found Oakley in her room, playing with the kitten.

"So, what is this grand gesture stuff you spoke of?"

She jumped up. "You mean it? You'll try to get her to take you back?"

"I'm going to try."

"She and Rebecca are crazy about you. Just tell her how you feel."

"You think so?"

Oakley rolled her eyes. "How could you doubt it? Anyone with eyes in their head could see how she looks at you. It's a bit obscene, if you ask me."

"Well, no one asked you."

"And when you two are together the sexual tension between the two of—"

"Hey, hey. I am not, repeat not, discussing *that* with my fifteen-year-old niece." He needed to get Libby back to help him navigate the teen years.

"Aw, gee, does that mean you won't be lecturing on the birds and the bees?"

"I won't need to because while you're living with me, you're not going to need to know about the birds and the bees because any guy will have to get through me first."

Oakley gave an exaggerated eye roll. "Oh, please."

Nick narrowed his eyes as he studied her. For all her protesting, he suspected she enjoyed the protective stance he was taking. He recalled a conversation he'd had with Libby. According to Libby, Oakley was grateful for the boundaries he had set. It showed he cared.

* * *

Nick roared into town on his bike and parked as close as he could get to Adventures in Quilting. He hoped the store wasn't too busy. He'd prefer to do his groveling without an audience. But he was prepared to do it in front of a packed store of town gossips, if he had to.

He got off the bike and pulled the bag out of the saddlebag. Glancing down, he felt a moment of panic. This didn't feel as grand as whatever Oakley was referring to.

He started along the sidewalk to the store and spotted Rebecca coming toward him.

"Rebecca, it's nice to see you. Where's your mom?" Nick glanced around, expecting to see Libby close by. She was vigilant when it came to her daughter.

"She's on the phone with my grandma," she said and continued making her way across the town green.

Sparing another glance in the direction Rebecca had come from, Nick turned and caught up to her. What was going on? Where was Libby?

"Is your mom on her way?"

Rebecca shook her head. "I tole you, she's talking to my grandma on the phone."

"So you're here by yourself?"

"Uh-huh."

Damn. What was going on? "You shouldn't be out by yourself."

She turned on him and placed her hands on her hips. "Why not?"

"You're too young. Besides, I don't think your mom would like it. Does she know you're out here by yourself?" What had happened? He wanted to get to Libby. Was she hurt or something? But he refused to leave Rebecca alone.

"I'm not too young! Why does everyone think I'm a baby?"

"Look, I know you're not a baby, but I think you should be with an adult. Tell me where you're going. I'll go with you."

"No." She shook her head and pushed out her lower lip.

"What?" Nick was taken aback. From the start, Rebecca had only ever been loving and accepting toward him. He recalled the day he'd met her, when she'd thrown her arms around him in unabashed affection. "Why can't I go with you?"

"Because I don't want you to go with me." She crossed her arms over her chest and glared at him.

"Why not? I thought we were friends."

"We were, but then you made my mommy cry, so I don't want to be your friend no more."

Libby cried? He swallowed the bile that rose in his throat at the thought of her crying. Of it being his fault that she'd cried. God, he hated that so much. That right there was why he never should have gotten involved. He should have followed his initial instincts and stayed away. Why hadn't he? Because he couldn't help himself. And if he was going to show Oakley how to live, he needed to own up to his mistakes and go for that brass ring.

He rubbed a hand over his face. "I'm sorry that I made your mom sad."

"I don't like it when she's sad."

"And it's all my fault," he said as much to her as himself.

"Yes," she said and nodded, her arms still crossed. "So I'm very sorry but I can't be friends with you no more."

He bit the inside of his cheek to prevent a smile at her polite candor. She really was a great kid and he was extra sorry that the fallout from his actions with her mother had affected her.

What had you expected? his conscience demanded. He sighed and opened his mouth, but before any words came out, a frantic Libby came pounding down the sidewalk.

"Rebecca, what are you doing leaving the store like that? You are in so much trouble, young lady."

"I'm sorry, Mommy, but I heard a motorcycle and came out to see. I told you I was going but you was busy yelling at Grandma." She stuck her lower lip out. "And I forgot I'm not friends with Mr. Nick."

"I wouldn't have let anything happen to her," he told Libby.

God, it was so good to see her. He'd missed her so much.

Libby drank in the sight of Nick. Oh, God, how she'd missed him.

"Can we go inside?" he asked. "I need to talk to you. Please."

"Sure." She'd listen to what he had to say. Her first instinct was to punish him for the way he'd treated her, but she'd had time to see her actions from his point of view. She couldn't place all the blame on him for not understanding. Her actions had hurt him and he'd lashed out.

Once inside the store, she turned the sign from Open to Closed. She nervously wiped her hands down her slacks. His appearance at her place didn't mean he was seeking a reconciliation. But she wasn't afraid to admit that she desperately hope that's what this visit meant. She couldn't imagine trying to live the rest of her life without him.

"Mr. Nick? What's in the bag?"

"Presents for you and your mom."

Did he think he could buy something and expect her to fall at his feet? Who was she kidding? She was ready to melt into a puddle just looking at him.

"Can I see?" Rebecca asked, bouncing on her toes. He glanced at Libby. She nodded and he handed the bag to her.

She reached in and pulled out two leather jackets, one adult and one child-sized.

Rebecca held hers up. "Look, Mommy, now we match with Mr. Nick."

"It's not grand like saving your sister's reputation by getting some jerk to marry her, but it's all I could think of." He shuffled his feet.

She frowned. "I don't have a sister."

"That's what I tried to tell Oakley, but she kept going on about it," he said on a sigh.

It dawned on Libby what he was talking about, and her eyes filled with tears.

"Look, Mommy, it fits." Rebecca had the jacket on and was doing a little dance. "What's it for?"

"For riding motorcycles. You two can't be proper biker chicks without them." His cheeks were red.

But it was his eyes that caught her. They were filled with hope and pleading.

"We're gonna be biker chicks?" Rebecca asked.

Libby covered her mouth with her hand. "It looks like it, sweetie."

"I don't know what that is, but I loves my new jacket. Can I go in back and look in the mirror?"

"Of course, sweetie." *Take your time.*

Rebecca gave Nick a hug. "I'm not mad anymore. Just don't make my mommy cry again."

"I promise." He returned her hug. "I will do my best to make your mommy happy for the rest of our lives if she'll forgive me."

"Are you gonna forgive him, Mommy?"

"I already have, sweetie."

"Goodie," Rebecca said and skipped off to the back room to admire her new jacket in the full-length mirror.

"You mean it?" he asked. "You forgive my terrible behavior that night?"

Her throat clogged with unshed tears; all she could do was nod.

"Goodie," he parroted and scooped her up. Hugging her tight, her feet dangling, he twirled her around.

"You truly forgive me?" he asked.

"If you can forgive me," she said. "You have no idea how much I've regretted ignoring you that night. I honestly thought I was protecting you and Oakley. I was afraid they might hurt you and that precious girl's feelings. I know how they can be."

He gave her a quick kiss. "Rebecca said you were on the phone yelling at your mother?"

"I told her I was in love with you and if you wouldn't forgive me, I was placing the blame on her." The thought of not having her parents in their lives anymore was sad. But not as terrible as the thought of not having Nick and Oakley in it. "I was going to come to see you tonight. Only I didn't have any grand gestures. Just myself, and maybe some red lace."

He groaned and said, "I can't believe you forgave me. I am so sorry for my boorish behavior."

"And I'm sorry for putting you in that position. I should have had the courage to introduce you no matter the consequences. I promise never to do anything like that ever again."

"I don't know what's going to happen in the future with your parents but I promise to stand by you whatever you decide." He squeezed her tight. "But if they try to hurt you, they'll have me to answer to."

"I've already decided. I love you and if they can't accept that, then it's their loss.

"I love you, Elizabeth Taylor, and I always will."

"And I love you. I never stopped, even when you said those things."

She couldn't wait any longer and threw her arms around his neck and pulled him in for a kiss.

They were still kissing when Rebecca came back in the room and threw her arms around both of them.

Epilogue

Six months later

Libby snuggled up next to him on the couch and admired the diamond he'd put on her left hand that evening. They'd gone for a romantic dinner and then to the lake after. In the moonlight at the lake, he'd gotten down on one knee and asked her to be his biker chick forever.

"I guess this means I won't be Elizabeth Taylor anymore," she said with a sigh.

"You can keep your name."

"What? No way. I will wear the Cabot name with pride."

"I figured it was about time…especially with this

bun in the oven," he said, placing his hand over her stomach.

She pressed her hand over his. "I know it's kind of soon and—"

"Considering I'm not getting any younger, I think it's not too soon."

"Didn't you know, forty is the new thirty."

He shook his head. "Not sure about that."

"Hey, I have no complaints."

"Of course this means no rides for you for a while."

"We'll be busy making more room," she said. "Are you sure you don't mind staying in this house?"

"Are you kidding? I took one look at this place and snatched you up." He laughed. "Oakley already loves the idea of making a bedroom in the basement. She'll have her own room and bathroom and some privacy. Of course if we put a television down there, we'll make sure there's no Netflix."

She scrunched up her nose in confusion. "No Netflix? I don't understand."

"There won't be any Netflix and chill under my roof."

"I still don't understand." What was he talking about?

He leaned over and whispered in her ear.

"What? No... Really? How did I not know this?"

He kissed her again. "You're such an innocent."

"Not anymore," she said and cupped her palm around his cheek. "I'm a biker chick now."

"Hmm, you certainly are."

Kissing him, she asked, "Happy?"

"Scarily so. I don't deserve—"

She pressed her fingertips against his lips. "Maybe neither of us does. Or maybe we both do. Either way, we're going to have it. Do you hear me?"

He started to say something, but she pressed harder and he nodded vigorously. He would have to be insane to let this amazing, wonderful woman go. And yeah, maybe he was punching above his weight class, but he was going to hold tight to the best thing that had ever happened to him.

"I'm so glad we're in agreement," she said and sighed. "We're going to give Rebecca and Oakley the family that *they* deserve."

"You're okay with Oakley living with us? I mean, I'm not sure what's going to happen with my sister, but the guardianship is permanent now. She's one of us. I have to be sure Oakley's not only safe but encouraged to reach her potential."

"That's the way I feel about Rebecca. Naturally, I feel the same way about Oakley. I see them as both our girls."

"She's already a teen, as you have pointed out on several occasions, with all that involves."

"I love you and I love her. You're a package deal and so am I."

"Then I say we consolidate our packages and— What?"

"Consolidated package?" She laughed. "As Rebecca would say, 'you sure talk funny,' but I find it terribly sexy, Mr. Nick. Consolidated package it is, with yours, mine and ours."

"Wrong," he said, shaking his head. "Just ours."

"You're right. Rebecca and Oakley are ours just as this one will be." She patted her stomach.

"You still don't mind taking on a teen?"

She shook her head. "Package deals don't bother me."

"Well, if you like that package, then…" He leaned down and whispered in her ear.

"You naughty man. I love it," she said and wound her arms around his neck, bringing his lips close to hers.

"What time did you say the girls would be home?"

She checked her watch. "Not for at least another hour."

He wiggled his eyebrows. "I can work with that."

"Does this mean we're going to Netflix and chill?"

"Absolutely." Not one to pass up an opportunity, Nick captured her mouth.

* * * * *

Chapter One

"Another drink for Maribel."

Maribel Del Toro held up her palm. "No, *thanks*. I might not be driving, but I have to worry about walking while under the influence."

For an establishment that was a historical landmark, the Salty Dog Bar & Grill had mastered the art of a modern twist. The ambience fell somewhere between contemporary and classic, with a long bar of gleaming dark wood, one redbrick wall and exposed ceiling beams. Separate and on the opposite side of the bar the restaurant section was filled with booths. To top it all off, a quaint sense of small coastal town community infused the bar. Maribel loved it here.

Her brother, Max, was the occasional bartender and full-time owner. Situated on the boardwalk in the quiet town of Charming, Texas, it was the kind of place where everybody knew your name.

Especially if you were the younger sister of one of the three former Navy SEALs who owned and operated the establishment.

"You had one beer. Even I think you're skilled enough to make it to the cottages without falling." Max grinned and wiped the bar.

"Ha ha. My brother, the comedian. I'll have a soda, please and thank you."

Afterward, she'd take a leisurely walk down to her beach rental a short mile from the boardwalk. Lately, she'd been digging her toes in the sand and simply staring off into the large gulf. Her father had once said if she ever got too big for her britches, she should consider the vastness of the ocean. She often had from her childhood home in Watsonville, California. The Pacific Ocean was an entirely different feel from the Gulf Coast, but both reminded her of how small her own problems were in comparison.

The doors to the restaurant swung open and some of the customers called out.

"Val! Hey, girl."

"When are you gettin' yourself back to work?"

"Soon as my husband lets me! Believe me, I miss y'all, especially your tips." Valerie Kinsella stopped to chat with customers and let a few of them check out the bundle in her front-loaded baby carrier.

She sidled up to the bar, her hand protectively cradled on her son's head of espresso brown curls that matched his mother's. "Hey, y'all. How's it goin'?"

"Hey there." Max hooked his thumb in the direction of the back office. "If you want Cole, he's in the back checking the books. We want to give the staff a nice bonus around the holidays."

"Well, dang it, I'm going to miss out on that, too. But I didn't just come by to see Cole. I sleep next to him every night." Valerie elbowed Maribel. "How are you enjoying your vacation?"

"Loving it. The beach rental unit is just perfect."

"And even if it is hurricane season, the weather seems to be cooperating."

Oh yeah. By the way, somebody should have told Maribel. When she'd eagerly booked this vacation for November, everyone forgot to mention the tail end of hurricane season. But this part of the Gulf Coast hadn't been hit in many years, so it was considered safe. Or as safe as Mother Nature could be. In any case, the lovely row of cottages near the beach were being sold to an investor, according to her sister-in-law, Ava, and this might be Maribel's last chance to stay there.

She nodded to Valerie's baby. "What a cutie. Congratulations again."

"Wade is such a sweet baby. We're lucky." Valerie kissed the top of his head.

He was a healthy-looking kid, too, with bright blue curious eyes the same intense shade as his father's. Maribel didn't have any children of her own, but she had plenty of experience. Loads. More than she'd ever wanted, thank you. In a way, that was why she was here in Charming, taking a sabbatical from all the suffering and gnashing of teeth. It went along with her profession like the ocean to the grains of sand.

"When do you go back to teaching?" Maribel gently touched Wade's little pert nose.

"Not until after the holidays. I've had a nice maternity leave, but it's time to get back to my other kids. The students claim to miss me. I have enough cards and drawings to make me almost believe it."

Maribel spent a few more minutes being treated to Valerie's "warrior story," i.e., her labor and delivery. She was a champ, according to Cole. Valerie claimed not to remember much, which to Maribel sounded like a blessing in disguise. Mucus plug. Episiotomy. Yikes. Maribel had reached her TMI limit when Cole, the former SEAL turned golden surfer boy, came blustering out of the back office looking every bit the harried father of one.

"Hey, baby." He slid his arm around Valerie, circling it around mother and child.

Maribel had known Cole for years since he'd been a part of the brotherhood who for so long had ruled Max's life. She imagined Max and his wife would be headed to Baby Town soon, as well. And though it was information still being held private, Jordan and Rafe were newly pregnant. Maribel had been given the news by a thrilled Jordan just last week.

Maribel slid off the stool. "Well, folks, I'm going to head on back to my little beach shack now."

Shack wasn't quite the right word. She'd been pleasantly surprised to find a suite similar to resort hotel villas. It contained a separate seating area and flat-screen, attached kitchenette and separate bedroom with a second flat-screen and a king-size bed. The bedroom had sliders opening up to a small patio that led to the private beach.

"Need a ride?" Cole asked.

"Nah. Part of the ambience of Charming can only be enjoyed by strolling."

Max gave a quick wave. "Don't forget, Ava wants you over for dinner soon."

"I'm here two weeks. Plenty of time." She slid a pleading look Valerie's way. "I'm hopeful for another invite to the lighthouse, too."

"Anytime!" Cole and Valerie both said at once, making everyone laugh.

Max rolled his eyes, but he should talk. He and Ava often finished each other's sentences.

Outside, the early November evening greeted her with a mild and light wind. Summers in the gulf had resembled a sauna in every way, but autumn had so far turned out to be picture perfect. Except for the whole hurricane season thing. Still, it was warm enough during the day for trips to the beach. When she dipped her toes in, the gulf waters were less like a hot tub and more like a warm bath. Maribel ambled along the seawall, away from the boardwalk side filled with carnival-style rides for children. The succulent scent of freshly popped kettle corn and waffle cones hung thickly in the air. She passed by shops, both the Lazy Mazy kettle corn and the saltwater taffy store. The wheels of an old-fashioned machine in front of the shop's window rolled and pulled the taffy and entertained passersby. In the distance, Maribel spotted a group of surfers.

The views were everything one would expect from a

bucolic beach town with a converted lighthouse, piers, docks and sea jetties. The first time she'd been here was for Max and Ava's wedding six months ago, and she'd fallen in love with the area. It was the only place she'd considered escaping when she'd decided to resign from her position as a social worker. The offer from a multi-author doctor corporation was one she'd consider while here. They wanted a psychologist on board to assist with their heavy caseload, and that meant Maribel would put her hard-earned PhD to use. Although she wasn't excited by the prospect. Maybe after this vacation, she'd be able to clear the decks and finally make a firm decision. The offer was attractive, but it would be a huge change for her. She wasn't sure she'd be able to do much good and felt at a crossroads in her life. And this was the perfect location to decide what she'd do for the rest of her professional life.

The small row of beachfront cottages were rented year-round by both residents and tourists. Maribel had lucked into a rental during the off-season, meaning she had the peace and quiet she craved. As far as she could tell so far, she had only one neighbor, immediately next door. He was the most irritating male she'd ever had the misfortune of meeting. Sort of. There was, in fact, quite a list. He was, at the moment, in the top five.

On the day she'd arrived, she'd been to the store to stock up on groceries for all the cooking she'd planned to do. Hauling no less than four paper bags inside, she'd set one down just outside the heavy front door, propping it open.

When she'd returned for it, a huge cowboy stood outside her door holding it.

"Forgot something." He'd brushed by her, striding inside like he owned the place.

"Hey," she muttered, following him.

The man spoke in a thick Texan drawl, and he hadn't said the words in a helpful way. More like an accusatory tone, as in "You dingbat, here's your bag. If you need any other help getting through life, let me know."

She'd caught him looking around the inside of her rental as if apprising its contents. But he didn't *look* like a burglar.

"I didn't forget." Maribel snatched the shopping bag from him, deciding in that moment he'd made it to the top five. Of all the nerve. She hadn't been gone a full minute.

"You might not want to just leave anything out here unattended. Unless you want someone to steal it."

Steal? Here in the small town of Charming, Texas?

She flushed at the remark. "I don't think anyone is going to steal my box of cereal or fresh fruit."

"Regardless, you should care for your property. Don't invite trouble."

Okay, so he'd figured out she was a single woman and wanted to look out for her.

"Great. If you're done with your mansplaining, I'm going to cook dinner."

"Are you liking this unit well enough? Everything in working condition?"

Now, he sounded like the landlord. *Good grief.* Top three most irritating men, easily.

"Yes, thank you, I have located everything I need." She rolled her eyes.

"I'm next door if you need anything else."

"I won't."

He'd tipped his hat, but she'd shut the door on him before he could say another word.

Since that day, she saw little of him, and that was fine with her.

Twenty minutes of an invigorating walk later, she arrived at her cottage. There was her neighbor again, the surly surfing cowboy, coming up from their lane to the beach carrying a surfboard under his arm. He might be irritating as hell, but he looked like he'd emerged from the sea shirtless, ready to sell viewers the latest popular male cologne.

She wondered whether he was attempting to cover two hero stereotypes at once. He wore a straw cowboy hat, and though this was Texas, after all, the hat didn't *quite* match with the bare chest and wet board shorts he wore low on his hips. A towel slung around his neck completed the outfit of the salty guy who once more simply nodded in her direction. Before she could say, "Howdy, neighbor," he stared straight ahead like she no longer existed.

No worries. She hadn't come here to make friends. Even if he resembled a Greek god. Thor, to be more specific—who wasn't actually from Greek mythology. This demigod had taut golden skin, a square jaw and a sensual mouth. His abs, legs and arms were chiseled to near perfection. But she was going to ignore all this because it didn't fit into her plans.

Focus. Men were not part of the plan. Even sexy irritating males, her weakness. She was here to unplug and had turned off her cell, giving her family the land-line for emergencies. In her plan for mindfulness and peace, she was practicing yoga every morning before sunrise. And reading. Not from her e-reader but actual print she had to hold in her hands.

Rather than dwelling on her problems, Maribel would set them aside for now. Since months of dwelling on her problems hadn't given any answers, she was trying this new approach.

Once she'd spent enough time away from her situation, her mind would produce fresh results and ideas.

Because she had to decide soon how she would spend the rest of her life.

Dean Hunter hopped out of the shower and wrapped a towel around himself. Another day completed in his attempts to hit the waves and master the fine art of surfing. All he had to show for it? Two more fresh cuts, five new bruises and a sore knee. He had to face facts: he was a disaster on the water, having spent most of his life on a working cattle ranch. He'd been bucked off many a horse, and how interesting to find it wasn't any less pleasant to slam into the water than the ground. Seemed like water should give a little, and of course it did, more than the ground ever would. Still hurt, though, equal to the velocity with which a person slammed into a wave.

Why am I here?

A question he asked himself twice a day.

He should have simply backed out of this vacation and lost his deposit. This time was to have been a getaway with Amanda, where he'd get down on bended knee and pop the question. The cottages were going to be a surprise wedding gift to her. A way to show her all he'd accomplished. They'd have a vacation home every summer, a whole row of them. He was a damn idiot thinking that maybe he'd finally found the right woman. He and Amanda were both part of the circuit and had been for years. They had a great deal in common, and eventually they'd decided moving out of the friend zone made sense.

Then, six months ago, he'd walked in on Amanda showing Anton "The Kid" Robbins the ropes. And by "the ropes," he meant he'd walked in on her and the twenty-six-year-old, Amanda straddling him like a bucking horse. No way a man could ever unsee that. He'd walked out of his own house and moved into a hotel room. One more race to win, he'd told himself, and maybe then he'd go out on top. But that hadn't happened.

To think that Anton had been his protégé. Dean hadn't been ready to retire, but he saw the sense in training the new kids, giving them a hand up. Someone had done this for him, and he would return the favor. He couldn't ride forever, but he'd thought he would have had a little more time. Now Dean was the old guard and Anton the new. He didn't have as many injuries (yet) as Dean and was also ten years younger.

Dean still had no idea how he'd gotten it all so wrong. He hadn't been able to clearly see what had been in front of him all along. His manager had warned him about Amanda, who was beautiful but calculating. Dean had wanted to believe he'd finally found someone who would stick by him when he quit the rodeo. He'd had about six months with her, during which time she convinced him he'd found the right woman. *Yeah, not so much.*

Their breakup happened right before his last ride. He'd already been reeling when he'd taken the last blow, this one to his career. In some ways, he was still trying to get up from the last kick to his ego. At thirty-six, battered and bruised, he'd been turned in for a newer model. Anton still had plenty of mileage left on him, time to make his millions before a body part gave out on him.

So Dean should have let the opportunity to buy this investment property go. There were ten cottages, and in anticipation of his stay here to check them out thoroughly, they'd kept them vacant for him. All except Cute Stuck-up Girl next door. The moment he'd noticed he wasn't here alone as expected, he'd phoned the real estate agent.

"Thought I was going to be here by myself."

"You were, but Maribel Del Toro apparently has some influential friends in this town, friends who know the current owner and have some pull. We thought it best not to reschedule her reservation like we did the others."

"How am I supposed to inspect her unit?"

He'd already found an excuse by hurrying to help bring in a grocery bag in before she had a chance to say anything. You would have thought he'd wrecked the place instead of tried to help. He'd obviously insulted her in the process, but how else was he supposed to check inside? He never bought a dang thing before he inspected every nook and cranny, and that included a horse.

"We will give you a clause to back out if something is wrong in that unit. These deals fall apart all the time."

"And why is she right *next* to my unit?"

The real estate agent sighed. "Remember, you asked for new storm windows if you were even to consider buying. Progress on the others was not complete, and hers was the only unit available when she arrived."

By nature, Dean was a suspicious sort, and he couldn't help but wonder why these units were going far too cheaply for ocean-front property. But as a kid who'd grown up in Corpus Christi to a single mother who never had much, it would be a nice "full circle" gesture to buy this. And after years of punishing his body and garnering one buckle after another, he was a wealthy man. Still, he didn't like anyone to know it, least of all women. So he dressed like a cowboy even if he was technically a multimillionaire. At his core, he was a cowboy and always would be.

While the injury was said to be career ending, he could have gone through rehab and come back stronger than ever. Having come from nothing, he'd been wise about his investments, and while others enjoyed buckle bunnies, gambling and drinking, Dean had socked away every nickel. He had investments all over Texas, including his ranch in Hill Country.

In the end, he'd forced himself to walk away from the rodeo before he didn't have a body left to enjoy the other pleasantries in life. Oh yeah. That was why he was here in Charming trying his hand at surfing in the Gulf of Mexico during hurricane season. It was just the shot of adrenaline a junkie like him needed.

He would find his footing in his new world with zero illusions he'd find a second career as a competitive surfer. Instead, it was time for the second part of his life to begin, the part that was supposed to matter.

Life *after* the rodeo. Life after poverty.

He'd already been coming here for a short time every summer just to remember his roots. He'd drive from Corpus Christi to Charming, counting his blessings. Enjoying the coastal weather.

Remembering his mother.

Once, he could recall having ambitions that went beyond the rodeo. An idea and a plan to fix for others what had been broken in his own life. Somewhere along the line, he'd forgotten every last one of those dreams. He was here to hopefully remember some of them in the peace and quiet of this small town. Here, no one would disturb him. No one except his feisty neighbor, that is, who behaved as if he'd deeply insulted her by carrying in her groceries. She'd immediately put him on the defensive, seeing as it had merely been an excuse to get inside her unit. It was as if she could read his mind. He didn't like it.

He often watched Cute Stuck-up Girl from a distance as she sank her feet in the sand and read a book. Two days ago, he'd seen her fighting the beach umbrella she'd been setting up for shade. It was almost bigger than her, which was part of the problem. She'd cursed and carried on until Dean was two seconds away from offering his help. He'd walk over there and issue instructions on how to put the umbrella up until she got all red in the face again with outrage. The thought made him chuckle. He'd put the umbrella up *for* her if she'd let him. Not likely.

Finally, she got it to stay up and did a little victory dance when she must have assumed no one was watching.

And he'd found a laugh for the first time in months.

After changing clothes and towel-drying his hair, Dean plopped on his favorite black Stetson and headed to the local watering hole. A little place along the boardwalk that he'd discovered a few years ago sandwiched between other storefronts and gift shops. At the Salty Dog Bar & Grill, the occasional bartender and owner there was a surfer who'd given Dean plenty of tips. Cole Kinsella had even offered Dean one of his older boards, since as a new father, he wasn't taking to the water as often.

Safe to say, Dean liked the bar and the people in it from the moment he'd strode inside and momentarily indulged in one of his favorite fantasies: buying a sports bar. It was one of the few investments he didn't have because he'd been talked out of it too many times to count. This place resembled a sports bar, but was more of a family place that also happened to have a bar. The restaurant section sat next to the bar separated only by the booths. Instead of huge flat-screens on every spare amount of space, there were chalkboards with the specials written out in fancy white cursive.

Everyone was friendly and welcoming. The first night Dean had come in, he'd met a group of senior citizens who were having some kind of a poetry meeting.

The only gentleman in the group, Roy Finch, had offered to buy Dean a beer.

"Don't mind if I do." Dean nodded. "Thank you, sir."

"You're a cowboy?"

"Yes, sir. Born and bred." Dean tipped his hat.

"Don't usually see that many of you here on the gulf."

"Our profession usually keeps us far from the coast."

"What you doin' in these parts?'

"Good question." Dean took a pull of the beer the bartender had set in front of him. "I guess I'm lookin' for another profession."

"All washed out?"

"That obvious?" Dean snorted. "I was part of the rodeo circuit longer than I care to say."

"Thought I recognized you. Tough life."

They'd discussed the rodeo and the current front runners, which unfortunately included Anton. The man thought he was God's gift to women, overindulging in buckle bunnies and earning himself quite a reputation both on and off the circuit.

Dean had gone over a few of his injuries with Roy, but held back on the worst ones. Mr. Finch had introduced him to his fiancée, Lois, and some other women who were with him and were all part of a group calling themselves the Almost Dead Poets Society. Every night since then, Dean met someone new.

Now, he sidled up to the bar, but the surfer dude wasn't behind it. A dark-haired guy named Max, going by what everyone called him, was taking orders.

"What can I get you?" he asked Dean in an almost-menacing tone.

"Cold beer."

"We have several IPAs, domestic and imported." He rattled off names, sounding more like a sommelier than a bartender.

"Domestic, thanks."

"Here you go," he said a moment later, uncapping a bottle and taking Dean's cash.

This guy wasn't quite as chatty and friendly as Cole had been. He was also busy as the night wore on and, after a while, got grumpy.

"Max," someone called out. "C'mon! I ordered a mojito about an *hour* ago."

This was a great exaggeration, as Dean had listened to the man order it no more than fifteen minutes ago.

"And if you ask me again, you're not getting it *tonight*."

Dean would go out on a limb and guess this man was one of the owners of the bar. Cole had explained they were three former Navy SEALs who had retired and saved the floundering bar from foreclosure.

Turning his back to the bar, Dean spread his arms out and took in the sights. A busy place, the waitresses in the adjacent dining area flitted from one table to the next. He saw couples, families and a group of younger women taking up an entire table.

"Hey there, cowboy," a soft sweet voice to his right said. "I'm Twyla."

Dean immediately zeroed in on the source, a beautiful brunette who looked to be quite a bit younger than him. He shouldn't let that bother him, but for reasons he didn't understand, only younger women hit on him. He guessed it to be the fascination with the cowboy archetype, which usually happened when traveling in urban cities or coastal areas. He happened to know men who'd had nothing to do with ranches or rodeos who wore Western boots, a straw hat and ambled into a bar. They never left alone.

But a beautiful woman would only take time and attention away from Dean's surfing. Besides, were he to take up with any woman, it would be with the girl next door. Literally. She was as gorgeous a woman as he'd ever laid eyes on. Dark hair that fell in waves around her shoulders, chocolate brown eyes that made a man feel…seen.

"Dean. It's a pleasure." He nodded, failing to give her a last name. She didn't seem like the type to follow the rodeo, but one never knew.

He intended to remain anonymous while in Charming, though a few had already recognized him. The night before, he'd given out his autograph and taken a few photos with a family visiting from Hill Country. He ought to ditch the hat and shoot for a little less obvious.

"You're on vacation?" Twyla asked.

"How did you guess?"

"Not many cowboy types around here."

"Actually, I'm a surfer."

Speaking of exaggerations…

"You're kidding. Well, you're in the right place. Pretty soon the waves are going to kick up, depending on whether a system hits us. But don't worry, we haven't had a direct hit in decades." She offered her hand. "I own the bookstore in town, Once Upon a Book."

Her hand was soft and sweet, making Dean recall just how long it had been since he'd been with a woman. *Too* long. And even though it seemed like bookstores had become as out-of-date and useless as broken-down cowboys like him, he didn't feel a need to connect with this woman.

She had a look about her he recognized too well: she had a *thing* about cowboys. He wasn't interested in indulging in those fantasies. Been there, done that, bought the saddle. He was done with women who were interested in the part of him he was leaving behind. Rodeo had been fun, his entire life for two decades.

And now it was over.

They chatted a few more minutes about nothing in particular, and then Dean set his bottle down on the bar, deciding to call it an early night.

"Nice meeting ya."

"I'll see you around?" she asked.

"You will." He waved and strode outside.

The sun was nearing the end of its slow slide down the horizon, sinking into the sea, assuring him the sky would be dark by the time he drove to his rental. He looked forward to another night of peace and quiet, retiring to bed alone and hogging the damn covers. There were good parts of being alone, few that they were, and he needed to remember them lest he be tempted to remedy the situation.

He arrived to find a basket in front of Cute Stuck-up Girl's house she'd obviously forgotten to bring inside, again, and Dean figured he'd knock on the door and finally introduce himself. This time, he wouldn't be as irritated and try on a smile or two. Maybe even apologize for their rough beginning.

Just a quick hello, and he'd be home lickety-split.

He stepped over the crushed shell walkway between them, heading toward the front door.

Then the basket made a tiny mewing sound.

What the hell?

Dean approached and bent low to view, with utter horror, that his neighbor had left her baby on the doorstep.

Chapter Two

Maribel was in the middle of chopping onions for her mother's arroz con pollo recipe when she heard a loud pounding on the front door. This was odd, because everyone she knew in Charming would call or text first. But she'd told Ava to drop by anytime. Maribel dried her hands on a dish towel, then walked toward the door. The pounding had become so fierce it could not possibly be her sweet sister-in-law. This was more like a man's fist. Or a hammer.

There was urgency in the knocking. She could feel it, like a pounding deep in her gut. With an all too familiar deep sense of flight-or-fight syndrome coursing through her, she swung the door open.

There stood her neighbor, holding a large basket.

His expression was positively murderous. "Forget something?"

Wondering why he was still so concerned about her forgetting stuff and ready to tell him off, she peered inside the basket. "Oh, you have a baby."

"Your baby." He snarled, then pushed his way inside, setting the basket down.

"*Excuse* me?"

"It was right on your doorstep. This is dangerous. How absent-minded are you, exactly? Are you going to tell me you didn't even realize?"

Her hackles went up immediately at even the suggestion that she, of all people, would forget a *baby*. He didn't know her or her history. He quickly went from top five to number one most irritating male she'd ever met.

"Number one!" she shouted.

"*Excuse* me?"

"I don't have a baby, *sir*!"

"Well, it's not *my* baby!"

They stared daggers at each other for several long beats. His eyes were an interesting shade of amber, and at the moment, they were dark with hostility. Aimed at her, of all people. Because he didn't know her and that she'd sooner be roasted over hot coals than put a child at risk.

Her mind raced. In the past few days, she'd never seen him with a baby. No sign of a woman or child next door, so her instinct was to believe him. It probably wasn't his baby. And either he was certifiably insane, or he really was indignant that she would have forgotten her baby.

Which meant… Realization dawned on Maribel and appeared to simultaneously hit him.

They both rushed out the front door, him slightly ahead of her. Maribel ran to the edge of the short path in one direction, and Cowboy went in the other.

"Hey!" he shouted after whoever would have done this terrible thing. "Hey! Get back here!"

"Do you see anyone?"

"You go back inside with the baby. I'll go see if I can find any sign of who did this." He took off at a run, jogging down the lane leading to the beach.

Her breaths were coming sharp and ragged. Maybe this was a joke. Yes, a big practical joke on Maribel Del Toro, the burned-out former social worker. But she didn't know of anyone who'd leave a baby unattended outside as a joke. It wasn't funny. Who would be this stupid and careless?

Inside, the baby lay quietly in the basket, kicking at the blanket, completely unaware of the trauma he or she had caused. Why *Maribel's* door? And who was this desperate? Almost every fire department in the country had a safe haven for dropping a baby off, no questions asked. Of course, Charming *was* small enough to only have a volunteer fire department, and she wasn't sure they even had a station in town. But Houston was only thirty minutes away and had a large hospital and fire department.

Dressed in pink and surrounded by pink and white blankets, a small stack of diapers was shoved to one side of the basket. The baby looked to be well cared for. Two cans of formula and a bottle were on the other side. Obviously, a very deliberate, premeditated attempt to get rid of a baby. Maribel unwrapped the child from the soft blanket and unbuttoned the sleeper. As she'd suspected, due to the baby's size, she found no signs of a healing umbilical cord. Not a newborn. The belly button had completely healed. Maribel's educated guess would make the infant around two to three months old.

Someone had lovingly cared for this baby for months and then given up. Why?

The question should be: Why this time?

Drugs? Alcohol? Homelessness? An abusive home? For years, Maribel had witnessed situations in which both children and infants had to be removed from a home. Usually, the need became apparent at first sight. Garbage inside the home, including drug paraphernalia. Empty alcohol bottles. Both kids and babies in dirty clothes and overflowing diapers. No proper bed for the child or food.

But she'd never seen a baby this well cared for left behind.

"Where's your mommy?" Maribel mused as she checked the baby out from head to toe.

A few minutes later, Cowboy came bursting through Maribel's front door slightly out of breath.

"I couldn't find anyone."

"I don't understand this. Why leave the baby at *my* front door?" Then a thought occurred out of the blue, and she pointed to him. "Hang on. What if they meant to leave the baby at *your* front door but got the wrong house?"

"Mine?" He tapped his chest. "Why *my* house?"

"Let's see. What are the odds somewhere along the

line you impregnated a woman? Maybe she's tired and wants *you* to take a turn with your child."

Even as she said the words, Maribel recognized the unfairness behind them. She'd made a rash conclusion someone this attractive had to be a player with a ton of women in his past. And also, apparently, someone who didn't practice safe sex.

And from the narrowed eyes and tight jawline, he'd taken this as a dig.

"That's insulting. I don't have any children. If I had a baby, believe me, I'd *know* about it."

"It doesn't always work that way, Cowboy." She picked up the baby and held her close, rubbing her back in slow and even strokes.

"My name's *Dean*, not Cowboy." He pointed to the diapers. "What's that?"

"Diapers," Maribel deadpanned. "Are you not acquainted with them?"

"This." He bent low and, from between the diapers, picked out a sheet of paper.

"What is it?" Maribel said.

Dean unfolded and read. As he did, his face seemed to change colors. He went from golden boy to gray boy.

He lowered the note, then handed it to Maribel. "It's not signed."

Maribel set the baby in the basket, then read:

Her name is Brianna, and she's a really good baby. Sometimes she even sleeps through the night. The past three months have been hard, but I want to keep my baby. I just need a couple of weeks to figure some things out. Please take

care of her until I come back. Tell her mommy
will miss her, but I promise I'm coming back. I
left some formula and diapers, and I promise to
pay you back for any more you have to buy. She
likes it when I sing to her.

"Figure a few things out" could mean anything from
drug addiction to a runaway teen.

And this troubled girl had left the baby...with Maribel.

"I swear, I... I don't know who would have done
this. I don't even live in Charming. I'm here on vacation."

"She must know you somehow. More importantly,
she trusts you with her baby."

"She's trusted the wrong person if she thinks I'm
going to allow this to happen."

He narrowed his eyes. "What does that mean?"

"We have to call the police."

"No. We *don't*."

"Just one week ago, I was an employed social worker
with the state of California. I know about these things."

"Sounds like you're no longer employed, and we're
in the state of Texas, last I checked."

"That doesn't change facts. This is child abandon-
ment, pure and simple."

"Except it's *not*." He snapped the letter out of Maribel's hands and tapped on the writing. "It's clearly
written here that she'll be back. She's asked you to
babysit. That's *all*."

"Are you kidding me? She left the baby on my *doorstep*. Babysitting usually involves *asking* someone first.

An exchange of information. Anything could have happened to her baby. You were upset when I left a bag of *groceries* on the doorstep."

"Is it possible she rang the doorbell, and you didn't hear? You took your sweet time coming to the door for me, and I was about to knock it down."

"It's…possible." She shook her head. "I don't know. We should call the cops. At the very least, get her checked out at the hospital and make sure she's okay."

"No. If we take her to a hospital, too many questions will be asked."

"Those questions *need* to be asked! We don't know what we're dealing with here."

"We know *exactly* what we're dealing with here, thanks to the note. A probably young and overwhelmed single mom is asking you to babysit. You're the one person who could stand between her ability to ever see her baby again."

You're the one person who could stand between her ability to ever see her baby again.

His words hit her with sharp slings and a force he might have not intended. They felt personal, slamming into her, slicing her in two.

"Nice try. But I refuse to be guilt-tripped into abandoning my principles."

He snorted. "Principles. That's funny."

"What's funny about principles? Don't you have them?"

"Principles won't work if there's no real intent behind them. Or is family reunification a myth?"

She crossed her arms. Interesting. Her analytical

brain took this tip and filed it away for future use. The man seemed to know a few things about the system.

"Of course it's not a myth. It's the goal, but too many times, the parents are unable to meet their part of the deal. The children come first. Always."

"And the children want to be with their parents. It's the number one truth universally acknowledged. If you call law enforcement, that's going to complicate everything."

"That will simply start the clock ticking, and she'll have forty-eight hours to return."

"I can't let you do that. This mother clearly wants her baby back."

Everything inside Maribel tensed when this total stranger told her what she could and couldn't do. He didn't know how many times she'd had faith in a parent, worked for their reunification, only to be burned time and again. The last time had nearly ruined her. She was done rescuing people.

"I can't... I can't take her."

"You're choosing not to. Do me a favor? Stay out of this. I'll take the baby."

"*You* will. You?"

For reasons she didn't quite understand, the surfing cowboy had strong feelings about this. And she got it. A baby in need brought out universal emotions. She wanted to help, but the right thing to do was to call the authorities. Eventually, if the mother *proved* herself to be worthy, she'd get her baby back through the proper channels. Parents should prove they were capable of caring for their children. That way, all could be reassured this wasn't simply a temporary lapse in the girl's judgment. Everyone could be certain the baby was returned to a safe environment.

Dean took the baby from Maribel, then bent to pick up the baby's basket. He moved toward the front door. "Don't let us bother you."

"Wait a second here. What do *you* know about babies? Have you ever had children?"

"No, but I know enough. The rest I'll learn online."

"Online? So, you're going to *google* it?"

"Listen, there are YouTube videos on everything. I guarantee you I can figure this out. You don't need a PhD to change a diaper."

Her neck jerked back. It was unnerving the way he seemed to read her, to know her, before she'd told him a thing. No, you didn't need a *PhD* to change a diaper, but to understand why people reacted in the ways they did. To meet them in their dysfunction and try to help. The problem was all bets were off when addiction was part of the picture. Then parents didn't behave logically. They made decisions not even in their *own* best interest, let alone a child's. And Maribel didn't know whether this mother was an addict who could no longer care for her child. She didn't know anything at all about this mother, and the thought filled her with anxiety.

She cocked her head and went for logic. "This is going to interfere with your precious surfing time, you know."

She'd noticed him on the beach with his board every day, like it was his religion.

"Not a problem." He turned to her as though giving her one more chance to reconsider. "But if that's an offer to babysit a time or two, I'd take you up on it."

"Babysit? For all practical purposes, that's *my baby* you're holding. She left her for me to take care of."

"And you've said you can't violate your principles, so…"

"I also don't know whether I can trust you to watch YouTube videos and figure out how to take care of a baby."

"Well, damn. Looks like your principles are in conflict with one another."

Really? Tell me about it!

Not long ago, this had been her life. A desire to help but forced to follow rules set in place with the best of intentions. Foster care was never the horrible place pop culture and the news media led people to believe. It was only meant to be a temporary and safe home. Too many negative stories made the press, and did not acknowledge those angelic foster parents who cared for children with what amounted to a pittance of a salary.

"While you cuddle up with your principles tonight, I'll be next door with Brianna." Then he left with the baby.

"Number one!" she shouted behind him, but either he hadn't heard or decided not to acknowledge it.

She wasn't cuddling up to her principles, she was *living* with them. Doing the right thing. And yet…procedure would involve alerting the police. The problem was she seemed to be in a gray area, but ethics were always important, regardless of whether legalities were involved.

You're here to unplug. Mindfulness is the key. You're going to teach yourself to cook. Read feel-good fiction.

Stay off your cell, all social media and recharge. You have a major decision to make.

Last month, an old headhunter friend had approached and offered Maribel a position with a six-figure salary. She'd be taking over the caseload of a therapist who had counseled the children of the Silicon Valley elite. Anxiety, depression and ADHD were core issues. Maribel had a knee-jerk reaction to the proposition: no. But maybe she could do some good there. It would be something so different from what she'd been doing for years. A chance to use her education and experience in a different way.

She only had a few more weeks to decide before they looked for someone else.

Maribel went back to her dinner of arroz con pollo, so rudely interrupted by both her neighbor and a baby. As she opened cans of tomato sauce and stirred them into the rice, she relaxed and unwound. Her breathing returned to normal, and her shoulders unkinked. Routines were good to employ in the aftermath of shock. They soothed. They reminded a person life would go on.

On the day Maribel discovered the toddler she'd helped reunite with his mother had been rushed to the hospital with dehydration, she'd brushed her teeth in the middle of the day. Later, she would come to doubt every decision she'd ever made, including the one to become a social worker.

Despite the fact Dean had let Maribel off the hook, she couldn't ignore the mother's request. The baby was her responsibility, and she never shirked her duties. Not from the time she was working with her parents in the strawberry fields of Watsonville to the moment of her PhD dissertation. She, Maribel Del Toro, was no quitter.

She didn't want a surfing cowboy dude who had to google *diapering* to take care of the baby. And even if Maribel had a good sense of people, she didn't know this man. She'd let him take a baby next door, where he might hopelessly bungle it all. In all good conscience, she couldn't just stand by.

Ten minutes later, she turned off the stove and banged on the door to *his* cottage.

He opened the door, almost as if he'd expected her. But then he walked toward the connected bedroom with barely a glance, simply leaving it for her to choose to walk inside or not.

"I can't walk away from her. It's my responsibility," she said.

Since he didn't say a word, she closed the front door and followed him past the sitting room area, the kitchenette and into the bedroom. He'd emptied a dresser drawer and placed Brianna in it, surrounded by her blankets.

"This is a temporary bed for her." He ran a hand through his hair, looking more than a little out of sorts. "Maybe I should buy a crib."

He'd removed the hat, and she wasn't surprised to find golden locks of hair had been under it, curling at his neck and almost long enough to be put in a short ponytail.

Hands in the pockets of his jeans, he lowered his head to study the baby as if mulling over a complicated algebra word problem.

Brianna cooed and gave him a drooly smile. Aw, she was such a cute baby. Beautiful dark eyes and curls of black hair. Her beautiful skin was a light brown. She could be African American, Latina or multiracial.

"As you said, babysitting her is temporary. You don't need to invest in a crib. Maybe this, um, drawer will do for now."

"You *approve*?"

The corner of his lip curled up in a half smile, and something went tight in Maribel's belly. The cowboy's eyes were an interesting shade some would call hazel, others might simply call amber. But they were no longer hot with anger.

She tilted her chin and met his eyes. "Let's just say I'm in new territory here, but so far, so good."

"You're going to help me?"

"It would be irresponsible of me to let you do this on your own."

He shook his head. "Those principles in conflict again. Pesky little things."

"Don't make fun of me. This is serious."

"Yeah, it is. A baby needs you. I know what I'm going to do. What about you?"

She still didn't know, but maybe she didn't *have* to make an immediate decision. It was entirely possible the mother would be back by tomorrow at the latest, regretting what she'd done and missing her baby. Unfortunately, Maribel was too jaded to believe this a real possibility.

But she wanted to.

"We don't even know if she'll be gone the full two weeks. She could come back sooner."

"Exactly." Dean picked up a diaper. "The way I look at this, Brianna is going to need more diapers. I already went through two of them."

"*Two?* You've been in here for fifteen minutes."

He scowled and scratched his chin. "She wet while I was changing her. Is that…normal?"

Oh boy. This guy really didn't know a thing. Then again, how often did men babysit siblings, nieces or nephews even if they had them? Not often, at least not in her family.

Dean had already explained he had no children of his own. *That he knew of.*

"It's normal. You're lucky Brianna isn't a boy. Sometimes the stream goes long and wide."

"Okay." Dean crossed his arms and gazed at her from under hooded lids. "Thanks for the four-one-one."

"Um, you're welcome." Self-consciously, Maribel pulled on the sleeve of her sundress and chewed on her lower lip.

She didn't usually wear dresses, and that might be the reason she was so ill at ease here with him. Usually she wore pantsuits, her hair up in a bun. Men were still occasionally strange creatures to her, who had ideas she didn't quite grasp.

Watching this particular man from a safe distance had been comfortable. Easy. She could ogle him all she wanted from the privacy of her own cottage and realize nothing would come of it. Now, standing next to him, there was a charge between them. He'd really *noticed* her. She suddenly felt a little…naked. And a lot…awkward.

"You mind watching her while I go buy some diapers and formula?" he said.

"Go ahead."

A perfect opportunity. While here alone, Maribel planned on surreptitiously checking out Dean's unit. It wasn't that she had trust issues, no sir, but if he was going to watch the baby *she'd* been entrusted with, she should make sure he could be relied on with any child. She wouldn't call it snooping, exactly. More like a light criminal background check.

"Be right back." He grabbed his keys.

"And don't forget baby wipes."

"Okay. Wipes."

She pointed. "*Baby* wipes. Don't get the Lysol ones."

"Speaking of mansplaining." He quirked a brow and gave her the side-eye before he walked out the door.

Snooping commenced immediately. First, she checked on Brianna, who, with a clean diaper, had gone back to snoozing. Admittedly the drawer was an ingenious and scrappy idea from a man who'd probably had to figure things out in the wilderness when all he had for supper was a stick and a rabbit.

Okay, Maribel, he's a cowboy, not Paul Bunyon.

She knew little of life on the range, where she assumed he lived. Checking through his luggage, she found plenty of shirts and jeans. Interesting. He wore dark boxer briefs. Not even white socks but dark ones. Wasn't that against cowboy regulations?

Put the underwear down and back away, Maribel.

His underwear and clothes told her nothing about the man. Importantly, she hadn't found a gun or a buck knife. She rifled through drawers in each room, finding real estate flyers and Ava's "Welcome to Charming" Chamber of Commerce handout. But nothing embarrassing, dangerous or disgusting. She checked the medicine cabinet and under the mattress for those pesky recreational drugs. On her principles, she'd whisk this baby away in a New York minute even if she found the (ahem) legal stuff. Nothing. So far, he checked out.

Then she found a pack of condoms in his nightstand drawer, and it snapped her back to reality.

What am I doing?

She sat on the bed and stared at the wall, covering her face. If only her colleagues could see her now. They'd no longer have any doubts that she'd done the right thing by resigning from the California Department of Social Services.

They'd no longer have any doubt that she'd lost all faith in humanity. She no longer believed in people. She no longer believed in second chances.

This poor man was trying to do a good thing here, and she'd found his condoms, violating his privacy in every way. None of her business. Hey, at least he was prepared. She could find nothing wrong with the man who'd offered to care for the baby, so she didn't have an excuse to call the authorities. He was right to hope. Maybe. There was a memory nagging at the edge of Maribel's mind, but she couldn't pin it down. Last week, when she'd been to the Once Upon a Book store with Stacy Cruz, Maribel might have mentioned her former career in social services. There had been a teenage girl there looking through the mystery section.

She could give this mother at least twenty-four hours.

One day to regret her decision and come running back for her baby.

The mother would be back, and if she didn't return, *then* Maribel would call the police.

Chapter Three

Dean stood in the middle of aisle fourteen, feeling like a giant idiot. He'd asked for wipes and the clerk sent him straight here, but this wasn't right. These were the Lysol cleaning wipes Maribel had warned him about, as if he didn't know any better. The clerk had simply assumed *he* didn't have a baby, but obviously must have a bathroom or a kitchen to clean. And he hadn't been specific enough. *Baby* wipes.

Maybe babysitting Brianna wasn't such a great idea. If only his pretty neighbor would have agreed to watch the baby and let him off the hook. What was wrong with her, anyway? He expected most women would want to babysit a cute baby, but then again, he'd wager she wasn't most women. It turned out she was a social worker with an inherent bias to mothers who made mistakes.

People like Maribel had changed the trajectory of Dean's life.

He wandered down the aisles and finally found the baby stuff. There were packages of diapers in all manner of sizes. Newborn, the smallest, and then differing numbered sizes by weight. He had no idea how much the baby weighed. In two seconds, he was overwhelmed. He didn't even know how old this baby was and hadn't thought to get Maribel's cell number so he could text her from the store. What *size*? He wanted to get eight to fourteen pounds because that made sense, but maybe over fourteen pounds would be best. Better to have a bigger size than too small, right? He knew that much, anyway.

The formula deal was a lot easier to figure out, so he picked up a case. The baby wipes, once he found them, also easy. Did not require a size, only choosing between scented, unscented, with added aloe vera and hypoallergenic. He chose the ones for sensitive skin, just in case.

As Dean was holding the newborn size diapers in one hand and the next larger size in the other, a man came rushing into the aisle and began snatching pacifiers off the rack like there might soon be a shortage of them. Pacifiers! Dean should have thought of that. Before the dude grabbed them all, Dean reached for one.

"Those are the best. Orthodontists recommend them," the man said, noticing Dean.

"Is there a sale going on?"

"Is there? Hope so. We're trying to wean her from these, but it's not working. And no matter what we do, we can never have enough of these on hand. We've lost so many of them under furniture, beds, cars, anywhere. I figure when we move, we're going to find a treasure trove of old and hairy pacifiers. They didn't just *disappear*. Must be hiding somewhere. It's like losing a sock in the dryer. No one has figured out where the other one goes. It's a mystery. Well, pacifiers are like clean socks."

"Uh-huh." Dean cleared his throat and examined the packaging. "How many should I get for my baby?"

"How old is she?"

"Um, she's really...*young*."

The man quirked a brow, thankfully accepting Dean's ignorance as to the age of his pretend child.

"You look familiar. You're that beginning surfer who hangs out at the Salty Dog, aren't you? Cole told me about you."

Dean's hackles went up at being referred to as "beginning" anything, but it was an unfortunately fair assessment.

"I'm Dean Hunter. And you are...?"

He offered his hand in a firm grip. "Adam Cruz. Nice to meet you. I'm one of the Salty Dog owners."

"Pleasure." Dean tipped his hat and reframed his story. "I'm, uh, babysitting? My niece. For my sister, she...she forgot to..."

Tell me how old her baby is?

Adam eyed the diapers Dean held. "Leave enough diapers? They go through those fast. My wife and I have a daughter, too. That's nice of you to babysit. I take people up on that every chance I get. I love my daughter, but holy cow, I need more time with my wife. Ya know?"

"Um, yeah. That's actually why I'm doing this. My sister needed some time with the wife." Dean winced, realizing he'd outed his nonexistent, invisible sister.

"And you're probably wondering what you got yourself into now."

Dean chuckled and rubbed his chin. "Ha, yeah. You could say that."

"Don't worry. I was terrified the first time I held my baby, afraid I'd break her."

"Yeah, that's how I feel."

Since the moment he'd called Maribel's bluff and hauled the baby with him next door, he had no idea what he was doing and if he'd somehow do more harm than good. Add to that the anxiety of wondering if the mother would come back as promised or if his next-door neighbor would get to be right. She would then turn him into the authorities right along with the baby.

He took the baby, she'd point and say. *And then proceeded to watch YouTube videos on how to take care of her. It was a recipe for disaster from the get-go. I tried to stop him!*

He could almost see *Rodeo Today*'s front-page headline:

Four-Time World Champ Quits Rodeo Circuit to Steal Someone's Baby

Dean held up the two different sizes of diapers. "Which one?"

"Easy. Unless your baby was delivered just today or premature, the newborn size is going to be too small. I made the same rookie mistake. She didn't fit into newborn by the time she was three days old. I'd get the next one up, twelve to eighteen pounds."

"Hey, thanks, buddy. I appreciate it."

Adam waved and rushed away, taking ten pacifiers with him.

When Dean arrived back to the cottage a few minutes later, the noises from inside sounded like *ten* angry babies in there, not *one*. Panic roiled inside of him, but he had nowhere to run. He was going to have to go inside and deal with this mess.

Maribel paced the floor with the screaming child. "Oh my God, you're back! Help!"

Her face flushed and pink, her eyes were nearly popping out of their sockets.

"What did you *do*? What's wrong with the baby?"

"You assume I did something to cause this? How about if you don't accuse me, and I won't accuse you?"

Somehow, he expected her to be better at this, though it might be unfair of him to assume so because she had a uterus. In his case, he would have done better at delivering this child than he probably would taking care of it. It couldn't be much different than assisting in the birth of a calf. And as a bonus, baby cows didn't cry.

"Make a bottle! Quick! She could be hungry. I've already changed her. You did buy more bottles, didn't you?"

Bottles. He forgot the bottles. Stupid Adam leading him to the pacifiers like they were made of gold when Dean should have focused on more bottles instead.

"She left one in the basket. Get it! Now!"

"Stop ordering me around."

He grabbed the bottle and a can of formula, grumbling the entire time.

What had she been doing when he'd been sweating in the store aisle over diapers? All she'd had to do was watch the baby. How hard could that be? She was a sweet little angel the whole fifteen minutes she'd been in his dresser drawer. Following the directions, he mixed the powder with water and poured it into the bottle, shook it then carried it over to Maribel.

"Did you warm it?"

"I was supposed to warm it? Here, give it back. I'll use the microwave."

"Not the microwave!" She hissed. "Good lord, you don't know *anything*. Here, you take her. I'll warm the bottle."

Dean took the baby, who didn't look anything like the angelic little bundle from earlier. Now she was a wriggling mess with a wail that would kill most grown men. Her little hands were curled into fists like she was mad as hell. He swore he could see her tonsils.

"Hey, hey. Listen, I'm trying to help you. Look, I know you're mad your mama left, but that's not my fault. She'll be back. I hope."

She better come back. He was willing to give the mother the benefit of the doubt, but someone who would abandon her baby and never return was lower than dirt. He hoped she had a damn good excuse.

Dean did his best to pace, shuffle-walk and swing, imitating Maribel. Brianna stopped crying for one second when she opened her eyes, as if shocked someone else was holding her. Still clearly not the person she wanted. Her silence was a momentary lapse, as if taking a breath and gaining strength. She went right back to crying with rejuvenated energy.

"Okay." Maribel appeared with the bottle and pointed to his couch. "Already tested for temperature. Just sit down with her."

He'd never been this awkward and bumbling in his life, but did as Maribel ordered, resenting every second of her authority. Balancing Brianna in the crook of his elbow, he eased the rubber tip of the bottle into her open mouth. She sucked away at the bottle with fervor.

Maribel collapsed on the couch next to Dean. "Guess she was just hungry."

"Why didn't you feed her while I was gone?" The mother had left one can of formula and a bottle after all.

"Are you *kidding* me? You don't know how hard this is! I couldn't hold her and make the formula. I only have two hands, and she cried louder every time I put her down."

More and more, Dean worried he couldn't do this on his own. And she obviously couldn't, either.

"Are all babies this *loud*?"

"She has a good set of lungs on her. I thought she'd never stop." She leaned back. "Oh, would you listen to that?"

"What?"

"Silence. I never knew how much I loved it until it was gone."

He eyed Maribel with suspicion. "How long has she been crying? She was fine before I left."

"She just took one look at me and started wailing. It's hard not to take it personally." Maribel leaned forward, watching the baby take the bottle.

This put Maribel at his elbow, dark hair so close to him he could smell the coconut sweet flowery scent. Cute Stuck-up Girl smelled incredible. His irritation with her ebbed.

"Aw, she's so cute. Check out her perfect skin." She caressed the baby's cheek with the back of her hand.

If it could be said they were staring at the baby, which they probably were, she stared right back. Her dark eyes were wide as she took them both in. This was one smart baby, alert and aware *something* had changed.

"Thanks for helping me," Dean finally said. "I'm sorry if I sound grumpy. Obviously, I couldn't have done this without you."

"I saw how strongly you felt about this."

"I'd say we both have equally strong feelings."

She sighed and offered Brianna her finger, and the little hand fisted around it. "It's just… I've seen this kind of thing before too many times, and it doesn't end well."

"Never?"

Dean didn't want to hear this. He wanted to believe the mother would return. Sometimes all a mother needed was for someone to have a little faith in her.

Sometimes that's all anyone needed.

"Not with abandoned babies. There's generally abuse in the home, a teenager trying to hide the unwanted pregnancy." She shook her head. "You don't want to hear the rest."

Dean swallowed hard. "But did anyone ever leave a note saying they'd be back for her baby?"

To Dean, the note the mother had left was filled

with hope. He remembered too well the taste of hope.
No one should be denied a second chance.

"Not to my knowledge."

"Then it's possible. You just haven't heard of any
instances. Granted, I agree this is unusual."

"I want to believe she'll come back, but there have
been too many disappointments along the line for me.
Addiction is powerful. It overcomes love."

That was one belief Dean would never accept. Not
in his lifetime.

"Sorry, no. Nothing can overcome love."

Maribel turned her gaze from the baby to him, forcing him to realize how close she was. She had a full
mouth and deep brown eyes that shimmered with the
hint of a smile. Damn, she was…breathtaking. Much
better-looking close up. He'd noticed her, of course,
on the beach wearing a skimpy red bikini, displaying
long legs and a heart-shaped behind. They often passed
each other: her sitting under the umbrella reading, him
coming back from his surfing day. After their disas-
trous first meeting, she'd been easier to dismiss from a
safe distance with a curt nod. Far easier than to remind
himself he didn't need or want any complications like
the type a beautiful woman would bring into his life.

*Get your act together before you even think to ask
someone to tag along.*

Her lips quirked in the start of a smile. "That's…
certainly not what I expected you to say."

"Why? You think cowboys don't believe in love?"

"Honestly, you'll have to forgive me because I'm
not sure most *men* believe in love. Or at least, I'm not
meeting them."

"Not sure who you've been dating, but that's a pretty sad statement."

"It is, isn't it?" Maribel leaned back, putting some distance between them, as if only now aware of how close she'd been. "I'm sorry to make such a blanket statement. You're right, there are some men who believe in love."

"But these are not the men you're dating. Why not?"

"Well, it's not like they wear a sign."

He snorted. "They don't wear a sign, but there are *signs*."

She simply stared at him for a moment as if she was still trying to decide whether or not he could be trusted.

"What are we going to do tonight?" She nudged her chin to Brianna. "About her?"

"We? I'll let her sleep in the drawer, or maybe I'll just lay her on the bed next to me."

She narrowed her eyes like she thought maybe this was a bad idea. "Are you a light or heavy sleeper?"

"Light." And lately, he hadn't been sleeping at all. But that was a story for another day. "It's a big bed. I won't roll over on her."

Maribel stood. "Okay. You take the first night, and tomorrow I'll take the second."

"You trust me? What if I'm some weirdo?"

"Some weirdo who wants to take care of a baby so her mother won't lose custody? I guess you're my kind of weirdo."

That wasn't enough for him. He pulled out his wallet and opened it to his driver's license, pointing to the photo. "This is me. Take a photo if you'd like."

She glanced at the ID. "That's you. But I…left my

phone next door. I'm actually unplugging this vacation."

Unplugging. What a concept.

"I need your cell number anyway. What if I need you in the middle of the night because I'm in over my head here?"

"Just walk over and knock on my door. But…loudly. *I'm* a heavy sleeper."

"Lucky you." He walked her to the door. "Can we agree not to tell anyone else about the baby?"

"I think that's best. I'll check on you two in the morning."

But between old memories, a helpless baby and a beautiful woman next door, Dean would be lucky to get a wink tonight.

Nothing can overcome love.

He certainly wasn't like the men Maribel met on dating apps.

Maribel mulled those words over as she brushed her teeth and got ready for bed, changing into her 49ers long T-shirt. If she hadn't known any better, she'd have thought those words had come out of her own mother's mouth. Her mother often made such sweeping and general statements, seemingly drawing the world into patches of black and white. No gray.

But Maribel certainly did not expect this Greek Adonis–type man with the chiseled jawline and broad shoulders to utter such words. Or to behave with such tenderness and concern toward a baby. Her heart had squeezed tight watching this big man holding a tiny infant close against his chest, as if he'd single-handedly protect her from the world. He might think he could, but Maribel had news for him. It wasn't going to be easy and almost inevitably result in a pain not easily overcome.

He'd been surly with her since the moment they met, his physical countenance often matching his sharp and pointy words. Narrowed eyes, tight jaw. Rigid shoulders. Until that one sentence, laid out for her like a truth bomb. When he'd said the words, his eyes were soft and warm, his voice rich and smooth as mocha.

Is family reunification a myth?

With those words, he'd poured a metaphorical bucket of ice water over her.

Because she used to believe in families. She once believed parents could be reunited with their children simply because of the deep bonds of unconditional love. Parents were hardwired by biology to love their babies and protect them. She'd believed with all her heart before she came front and center with the gray area: addiction. Mental Illness. Poverty. Now, she still lived in those murky shadows. She wished she could see things differently and, as she had in the beginning, with a hope and belief that she could change the world. She now realized she could not.

And if the mother hadn't returned by tomorrow night, Maribel would call the police. Dean wouldn't take it well, and there was no point in preemptively starting an argument by revealing her plan. For now, she'd agreed to do this his way. It certainly didn't mean he would *always* get his way. By tomorrow night, maybe this wouldn't be an issue. The mother would be back, or the baby would be on her way to a competent foster home with a loving couple prepared to keep and nurture a baby.

She settled on her bed, pulling out her book to read before she went to sleep. Recently, on the advice of a friend who wrote a book and ran a website on avoiding burnout and rediscovering your purpose, Maribel had returned to print. Normally she read everything from her phone app, but according to her friend, she'd inadvertently zapped herself out of the joy of reading. Her goal here was to slow down, take her time, touch the paper pages and flip through them. Reading was an experience for more than one sense. It could be both tactile and visual. She'd somehow lost the joy of taking her time with something she loved.

Last week she'd visited Once Upon a Book with Stacy and loaded up on novels with happy endings. If it had a dog on the cover and a couple lovingly smiling, it got purchased. Some of her friends loved the raunchy and realistic stuff about the agonizing pain of breakups. If a book made them ugly cry, it became a forever favorite. Not Maribel. She'd had enough of real life. When she'd wanted to cry, when she wanted a knot in her stomach that wouldn't go away, all she'd had to do was read her case files.

In the first few days of reading print books again, she became aware of two things: her focus was lacking, and she almost didn't have the patience to slow down enough to *read*. So she continued to work at it one page at a time. This week on the beach under an umbrella. In fact, she'd had a quiet week until the baby showed up.

Outside, the sounds of soothing waves rolled in and out, and Maribel focused on turning the pages of her book. In no time at all, she was in the mountains of Humboldt County, where a handsome farmer had taken in a divorced mother of two looking for a new start. Sleep came easily, enveloping her in warmth.

The next morning, Maribel blinked, stretched and listened through the thin wall connecting both cottages. No baby crying. Hardly any noise at all outside. Only a sense of disturbing awareness pulsing and buzzing through her body that she couldn't ignore. Maribel could almost hear her sister Jordan's voice in her head.

Time to admit a few things.

Okay, yes, I'm attracted to the grumpy man. So what? Who wouldn't be?

He exuded alpha male confidence, and it had always been her lot in life to fall for the difficult men. For the ones with permanent scowls and surly attitudes. She couldn't seem to fall in love with someone sweet and kind like Clark, her nicest ex-boyfriend, who'd told her in no uncertain terms, "I'm sorry, Maribel, but you are sucking the life right out of me."

Ouch.

Maribel wasn't great at dating, having spent most of her childhood studying. It wasn't that she was trying to prove something, but early on, Maribel realized her strengths were in textbooks. Whether it was science, math or history, she slayed it. Testing wasn't an issue for her. Blessed with a nearly photographic memory, academia wasn't difficult. Boyfriends, at the time, were. This meant that essentially, she was a little socially hindered when it came to romantic relationships.

She'd tried online dating, setting up her profile on Tinder and the others. One of the men had turned out to be married, making her paranoid enough to check for wedding ring tan lines from that point on. One man had arrived at their coffee date looking perfectly presentable. Slacks, dark button-down, loafers. A face with good character, if not particularly handsome. No tan line. After ordering, he called himself a naughty boy, said he had to be punished from time to time and wanted a dominant woman.

She left without finishing her coffee, went home and removed her profile from that particular dating app.

Now, she went to the kitchen to make coffee, the quiet of the morning reverberating all around her. Dressing quickly, she walked next door to check on the baby. Dean had left the door unlocked, so she let herself inside. Tiptoeing through the connected rooms to the bedroom, she found the baby sound asleep in the drawer wrapped in blankets, her little fisted hands bracing her face, her sweet mouth softly suckling in her sleep.

Dean lay on his back on top of the blankets, wearing board shorts and—*oh my*—no shirt. He'd thrown one arm over his face like he wanted to block everything out. Suddenly, he sprang up on his elbows, eyes squinting into the brightness.

"What? *What?*"

Maribel startled and took two steps back. She hadn't said a word and, in fact, was barely breathing. He wasn't kidding about being a light sleeper.

"It's just…me," Maribel squeaked and held up both palms, surrender style. "Sorry. I woke up early and wanted to check on you two. Go back to sleep."

He ignored her and instead walked around the bed to check on the baby.

"She's doing fine," Maribel whispered. "You can relax."

"Now she's sleeping better than I did." He ran a hand down his face. It was only then she realized he'd gathered his hair into a short ponytail.

He had a good face, chiseled jaw and irresistible stubble.

Down, girl.

"Rough night?" She swallowed.

"She was up at two in the morning wanting…something. Gave her a bottle, but she just wanted to be… I don't know…held?" He scratched his chin, and the stubble made a low sound.

"So, you didn't get much sleep?"

"No big deal. Haven't slept well in a while. You?"

"Like a baby. A very nice rest, thanks."

It wasn't entirely true. She'd lain awake for an hour thinking about the baby. About Dean. The mother and whether or not she would return. Whether or not Maribel was doing the right thing giving her a chance to return before involving the authorities.

"Got news for you. Apparently, babies don't sleep. Kind of like me. If you slept well, you did *not* sleep like a baby."

"That could be why you're grumpy all the time." She cleared her throat when he gave her the side-eye. "What do you do about it?"

"I don't take medication if that's what you're asking."

"No, there's melatonin, which is natural. Personally, I recommend reading before bedtime. Something light and happy."

He turned to study her then, his amber eyes appearing darker near the irises. Well, if he was going to stare, she would stare right back. She wasn't intimidated by good-looking dudes with hot bodies. If someone looked away first, it wouldn't be *her.*

Let that be him. She met his eyes. With a baby between them and the fact it was morning, she couldn't escape the unnatural intimacy of the moment. She was in his bedroom just as he'd rolled out of bed. He stood at her elbow, arms crossed, so close her bare elbow brushed against his naked and warm skin.

And it seemed that a live wire lay sparking between them.

One half of his mouth tipped up in a smile. "How did I do? Did I pass the health inspection?"

Still meeting his gaze, she cleared her throat. "You did fine, obviously."

The gaze he slid her made bells and whistles go off in her head. Her body buzzed, and her legs tightened in response to the hint of a smile on his lips. Smiling, she'd decided, was overrated. Better than a smile was the start of one. The way it began in the eyes, moving slowly. Like a teaser of "coming attractions."

Damn it!

She looked away first, too unnerved by the blatant invitation in his eyes.

"Okay! I see everything is good in here. I'll make her a bottle for when she wakes up, and I can take her next door."

She thought she heard him mutter, "Chicken," as she quietly walked away.

Don't miss
A Charming Doorstep Baby
by Heatherly Bell,
available September 2023 wherever
Harlequin Special Edition books and
ebooks are sold.

www.Harlequin.com

#3007 FALLING FOR DR. MAVERICK
Montana Mavericks: Lassoing Love • by Kathy Douglass

Mike Burris and Corinne Hawkins's rodeo romance hit the skids when Mike pursued his PhD. But when the sexy doctor-in-training gets word of Corrine's plan to move on without him, he'll pull out all the stops to kick-start their flatlined romance.

#3008 THE RANCHER'S CHRISTMAS REUNION
Match Made in Haven • by Brenda Harlen

Celebrity Hope Bradford broke Michael Gilmore's heart years ago when she left to pursue her Hollywood dreams. The stubborn rancher won't forgive and forget. But when Hope is forced to move in with him on his ranch—and proximity gives in to lingering attraction—her kisses thaw even the grinchiest heart!

#3009 SNOWBOUND WITH A BABY
Dawson Family Ranch • by Melissa Senate

When a newborn baby is left on Detective Reed Dawson's desk with a mysterious note, he takes in the infant. But social worker Aimee Gallagher has her own plans for the baby...until a snowbound weekend at Reed's ranch challenges all of Aimee's preconceived notions about family and love.

#3010 LOVE AT FIRST BARK
Crimson, Colorado • by Michelle Major

Cassie Raebourn never forgot Aiden Riley—or the way his loss inspired her to become a veterinarian. Now the shy boy is a handsome, smoldering cowboy, complete with bitterness and bluster. It's Cassie's turn to inspire Aiden...with adorable K-9 help!

#3011 A HIDEAWAY WHARF HOLIDAY
Love at Hideaway Wharf • by Laurel Greer

Archer Frost was supposed to help decorate a nursery—not deliver Franci Walker's baby! She's smitten with the retired coast guard diver, despite his gruff exterior. He's her baby's hero...and hers. Will Franci's determined, sunny demeanor be enough for Archer to realize *he's* their Christmas miracle?

#3012 THEIR CHRISTMAS RESOLUTION
Sisters of Christmas Bay • by Kaylie Newell

Stella Clarke will stop at nothing to protect her aging foster mother. But when sexy real estate developer Ian Steele comes to town with his sights set on her Victorian house, Stella will have to keep mistletoe and romance from softening her hardened holiday reserve!

Get 3 FREE REWARDS!

We'll send you 2 FREE Books plus a FREE Mystery Gift.

FREE
Value Over
$20

Both the **Harlequin® Special Edition** and **Harlequin® Heartwarming™** series feature compelling novels filled with stories of love and strength where the bonds of friendship, family and community unite.

YES! Please send me 2 FREE novels from the Harlequin Special Edition or Harlequin Heartwarming series and my FREE Gift (gift is worth about $10 retail). After receiving them, if I don't wish to receive any more books, I can return the shipping statement marked "cancel." If I don't cancel, I will receive 6 brand-new Harlequin Special Edition books every month and be billed just $5.49 each in the U.S. or $6.24 each in Canada, a savings of at least 12% off the cover price, or 4 brand-new Harlequin Heartwarming Larger-Print books every month and be billed just $6.24 each in the U.S. or $6.74 each in Canada, a savings of at least 19% off the cover price. It's quite a bargain! Shipping and handling is just 50¢ per book in the U.S. and $1.25 per book in Canada.* I understand that accepting the 2 free books and gift places me under no obligation to buy anything. I can always return a shipment and cancel at any time by calling the number below. The free books and gift are mine to keep no matter what I decide.

Choose one: ☐ **Harlequin**   ☐ **Harlequin**   ☐ **Or Try Both!**
                  Special Edition   **Heartwarming**   (235/335 & 161/361
                  (235/335 BPA GRMK)   **Larger-Print**   BPA GRPZ)
                                            (161/361 BPA GRMK)

Name (please print)

Address   Apt. #

City   State/Province   Zip/Postal Code

Email: Please check this box ☐ if you would like to receive newsletters and promotional emails from Harlequin Enterprises ULC and its affiliates. You can unsubscribe anytime.

Mail to the Harlequin Reader Service:
IN U.S.A.: P.O. Box 1341, Buffalo, NY 14240-8531
IN CANADA: P.O. Box 603, Fort Erie, Ontario L2A 5X3

Want to try 2 free books from another series! Call 1-800-873-8635 or visit www.ReaderService.com.

*Terms and prices subject to change without notice. Prices do not include sales taxes, which will be charged (if applicable) based on your state or country of residence. Canadian residents will be charged applicable taxes. Offer not valid in Quebec. This offer is limited to one order per household. Books received may not be as shown. Not valid for current subscribers to the Harlequin Special Edition or Harlequin Heartwarming series. All orders subject to approval. Credit or debit balances in a customer's account(s) may be offset by any other outstanding balance owed by or to the customer. Please allow 4 to 6 weeks for delivery. Offer available while quantities last.

Your Privacy—Your information is being collected by Harlequin Enterprises ULC, operating as Harlequin Reader Service. For a complete summary of the information we collect, how we use this information and to whom it is disclosed, please visit our privacy notice located at corporate.harlequin.com/privacy-notice. From time to time we may also exchange your personal information with reputable third parties. If you wish to opt out of this sharing of your personal information, please visit readerservice.com/consumerschoice or call 1-800-873-8635. **Notice to California Residents**—Under California law, you have specific rights to control and access your data. For more information on these rights and how to exercise them, visit corporate.harlequin.com/california-privacy.

HSEHW23

HARLEQUIN
PLUS

Try the best multimedia subscription service for romance readers like you!

Read, Watch and Play.

Experience the easiest way to get the romance content you crave.

Start your **FREE TRIAL** at
www.harlequinplus.com/freetrial.